Also By P

STAT: Special Threat Assessment Team

Wolf Under Fire
Undercover Wolf
True Wolf

X-Ops

Her Perfect Mate
Her Lone Wolf
Her Secret Agent (novella)
Her Wild Hero
Her Fierce Warrior
Her Rogue Alpha
Her True Match
Her Dark Half
X-Ops Exposed

SWAT: Special Wolf Alpha Team

Hungry Like the Wolf
Wolf Trouble
In the Company of Wolves
To Love a Wolf
Wolf Unleashed
Wolf Hunt
Wolf Hunger
Wolf Rising
Wolf Instinct
Wolf Rebel
Wolf Untamed
Rogue Wolf
The Wolf Is Mine

LOVING THE WOLF

PAIGE TYLER

Cover design by Patrick Kang
Cover image by Don Dean, Drobot/Shuttershock

Published by Sourcebooks Casablanca, an imprint of Sourcebooks
P.O. Box 4410, Naperville, Illinois 60567–4410
(630) 961-3900
sourcebooks.com

Printed and bound in Canada.
MBP 10 9 8 7 6 5 4 3 2 1

With special thanks to my extremely patient and understanding husband. Without your help and support, I couldn't have pursued my dream job of becoming a writer. You're my sounding board, my idea man, my critique partner, and the absolute best research assistant a girl could ask for. Love you!

CHAPTER 1

Senior Corporal Trevor McCall stood in front of the three-floor industrial building in the heart of Burbank, California, comparing it to the address on his phone, not quite sure if he was in the right place. This was supposed to be Jenna Malone's apartment, but on the outside, it looked more like a warehouse than a residential complex. Then again, this was Los Angeles. Maybe this was what passed for an apartment building out here.

Before he could step inside and find out one way or the other, the phone in his hand rang, making him almost drop the damn thing. He checked the screen, prepared to let the call go to voicemail, until he realized it was Hale Delaney, his SWAT teammate from back in Dallas. Hale was also his fellow conspirator in this wild scheme to sneak out to southern California so Trevor could spend some quality time alone with Jenna—the sister of one of his best friends, Connor, who also happened to be a member of Dallas SWAT team. And a werewolf. Just like Trevor and everyone else on the team.

Trevor thumbed the green button, then held the phone to his ear. "Hey. What's up?"

"Not much. Just calling to make sure your flight

arrived okay," Hale said. "And to let you know that the plan worked. Everyone in the Pack thinks you're in Richmond, Virginia, visiting family, exactly like you said you were doing. No one suspects a thing."

"Excellent. Thanks for covering for me," Trevor said. "I owe you big for this. I hate asking you to lie to the Pack—hell, I hate lying to them, too—but they've been so damn nosy lately."

"Well, you have to admit that asking for vacation time out of the blue to visit a family you've barely spoken to since joining SWAT five years ago is a little suspicious." Hale chuckled. "Then there's also all the time you and Jenna spent hanging out at the barbecue when she was here a few weeks ago. Trust me, your interest in her definitely didn't go unnoticed."

Trevor tensed, grip tightening on his phone. "Do you think Connor was one of those people who noticed? I mean, if there's one way this whole thing is going to blow up in my face, it's if Jenna's brother decides to follow me out here."

"I don't think you have to worry about that," Hale assured him. "I've been keeping a close eye on him, and it doesn't seem like he's suspicious. To be honest, he's been so focused on Kat, I don't even think he knows you left."

He let out a sigh of relief. "Thank God for soul mates." If Kat was simply some woman who Connor was dating instead of *The One* for him, the guy would probably be all up in Trevor's business. "I don't want to have to deal with him—not until I know if there's anything real between Jenna and me."

Trevor had only vaguely been aware Connor even had a "baby" sister and that she had witnessed the kidnapping of their other sister a decade ago. Connor refused to talk about what had happened but said that it had left Jenna mentally and emotionally scarred. Then, a few weeks ago, Jenna had shown up in Dallas to visit Connor. Trevor had been attracted to her on the spot. Like...seriously attracted. Unfortunately, he'd barely said two words to her before Connor lost his damn mind, telling Trevor to stay away from his sister because she was too "fragile" to handle any kind of relationship with someone after everything that had happened to her. Connor hadn't said it out loud, but Trevor was pretty sure there was also a certain amount of that you-aren't-good-enough-for-my-sister crap going on as well.

Considering the fact that Connor had been acting like a complete jackass, it wasn't shocking Jenna had gotten into an argument with her brother. What was surprising was that instead of going to a hotel, she'd asked Trevor if she could stay with him while she was in Dallas. He didn't have to think twice about agreeing.

"So," Hale's deep voice came through the phone,

startling Trevor out of his reveries. "Have you given any thought to what you're going to do if Jenna is *The One* for you—or how you'll break it to Connor?"

Trevor's mouth curved as he thought of how much fun he'd had hanging out with Jenna back in Dallas. They'd spent hours talking and laughing about the silliest things. And while it would have been easy to do a lot more than that together, he knew that in some ways, Connor was right. Jenna might put on a good face, but she was still dealing with the trauma of seeing whatever had happened to her sister. Trevor hadn't wanted to rush her into anything, but the whole time they'd been together, he couldn't stop himself from thinking about what could be...if they had time to explore it.

Which was why he'd jumped at the chance to come out to LA when Jenna had asked.

He stared at the warehouse building in front of him. "If Jenna is my soul mate, then I'll worry about telling Connor. Until then, I'm not going to think about him."

He expected pushback on that, waited for Hale to tell him he was being stupid...silly even. But his teammate, his pack mate, and his friend didn't do any of that.

"I wish you all the luck in the world then," Hale said. "And don't worry about Connor finding out before you're ready to tell him. I've got your back."

Trevor still wasn't sure how Hale had figured out he had a thing for Jenna or that she'd been staying at his place. He knew it wasn't because Hale had picked up her scent because, seriously, the guy had the worst nose in the Pack. But somehow, Hale had, and Trevor would be forever grateful. Coming out here to California to woo the woman who *might* be his soul mate was nerve-racking as hell. It helped to know he had someone on his side.

"I'll call you later and let you know how things go," Trevor said.

It was time to stop talking and do this.

Shoving his phone in the pocket of his jeans, Trevor took a deep breath, trying to psych himself up. He didn't know why he was so damn nervous. But talking to Jenna a few times a week since she'd left Dallas—even FaceTiming now and then when they got the chance—was one thing. Showing up in LA was another. It was a big step—even if his inner wolf insisted he was ready for it.

Well, ready or not, he was here.

Tightening his hold on the handle of the weekender bag in his hand, Trevor opened the door, walked inside, and headed for the steps.

The interior of the building was a lot nicer than the exterior, but it still had a decidedly industrial feel, with lots of exposed concrete and steel support beams. There was some splashy, colorful modern art on the walls here and there, which wasn't exactly

Trevor's thing, but it all came together in a way that seemed to work.

Jenna's delectable scent hit him the moment he reached the second floor. Then again, he supposed there was always a chance someone was simply burning candles in their apartment. That could explain the heavenly scent of honeysuckles filling the air. When he finally reached Jenna's door at the end of the hallway and breathed in the flowery fragrance wafting gently out from underneath it, he knew for a fact it could only be Jenna's scent. In all honesty, he'd already known that because it was the very same one that had enveloped him since he'd first met her back in Dallas. There was no mistaking it.

Heart beating faster, he rapped his knuckles on the door. It opened a few seconds later to reveal the most beautiful woman in the world he'd ever set eyes on. Maybe it was simply the fact that he'd been waiting for weeks to see her in person again, but she was even more gorgeous than she'd been the last time he'd seen her.

Slender and graceful, with perfect skin, soft pink lips, a button nose, and hazel eyes gazing out from under graceful arching brows, she looked like an elf who'd just stepped out of a *Lord of the Rings* movie. While in Dallas, she'd usually worn her hair up in a high ponytail, but now, her honey-blonde hair was loose around her shoulders, the silky waves hanging down to her waist. It was all he could do to not reach out and run his fingers through it and feel its softness. Hell, what he really wanted to do was bury his face in those tresses and breathe her in. The only urge stronger than that was the one demanding he sweep her into his arms and kiss her until they were both out of breath.

Crap. He'd been standing in front of Jenna for who knew how long, neither of them saying a word, and he was already about to lose it. Damn, he was in so much trouble.

Before he could open his mouth, Jenna rushed forward and threw her arms around him, squeezing him so tightly it practically choked the air out of him. Strangely, it was still the best hug he'd ever gotten. Not that he was like a big hugger or anything. But if he were, her hug would have been award winning. Easily two thumbs up and five stars.

The air was electric between them when Jenna finally stepped back, gazing up at him with expressive eyes that were filled with innocence and fire at the same time. His lips were tingling with the desire to bend his head and kiss her, even as it seemed she might do the same thing at any second.

But then the moment passed, and Jenna took a step back, a brilliant smile lighting up her face as he fought for the ability to breathe again. Yup, she would almost certainly be the death of him.

"I'm guessing your flight was horrible?" she

asked, glancing over her shoulder as she led him into her apartment. "I saw on the airline website that your takeoff was delayed multiple times. They didn't give any details though."

Closing the door behind him, Trevor followed her into the living room and set his bag down beside the comfortable-looking couch, then took a look around. Jenna's apartment continued with the industrial feel he'd taken note of in the lobby, but there was a warmth to it that had been missing downstairs. That was probably thanks to the old movie posters and soft wall hangings. They softened the otherwise harsh tone of the place. Her taste in decor had turned the apartment from cold to cozy. He could definitely get used to it, that was for sure.

Not that I'm assuming I'll have the chance to get used to it, he quickly told himself. *Just, you know, if things go that way.*

He was about to answer Jenna's earlier question about the delayed flight when a petite red-haired woman walked into the room from the kitchen, a glass of wine in her hand. It struck him then that he'd been so focused on Jenna that he hadn't even paused to check to see if there was anyone else in the apartment with her. Not to mention so wrapped up in Jenna's scent that he hadn't been able to smell anyone else.

Yet another indication that his inner werewolf had it as bad for Jenna as he did.

"Oh, I almost forgot." Jenna said, laughing as she pointed at the redhead. "This is my next-door neighbor—and very best friend—Madeleine Waller. She's been keeping me company while I waited for you to get here."

"Nice to meet you," Madeleine said with a smile, reaching out with her free hand to shake his. "Jenna has told me a lot about you. Honestly, that's the biggest reason I'm here. I had to see if you lived up to all the hype."

"Hype?" he questioned, throwing a quick look at Jenna, who seemed to be blushing a bit at the moment.

It was Madeleine's turn to laugh. "Don't worry about it. Just girl talk," she said with a wave of her hand before draining the last of her wine, then moving into the open kitchen to set the glass on the counter. "But now that you're here, I'll be on my way and give you two some time to catch up."

Jenna tried to get her friend to stay, saying something about dinner, but Madeleine simply waved her hand again as she headed for the door. "You know what they say about three being a crowd." She grinned. "I'll check in with you tomorrow so you can fill me in on your reunion."

It was impossible to miss the innuendo in Madeleine's tone, not to mention the sly look she gave Jenna as she left. Something told him that Jenna and Madeleine were the kind of friends who confided in each other about everything. Trevor had to admit that he wondered what they'd said about him.

"You never did answer my question about your flight," Jenna said, walking into the kitchen. Opening the oven, she reached inside to take something out. Something that smelled awesome.

How the hell had he missed the aroma of tomatoes, garlic, and cheese? Had this attraction to Jenna completely broken his nose?

"Yeah," he finally managed. "We were delayed on the tarmac because one of the planes ahead of us had mechanical issues. It ended up turning a three-and-a-half -hour flight into seven."

She set the casserole on the table, then glanced over her shoulder at him as she walked over to the fridge. "Ugh. That sounds dreadful."

His mouth edged up. "It was worth it."

He thought she might have blushed a little at that, but she ducked into the fridge before he could be sure. A moment later, she turned back around, holding up a bottle of beer in one hand and wine in the other, a brow raised in his direction. He pointed at the beer.

"This is the part where I'm supposed to say that you didn't need to go to the trouble to make me something to eat," he said. "But to be honest, it's been a long day, and I'm starving."

"It wasn't any trouble," Jenna said with a smile,

handing him the beer, then pouring some wine into a glass for herself. "I thought you might be hungry after the flight, so I'd already planned to have a big dish of baked ziti ready for you. Grab a seat while I get everything set out."

"Can I do anything to help?" he asked.

He wasn't going to be on *MasterChef* anytime soon, that was for sure, but he could find his way around a kitchen okay when he had to.

"I'm good," she said. "Sit."

Trevor opened his mouth to make the offer again, but Jenna was already shooing him over to the glass-topped table. He pulled out a chair and sat down, watching as she moved around the kitchen. A big bowl of salad and basket of garlic bread joined the table with the baked ziti, their combined aromas making his mouth water. He couldn't remember the last time someone had cooked dinner for him. Even if there was nothing serious going on between them—yet—it still made him feel good.

"Did my pain-in-the-ass brother give you a lot of grief about coming out here to see me?" Jenna asked as she slipped into the chair opposite him.

Trevor was too busy enjoying his first bite of the pasta, meat, and cheese combination to answer right away. To say it was delicious was an understatement. If he wasn't so focused on maintaining his cool, manly exterior, he might have groaned out loud.

"He probably would have…if I'd told him," Trevor finally said. "But Connor—and most of the SWAT team—think I'm visiting my family in Virginia."

Jenna regarded him for a moment, a forkful of salad halfway to her mouth. "I hope that doesn't mean you're embarrassed to be hanging out with me."

"Not a chance," he said firmly. "If you want, I'll pick up the phone and call your brother right now and tell him exactly where I am. But you know as well as I do that Connor will be on the next flight out here so he can do everything he can to keep us apart. I'd prefer to spend the week getting to know each other on our own terms without his interference."

She made a face, then nodded. "You're not wrong about that. Connor would definitely be sticking his nose where it doesn't belong. Which is why I don't have a problem keeping this from my brother, especially after the way he behaved when I was in Dallas. But you know that at some point, he's going to find out."

"Let him." Trevor reached across the table to rest his hand gently atop hers. "If we decide we want to see each other, that's our decision, not his. He can complain all he wants, but it won't change anything for us."

Across from him, Jenna smiled, her face

immediately lighting up. Her reaction did something silly to Trevor's insides, and he couldn't help but wonder if it was possible to become addicted to seeing someone else so happy.

While her brother should be the last thing either of them wanted to talk about, as they ate dinner, he and Jenna ended up exchanging funny stories about Connor, from the Halloween costumes he'd worn as a kid to all the silly things he'd done back in Dallas. They had so much fun that Trevor would gladly have stayed up all night talking, but a little while after they finished eating, Jenna yawned, her eyes looking tired. He glanced at the clock on the stove and saw that it was nearly eleven.

"Sorry," Jenna said, hiding another yawn behind her hand. "I've been working overtime for eight days straight so that I wouldn't have to go into the office while you're here. I guess all those late nights are catching up to me."

"No need to apologize. It was a long day, and I'm pretty tired, too," he said. "Come on. Let's go to bed."

Pushing back his chair, he got to his feet and collected their dirty dishes, ignoring Jenna's objections when she said she'd take care of cleaning up. It wasn't until Trevor was helping her load the dishwasher that he realized what he'd just said. It sounded like he was assuming they were going to sleep together. Which he didn't. He was more than ready to go there if that was something Jenna wanted, but he was definitely going to let her take the lead on that. He sent a covert glance in her direction to see if she'd read more into his comment than he'd intended and was relieved to see that she hadn't.

"Come on," Jenna said after they'd finished cleaning up. "I'll show you the guest room."

Trevor followed her through the living room and down the short hallway off it, grabbing his weekender bag on the way. The door to her bedroom was opened, and as they walked past it, he caught a glimpse of soft fabrics, plump pillows, and tranquil colors, along with more movie posters, graphic art, and framed photos all over the walls. The apartment's lone bathroom was ahead of them, at the end of the hall. He could just make out a counter with double sinks through the partially open door.

"Forgive the mess," Jenna said as she led him into the room on the left. "I use the guest bedroom as a home office. Or well...more of a workshop really. I do a lot of painting and sculpting work in here when the mood strikes, which is frequently. I cleaned up as much as I could, but it still smells like paint and clay."

He could definitely smell it. But then again, with his nose, Jenna could scrub the room for a month and he'd still be able to pick it up. Not that he cared. Something told him that when he fell asleep tonight, the only thing he'd be able to smell were honeysuckles.

He was about to tell her that he couldn't smell a thing to allay any worries she had, but the words got stuck in his mouth the moment he saw those paintings and sculptures she'd mentioned.

From their conversations back in Dallas, Trevor knew Jenna worked in the movie industry and that while she did some regular glamour makeup, as she called it, she mostly made her living by creating monsters. But while he'd understood that as a concept, it hadn't sunk in until now, when he saw all the scary crap filling the room.

The unframed paintings were startling to say the least. Creatures like nothing he'd ever seen or even imagined filled canvas after canvas. Blood-red eyes looked back at him, faces full of anguish, teeth so jagged and broken that they conveyed both terror and pity.

But as disturbing as the paintings were, it was the full-body sculptures that lined the far wall that genuinely gave him pause. Drawn to them, he crossed the room, studying each one as he came to it. There was a vampire, a zombie, a mummy, and even a traditional Hollywood werewolf, complete with a long snout, its lips pulled back showing off razor-sharp fangs. It was incredibly realistic, right down to the thick ruff of fur around the neck. For a moment, Trevor wondered what Jenna would say if she saw a real werewolf. If she saw *him* in his shifted form, four legs, tail, and all.

As he progressed around the room, the sculptures became darker and more twisted. He wasn't sure if they were supposed to be mythological creatures or simply something out of Jenna's imagination. Either way, it was astounding how someone as sweet as she was could create such messed-up stuff. And that was coming from a guy who'd seen his fair share of things that go bump in the night.

The last three creatures in line were shorter, but he couldn't make out any details, since all three were covered with white sheets.

"Those are works in progress," she said, coming over to stand beside him, her voice a little tense and her eyes darting to the side, like she was nervous that he'd want to see them or something. "I keep them covered until they're completely done."

Trevor was about as far away from an artist as a person could get, so he didn't even attempt to unpack what Jenna might mean by *works in progress* and why she wouldn't want anyone to see. So instead, he simply nodded.

"There are fresh towels in the bathroom if you want to shower first," Jenna said.

"Thanks."

He showered and brushed his teeth in something less than five minutes. As a cop, he got used to cleaning up fast. After toweling off, he put on a pair of shorts and a T-shirt, then called out to Jenna that the bathroom was free as he slipped back into the guest bedroom-slash-monster workshop.

In the bathroom, he heard Jenna turn on the water, then step into the tub. Seconds later, he picked up the scent of coconut shower gel, and unbidden, the image of foamy soap suds sliding down naked smooth skin popped into his head. The reaction going on in his shorts was immediate and intense and suggested he might need to go back for another shower. A cold one. It didn't help that the fragrance of the body wash Jenna was using seemed to combine with her own scrumptious scent, making him damn near drool. He had no idea how he'd ever get to sleep tonight.

Jenna finished showering a lot faster than Trevor thought she would. He'd barely gotten a chance to do more than pull down the blankets on the bed before she showed up at the door, looking positively mesmerizing in a pair of shorts and a tank top.

Don't stare...don't stare...don't stare.

"Do you have everything you need?" she asked, stepping into the room and glancing at the bed and the blankets he'd pulled down. "I can get you some more pillows or another blanket if you think you'll be cold."

"No, I'm good. Thanks," Trevor said, even as the voice in the back of his head whispered that the only thing he needed was right here in front of him.

"Sorry to put you through all this trouble. Making dinner—which was delicious, by the way—and cleaning up in here."

Jenna moved closer, coming to a stop right in front of him, her angelic face tilted up so she could gaze at him. "It was no trouble at all," she said softly. "I'm glad you came out to see me. It means a lot. More than you'll probably ever realize."

Trevor was about to ask what she meant by that last part, but as he opened his mouth to speak, Jenna went up on her toes, her warm lips landing lightly on his cheek.

As fast as it had come, the kiss ended, and Jenna was backing up with a slight smile tugging up the corners of her mouth and a blush coloring her face. "Good night."

"G'night," Trevor mumbled, standing there like a dimwitted twit as she walked out of the bedroom and across the hallway into her own, leaving him to think about what had just happened even as his face tingled where she'd kissed him.

As kisses went, it had to be the most chaste one he'd ever gotten, but he found himself smiling all the same, deciding he'd never trade that simple touch on the cheek for anything in the world.

Jenna was *The One* for him. There was no doubt in his mind of that. Now, he had to figure out how to explain to her that she was his soul mate. Without making her think he was off his rocker.

He walked over to the door to turn off the light, resisting as his inner wolf urged him to keep moving right across that hallway and into Jenna's room. Instead, he took a deep breath, breathing in her heavenly scent for a few seconds before heading back to his bed.

Sighing, he lay back on the soft mattress, listening to Jenna toss and turn across the hall. She seemed to find a comfortable position quickly enough, though, and within moments, he heard the rhythmic sounds of her even breathing as she fell asleep.

He stared up at the ceiling in the darkness, mind racing at the likelihood that he had truly found his soul mate. He'd been pretty sure even before coming out to California—hence the reason he'd come out here in the first place—but being *pretty sure* was drastically different from knowing. And now that he was here and feeling more alive than he had in the weeks since they'd been separated, he knew for certain. Jenna was *The One* for him, the woman he'd been waiting a good portion of his adult life for, even if he'd never known it.

Part of him wanted to run over to Jenna's room right this second and tell her the big news. Fortunately, it wasn't hard to resist that psychotic idea. He could only imagine how she'd react if he suddenly started spouting off lines about werewolves, fated love, and destiny. It wasn't a very pretty picture. No, he was going to have to take this slowly and let Jenna come to her own conclusions about the bond developing between the two of them.

Of course, there was one person who could screw up that extremely reasonable plan—Connor. His pack mate had damn near blown a gasket when Trevor had done nothing more than look at his sister. What would he do when he found out that she was Trevor's soul mate?

Would he attempt to get between them after knowing they were destined to be together? Considering how overprotective Connor was when it came to his sister, almost certainly, even though he'd just found his own soul mate.

Would it come to a fight between him and Connor? Yeah, probably.

Trevor was still thinking about that when he *felt* someone watching him. For half a second, he thought it was Jenna, but then he realized the sensation wasn't coming from the doorway but inside the room. Somewhere close, too. He darted a quick look toward the window, not sure how someone could get up to the second floor, much less do so without him smelling them.

But no one was there.

And yet he continued to feel eyes on him.

Lots of eyes.

It only took a few more seconds to realize that

the only things in the room with him were Jenna's clay sculptures. He glanced at them to see that all the creatures were facing his direction. And with the way the glow of the streetlamps came through the window and bounced off their deep-set eyes, it was like they were staring at him.

He felt silly for even admitting it to himself, but the damn things were creepy as hell. It was like they were sizing him up to eat or something. He rolled over onto his side so his back was to them, telling himself to forget about the sculptures and to focus on thoughts of Jenna. He'd fall asleep soon enough anyway.

But ten minutes later, he was still wide awake, the back of his neck tingling uncomfortably at the sensation of being watched. With a growl, he got up and turned all the sculptures around to face the wall, then got back in bed. There was no way he'd ever be able to get any sleep with them staring at him all night.

CHAPTER 2

"YOU'RE GOING TO LOVE THIS PLACE," JENNA SAID as Trevor held the door open for her and they walked into the downtown 1940s style diner. Decorated in cream and maroon, the old-fashioned counter and classic light fixtures gave it a vintage feel that made customers think they stepped back in time.

"I feel bad making you run around all over the place like this," Trevor said as he and Jenna slid into a booth in the back. "I'm sure it must be boring as heck for you to be doing all this tourist stuff when you've lived in LA your whole life."

She laughed. "Are you kidding me? I haven't done any of this stuff since I was a kid. I had an amazing time. Though I think I might have scheduled too many attractions for us to do in one day. I'm exhausted."

Trevor let out a deep chuckle, the sound making her feel warm all over. "Yeah. Visiting the Natural History Museum, Venice Beach, Santa Monica Pier, Hollywood Boulevard, Los Angeles Zoo, and the Griffith Observatory all in one day might have been a bit ambitious." He reached over to pluck two menus from the wire rack near the wall by their booth, holding one of them out to her. "Maybe tomorrow we should pick out one or two places to see."

"Deal," she agreed, taking the menu from him, even though she already knew what she was going to order.

She ate here on the reg, partly because the food was seriously ah-mazing, and partly because the diner was close to Skid Row with its maze of back alleys and the large number of unhoused people who frequented the area. But she couldn't tell Trevor that.

"Well, if you're looking for one big attraction that will keep us occupied all day tomorrow," she said, setting the menu aside and looking across the table at the extraordinarily attractive man she'd been lucky enough to spend the whole day with, "then you're talking either Universal Studios or Disneyland. Your choice."

"Either of those sounds good to me." Trevor placed his own menu on the table, then smiled and reached over to take her hand. "But honestly, it doesn't matter where we go. I'm having fun simply hanging out with you."

If they weren't in a crowded diner, Jenna would have probably thrown herself across the table and hugged the stuffing out of him. And kissed him, too. Yeah, there'd be a lot of that. What else could you do when you found a guy so completely perfect?

When she'd met Trevor in Dallas, the first word that had popped into her head was *gorgeous*. Tall and muscular with dark, silky hair, he had soulful brown eyes that pulled you in and a jawline perpetually roughened with sexy scruff. Seriously, Adonis would cry like a baby at the sight of this man.

It wasn't until her jackass brother had opened his mouth and insulted her that Trevor had shown her what kind of man he truly was, however. He'd given her a place to stay, someone to rant to, even a shoulder to cry on. All without asking a single question. He hadn't even inquired what her butt flake of a brother had said to make her so mad. He'd simply accepted that she needed his help and had provided it.

She'd be the first to admit that she developed a thing for Trevor incredibly fast. But she hadn't realized how strong her feelings were until she'd come home. That was when she found herself thinking about him all the time, even dreaming about him at night. Worse, she sometimes got this ache in her chest when she thought about how much she missed him. To be honest, it scared her a little to think about how quickly he'd found a place in her heart.

Still, when she'd suggested that he come out to LA to see her and he'd agreed, it had been like a weight she hadn't even realized was there had lifted off her chest and she could breathe again. And now that Trevor was here, all she could do was hope that he'd stay longer than the week they'd planned on. It was an extraordinary rush.

Their server showed up before Jenna could tell Trevor that she loved hanging out with him, too.

"Hey, girl," the dark-haired waitress said, giving Jenna a smile. "Want the usual?"

Jenna grinned. When you went to a restaurant as regularly as she came here, it was only natural to become friends with the people who worked there. And Cindy was one of the best. "Yup. Chili burger with cheese, fries on the side, and a glass of iced tea."

This place was known for comfort food, and that had been her go-to order since the first time she'd eaten here.

"And for you?" Cindy said, looking at Trevor.

"Sounds so good I'll take the same," he said. "But make mine two burgers and a double order of fries. Oh, and could you add a plate of onion rings, too?"

"Sure thing," Cindy said, jotting it down on her notepad. "I'll get those iced teas right out to you."

Trevor put their menus back in the holder as Cindy walked away, then looked at Jenna. "Since she knew what you were going to order, I'm guessing you come here frequently."

Jenna nodded, her lips curling into a smile. "Yeah. I found this place a couple months ago. I immediately fell in love with it and have been coming back once a week or so ever since."

As they ate, she and Trevor talked about the places they'd been to that day while out sightseeing. Jenna nodded and responded in all the right places, but at the same time, she found herself thinking about the real reason she came back to this part of town every week.

Two months ago, she'd been wandering the alleys of the nearby Skid Row, hoping against hope to find her missing sister, Hannah, among the hundreds of unhoused people who lived in that part of town. Finding someone who'd been missing for nearly a decade seemed impossible, but she'd never given up on her sister and she never would.

Then one night, Jenna had seen a woman she was sure was Hannah darting through the shadows. Before she even realized what she was doing, she called out her sister's name. The woman had whirled around to look right at her, and in the glow coming from a streetlight, Jenna recognized her sister's face. But instead of running over to her, Hannah had turned and headed in the other direction. Jenna had chased after her, frantically calling her name, but Hannah disappeared down a manhole into the sewer. Going after her wasn't an option. Jenna simply didn't do dark places like that. Claustrophobia had never been an issue for her when she was a kid, not until her sister had been kidnapped. Now, it was a major part of her life.

Jenna had been coming back to this same part

of town since that night, hoping to stumble across her sister again. This diner served as a great place to start from, since it provided takeout meals for the unhoused, which she took with her whenever she traveled the back alleys. The meals served two purposes—feeding people who could really use the help as well as providing cover for why Jenna would be wandering around that part of town so late at night.

"Maybe we should head back home after dinner," Trevor said, dragging Jenna out of her thoughts and back to the present.

She gave herself a mental shake. "What?" she asked.

How much had she missed? If the amount of food left on her plate was any indication, especially compared to Trevor's nearly empty one, she got the feeling she'd been zoned out for a while.

Trevor's mouth curved into a small smile. "I was saying that you seem a little out of it. Considering how much running around we did today, I'm not surprised you're tired. We can head back to your place after dinner if you want instead of going to a movie."

Jenna shook her head. "I'm fine. I was just lost in thought. That's all."

Trevor looked skeptical at that, but he didn't push, which Jenna appreciated. Whenever she ate at the diner, she always brought meals to the unhoused who lived there, and she didn't intend to detour from that tonight. And who could blame her if she looked for her sister while they were there?

Unable to tell him that, she hoped to distract him by reaching over and stealing a french fry off his plate. The expression of mock horror on his face at the move almost made her laugh.

"Hey! Why are you stealing my food when you still have plenty on your own plate?"

"I wasn't stealing," she corrected, nibbling on the fry in her hand. "I'm merely checking to see if your fries taste better."

Grinning, Trevor grabbed a fry off her plate and shoved it into his mouth. "Mmm. You might be onto something. Your fries so taste better than mine."

They both laughed at that, his earlier comment about going directly home completely forgotten, which was good. They couldn't go back to her place—or even the movie—without first going to Skid Row. Jenna felt a little bad about not being completely honest with Trevor about her motives for coming to this particular part of town, but it was for a good cause. At least that was what she told herself.

She ended up letting Trevor eat most of her fries. There were more than she could handle, and he definitely still looked hungry. Besides, sharing them with him made her feel a little better about fibbing to him. But in the end, he motioned for their server and ordered more fries for them anyway.

"So how did you get into special effects makeup?" he asked, dunking a handful of fries in ketchup. "It doesn't seem like a career I would have expected you to end up in."

"Why?" she asked with a snort. "Because I'm a woman instead of a Star Trek–watching fanboy who looks like he lives in his parents' basement?"

Trevor looked chagrined for all of a second. "Um…actually…that's pretty much exactly what I was thinking. Can you blame me?"

Jenna couldn't help but laugh. "Okay, if I'm being honest, you did just describe an extremely large percentage of the students taking the FX—special effects—track with me at the makeup school I went to here in LA. So I guess I can see your point."

"Makeup school? Is that like a college program or something?"

"Not quite," Jenna said, then went into her standard spiel about the special effects education industry, telling him that while there were some college programs for it, most of them were overly broad. "You can get a bachelors in filmmaking at a handful of universities and colleges, but if you want to specialize in movie makeup and effects, you need to go to a place like I did. It's expensive, but you end up learning from the people who do this stuff for a living. The FX track I received my diploma in consisted of nothing but makeup, creature design, and creature fabrication. With the connections I made there, I had a job in the industry before I even graduated."

"Okay, that explains where you learned how to do the stuff you do, but that still doesn't answer my original question," Trevor said. "What made you start down this monster-making path to begin with?"

Jenna hesitated, not really sure how much her brother had already told Trevor about the events following Hannah's disappearance. And if he didn't know anything about that, Jenna wasn't sure how much she wanted to get into it. She liked where the connection developing between her and Trevor was going, and she didn't want to mess it up by having him think she was mentally unstable or something.

"Art was always my thing when I was a kid," she said, sipping the iced tea Cindy had refilled for her when she brought the extra serving of fries. She was comfortable enough to reveal this part of her life. "I was drawing before I was five and sculpting by the age of eight. I had no idea exactly how it would work out, but I knew someday I'd make a living as an artist."

Trevor nodded but didn't say anything. It was the acceptance in his eyes that allowed her to keep going and reveal a little bit more of herself to this man.

"I'm not sure what, if anything, my brother has told you about the events surrounding the disappearance of our sister, Hannah," she said softly, raising a brow and waiting for him to respond.

"Not much," he admitted. "I know that you were there when your sister was kidnapped and that it was very traumatic for you. That's all he ever told us."

"That's enough for the purposes of this conversation," she said, relieved that Connor hadn't spilled all her secrets. "Suffice it to say, I had a hard time right after my sister disappeared, for a variety of reasons. I ended up in therapy, trying to find a way to cope with my feelings about that night. Long story short, my art became that coping mechanism. It allowed me to express my emotions without having to talk about them. It allowed me to get everything out."

Trevor regarded her thoughtfully, as if considering that. "Okay. But what about the creatures in your workroom? How did you get from a mechanism to help you cope with your trauma to that?"

Jenna finished the last of her burger before answering, using the time to come up with the best way to answer him. In the end, she gritted her teeth and went with the truth—or at least a version of it.

"The things I went through with my sister, and everything that happened afterward, left me with a different perspective on the world, I guess you could say. So now, I draw and sculpt the things I see in my head. I'm sorry if that alarms you or makes you think of me differently."

Trevor didn't say anything, but it was obvious from his expression that he was trying to work through everything she'd dumped on him. Jenna held her breath, waiting for him to say something. It was probably only a few seconds before he finally spoke, but it seemed like an eternity to her.

"I don't know the details, but it's obvious you went through something at a very young age that nobody at any age should ever have to go through," he said quietly. "There are a lot of people in the world who would have caved, but you found a way to deal with it and thrive. Why the hell should I ever be anything but impressed by something like that? Even if I do have to turn your creatures around to face the wall so I can sleep in the same room with them."

Jenna laughed a little, both because he didn't want her masterpieces to stare at him while he slept and because she hadn't freaked him out so badly that he wanted to catch the next flight back to Dallas. She counted that as a win.

After that big reveal, the tone of the conversation changed and became lighter. Trevor asked lots of questions about the kind of stuff she'd done in her FX program and how that compared to the work she was doing on movies and TV shows now. Jenna found herself relaxing and enjoying the chance to chat about what she loved doing without having to feel like she was being judged for it. Outside her colleagues and Madeleine, everyone seemed to think there was something wrong with her for the images that came out of her head. That included her brother and their parents, she was sad to say.

"You two leave room for dessert?" a feminine voice intruded, pulling Jenna out of the moment. She looked up to see Cindy standing there with a knowing smile on her face. "If it helps you decide, we just finished a batch of maple bacon doughnuts. They're still warm."

Jenna laughed at the expression that appeared on Trevor's face, which could only be described as enraptured. "I think we can take that as a yes," she told Cindy. "We'll take half a dozen with extra maple syrup."

"Coming right up." Cindy scribbled a note on her pad. "Will you also be ordering any takeout meals like you normally do?"

From the corner of her eye, Jenna saw the look of confusion on Trevor's face. She ignored it for the moment, instead nodding at Cindy. "I'll take a dozen meals. But can you hold them until we're ready to leave?"

"Definitely. And thanks a lot for the help." Cindy smiled. "I'll bring the meals out with the check."

Across from Jenna, Trevor gave her a questioning look. "Meals?"

"They're meals for the unhoused," Jenna explained. "A lot of the restaurants in this area offer them because there are a number of street people who call the back alleys of the Skid Row district home. I always buy meals anytime I'm here, then head over to hand them out. You don't mind, do you?"

Trevor shook his head. "Not at all. I think that's really awesome of you. I'd be happy to go with you and help. Do you normally do it on your own?"

Jenna didn't detect any of the harsh accusation in Trevor's voice she had when she'd told her brother she was walking around Skid Row at night, but there was definitely concern there.

"Normally," she said. "But I promise I'm always careful, and I always stick to the most well-lit parts of the district."

Honestly, very little of that was true, especially the last part, but Jenna didn't like the idea of Trevor worrying about her. Thankfully, Cindy showed up then with their dessert, which kept Trevor from asking for details, which would have certainly revealed how *not* careful she'd actually been lately.

"Enough about me," Jenna said as she helped herself to a doughnut, eager to keep Trevor from digging into her visits to Skid Row. "We've talked about me the entire day. Tell me something about you."

"What do you want to know?" he asked, taking

a big bite of the bacon-and-maple-syrup-covered doughnut, making little happy noises that were absolutely adorable as he chewed. She couldn't blame him. The sweet, sugary concoctions were to die for.

"Anything. Everything." She nibbled on her own doughnut. "Tell me about your family. Where did you grow up? How did you end up in Dallas? How long have you been a cop? How did you end up in SWAT? How long have you and my brother been friends?"

Trevor laughed, the sound a deep, sexy rumble. Jenna really liked it when he did that. It made her happy.

"I grew up in Virginia. Near Richmond, actually," he said, taking a much smaller bite of his second doughnut, apparently wanting to make it last. "I come from a big family with three brothers and two sisters, and we were all raised in a big farmhouse that has been in the family for over a hundred years."

"That must have been cool," Jenna said, even though she had a hard time imagining that many siblings. "Growing up on a farm, I mean."

He shrugged. "I guess it was, for the most part. Don't get me wrong. I had a great childhood. But if there's one thing I remember about growing up in a house full of six kids, it was the constant noise. There wasn't a day that passed when one of us wasn't shouting or arguing about something. After eighteen years of it, the constant noise started to get to me."

Jenna caught Cindy's eye across the diner and motioned for her to bring another serving of doughnuts. Trevor had already inhaled five of the things while she was still nursing hers, and he looked like he might reach over and nab a bite of hers any second.

"So...what, you left home and ran off to Dallas to join the SWAT team?" she asked him.

"You make it sound like I ran off to join the circus," he said with a chuckle. "But no, it wasn't quite like that. When I made the decision to leave home, I had no idea what I wanted to do or where I wanted to go. I only knew that I needed to get out of the town where I'd spent my whole life. College wasn't what I was looking for, so I ended up joining the army."

Huh. Jenna wasn't completely shocked at hearing he'd enlisted in the military. Well...maybe a little... but only because she'd stayed in Trevor's apartment for almost a week when she was in Dallas and had never seen any pictures or mementos that would lead her to think he'd ever been in the army. It hadn't come up in any of their conversations either. Though, if she was being honest, Jenna would have to admit that she'd been a little distracted most of the time she was there, upset by thoughts of

Hannah and the horrible things Connor had said during their argument.

"I didn't know you were in the army," she said. "Were you a cop? What are they called…MPs?"

"Yeah, they're called Military Police—MPs," he said with a smile, helping himself to another doughnut that Cindy had brought over.

She'd long since given up on trying to understand how a man could eat like Trevor did and have a body that looked like his. He must have the metabolism of a wild animal or something. It should have been a crime.

"But no, I wasn't an MP in the army," he added after taking a sip of iced tea. "I was a mechanic, actually. I always loved working on cars and the equipment on the farm, so I thought it would be a good fit."

"I guess that explains the sweet classic Ford Thunderbird you told me you refurbished." She smiled as she remembered how much fun she'd had riding around Dallas with him, the top down on that cherry-red car.

"I found that car shortly after I became a patrol officer in the Dallas PD," Trevor said, his mouth curving into a fond smile. "I'd been a cop for all of a month when I got called out to help search for a missing kid. I ended up finding her trapped in a rusted-out shell of a car buried in the middle of a dilapidated barn on the back side of her family's property. Her parents wanted the barn bulldozed immediately, so I asked if they'd let me haul out the old car and whatever parts I could find before they did. Six years later, that rusted shell is the mint 1957 Thunderbird you enjoyed riding around in so much."

Jenna had at least a hundred questions regarding that story but decided to start with the part he'd obviously skipped over. "Wait a minute, I think we missed a step. How did you go from the army to being a cop in Dallas?"

She could see the hesitation in his eyes, even as he attempted to hide it. That immediately spiked her curiosity, and she wondered what he could be hiding.

"I was in the army for four years," he said slowly, focusing all his attention on the last few pieces of his bacon-covered doughnut. "But I ended up getting hurt during a deployment and made the decision to get out."

"You got hurt?" Her heart started to thump uncontrollably for no reason that made sense to her. "Was it bad? Are you okay now?"

"Relax," he said, his expression soft as he gazed at her. "I won't try and pretend what happened to me was fun, but I got through it and I'm fine now. Afterward, staying in the army wasn't an option, though. I'd been assigned to Fort Hood prior to the deployment, which is only about two hours from Dallas, so when I came back to do all the out-processing paperwork, it made sense to look around there for something else to do. One thing led to another, and I ended up becoming a cop. A few years later, I got recruited by SWAT."

Jenna didn't miss the fact that Trevor seemed to be leaving out most of the story. Her first instinct was to ask an endless stream of questions about exactly how he'd been injured, how bad those injuries had been, why he hadn't gone back home to Richmond after getting out of the army, and why he'd become a cop instead of doing any other job.

But before she could open her mouth and start interrogating him, she took a second to remember that there had been a significant event in her own life that she didn't like talking about. This was probably the same kind of thing, and from her own experience, she knew that trying to get a person to talk about a subject they'd rather not was the fastest way to shut them down for good.

Deciding to table all her questions for the moment, Jenna instead asked him about his time in SWAT and the people he worked with. It was immediately obvious that his teammates were special to him. From the way he smiled when he talked about them, it was like they were a second family to him.

They chatted about that until Cindy showed up with the check and a cardboard box filled with the takeout meals. Jenna reached for the bill, but Trevor got to it before she did, swiping the paper away seconds before her fingers got close.

"Okay, you can pay for dinner, but I'm paying for

the takeout meals," she said firmly, even as Trevor handed Cindy his credit card.

"Let me pay. Please," he said when Jenna held out her own card. "It's the least I can do considering the fact that you're letting me stay at your place this week and eat up all your food. Besides, I'll never be able to thank you enough for introducing me to maple bacon doughnuts. I'm not exaggerating when I say you've quite likely changed my whole life."

Jenna snorted at that, especially the stuff about the doughnuts. Still, she couldn't come up with a way to argue his point, so she let it go. And if she was being honest with herself, she sort of liked the idea of him stepping up and paying for dinner. Guys she dated didn't do anything like that, not unless they thought they were going to get something out of it. Something told her that Trevor had never entertained a thought like that in his life.

A few minutes later, Cindy came back with his card, telling them to have a great night. Trevor stood, collecting up the box of meals. "All right, let's go hand out this food."

Jenna smiled as they walked out of the diner and started down the sidewalk. Then she remembered she was essentially lying to him about why they were going to the Skid Row district, and a good portion of her happiness faded. She tried to tell herself that the end justified the means, but that didn't seem to help.

CHAPTER 3

When he and Jenna got to Skid Row, the area cluttered with tents and makeshift lean-to shelters, she led Trevor toward the back alleys instead of the larger clusters of people scattered along the main street. She waved at a few people and said hello to others, handing out meals along the way. But mostly, she focused on where she was going, every step taking them deeper and deeper into the darkness as she moved her head from side to side.

Like she was looking for something in particular.

Or someone.

When she made a beeline for a small group of people huddled in an alcove, he realized that must be who she was searching for.

"Trevor, I want you to meet Ada Hawkins and her daughter, Nicole," Jenna said, handing takeout containers to the two dark-haired women, then distributing more to the other people gathered there before flashing him a smile. "You wouldn't know it by looking at them, but they're some of the nicest zombies you'll ever meet."

He reached out to shake the women's hands but then did a double take when Jenna's words finally registered. *Zombies*. Ada and Nicole didn't smell dead.

"Um...what?"

Ada laughed at the expression on his face, the lines around her gray eyes becoming more pronounced. "Jenna helped us get a job on the set of one of the TV series she works on a few months ago. The first roles we had were as zombie extras. The director liked us so much that she brought us back for other parts. It turns out that being a monster pays pretty good."

"I only wish I could find enough work to get you and Nicole into a better living situation," Jenna said sadly.

Ada took Jenna's hand and gave it a squeeze. "You're doing more than enough for us, hon. We're okay. If we can keep working and saving all our money, we should be able to find a place to live by next year. Maybe even get Nicole signed up for some of those college classes you mentioned."

Trevor listened as Jenna discussed other extra roles Ada and her daughter might be right for as well as second-set directors she wanted to introduce them to, even a few apartment complexes they might want to look at when they felt they had enough money saved up for a deposit.

It wasn't long before the other unhoused people gathered around them. Jenna knew each of them by name, and from the way she asked how they were feeling, if they were eating enough, and if they were staying warm at night, it was obvious she truly cared about all of them.

Trevor was talking to Nicole about what it was like being an extra on a TV show when he noticed Jenna and Ada move off to the side a few feet away from where he and the rest of the group were standing. Jenna leaned in close and whispered something to the older woman, who immediately nodded. With his keen werewolf hearing, Trevor could easily have eavesdropped on the conversation but didn't. Then he saw Jenna throw a covert glance over her shoulder, peeking his way without trying to make it look like she was. That was a guilty look if he'd ever seen one.

"Aaron saw one a few nights ago two streets over in the alley off Winston across from the Mission," he heard Ada say to Jenna, her tone full of fear. "The thing tried to grab Rubi. It would have gotten her, too, if she hadn't beat it off with that old, rusty walker of hers."

"Crap," Jenna said. "Is Rubi okay?"

"Yeah. She's still shaken up, though," Ada said. "She can probably give you some more information if you want to talk to her."

Jenna nodded. "Thanks. I'll talk to her before we leave."

Before Trevor could figure out what to make of all that, Jenna was already heading back over to him, a smile on her face. She picked up the cardboard box that was on the ground beside him, which still had three takeout containers in it.

"There are a few other people I want to visit tonight, including an older woman I'm worried about," she said, gazing up at him with an expression that was so innocent Trevor had to wonder if maybe he was wrong about something else going on here. "Just to make sure they get something to eat tonight. You don't mind, do you?"

"No problem," Trevor said, taking the box from her hands even as he decided he was definitely being played. While Jenna might care about the people living on Skid Row, she clearly had another motive for being here. He just didn't know what.

He wasn't shocked when Jenna led him to Winston Street and then continued into the back alleys near some kind of unhoused mission. He liked to think she simply wanted to check on the older woman like she claimed, but he got the feeling there was more to it than that.

Rubi was easy to find and impossible to miss. At least eighty years old with an aura of bustling energy about her, Trevor could easily imagine the woman beating on some attacker with the rusty metal walker she shambled around with. Jenna had introduced him, then handed Rubi all three of the takeout containers. She was in the middle of asking how Rubi was doing after the *bit of trouble* she'd had recently when a loud scream echoed through the alleys behind them.

Trevor immediately went into SWAT mode.

"Stay here," he said firmly to Jenna.

Not waiting for a reply, he turned and ran toward the sound. As he moved, his nose and ears began working overtime, pinpointing the source of the noise even among all the twisting and turning alleyways. He'd barely made it a block before realizing Jenna was following him.

Because of coursc she was.

The instinct to slide to a stop and tell Jenna to go back where it was safe was damn near impossible to resist. Unfortunately, he never got the chance to even seriously consider the action, since the next turn in the alley brought them both face-to-face with the woman screaming...and the thing dragging her across the asphalt like a she was a child's toy.

The creature's scent hit him even as Trevor attempted to comprehend what he was seeing. A combination of old dirt and oily musk, it was nearly overpowering to his sensitive nose. He'd never smelled anything like it. Probably because the creature was like nothing he'd ever seen before.

The thing stopped in its tracks, snapping its head around in Trevor's direction. It was maybe three feet tall—though it was difficult to be sure since it was hunched over. Trevor thought at first it was some kind of large baboon that had escaped from the zoo, but then he got a good look at the creature's thick shoulders, arms, and thighs. It was also pale and almost completely hairless except for a few wisps along its chest and belly. Nope, definitely not a baboon.

Trevor was still trying to figure out the best way to free the woman when the creature let out a possessive hiss and clamped its claw-tipped fingers around her lower leg even tighter. The woman, who couldn't be more than two or three years older than Jenna, fought like mad—kicking and punching at any part of the thing she could reach—and the creature didn't like it.

It snarled, lips peeling back to show canine fangs that were terrifyingly long for a creature of its size. It yanked on the woman's leg, like he was trying to tell her to shut up and stop fussing.

Trevor would have given anything to have his normal SIG 10mm with him, but bringing a handgun hadn't been an option for the trip out here, even if he had thought about needing one. Normally, not having a weapon wouldn't have been a major problem. As a werewolf, he came equipped with his own weapons.

Unfortunately, with Jenna right beside him and the unhoused woman in the creature's grasp, it wasn't like he could wolf out right there in the middle of the alley. He glanced around, looking for something he could use as a weapon, but didn't see anything.

As if the creature knew exactly how limited

Trevor's options were at the moment, it began to drag the struggling woman farther down the alley, ignoring her futile punches and kicks.

"Stay back," he said over his shoulder to Jenna, praying she paid attention to him this time.

Then he was off and running, charging forward at full speed. Well, as fast as he could go without shifting. He slowed just long enough to scoop up the heavy piece of wood lying on the ground in his path. It wasn't much, but the makeshift stake was the only thing in the alley that even came close to a weapon.

The creature must have taken Trevor's charge seriously because it tossed its would-be victim aside like a rag doll and moved to close the distance between them. At the same time, it spread its long, muscular arms wide and let loose a gut-twisting shriek that reverberated off the buildings to either side, echoing back at them over and over again.

Trevor launched himself at the creature, coming in high as he brought the wooden stake down toward the thing's chest. He didn't like the idea of taking out a living thing he knew absolutely nothing about, but the creature's actions in regard to the woman had clearly been harmful. Trevor couldn't take the chance of letting this thing go.

The creature tried to slash him on the way down but missed. Trevor's stake didn't, the roughly shaped point striking dead center in the middle of its chest with all the force his werewolf-enhanced strength could apply. The piece of wood, as blunt as it was, should have still pierced right through the creature's chest and come out the other side. Instead, it shattered into a dozen splinters right in Trevor's hand, not even scratching its pale and mottled skin.

He and the creature went down in a pile of limbs, the thing slashing out at him with claws that whistled as they cleaved the air. Trevor got an arm up just in time to block the incoming blow, and the move damn near broke his bones.

A punch to the creature's face felt like hitting a brick wall, with no damage to show for it. In desperation, he shoved against the thing's chest, sending it flying, only to see the creature bounce gracefully off the nearest wall to land on all fours a little farther down the alley. The thing's lips pulled back from its fangs once again, almost as if it was challenging Trevor to try again.

Trevor jumped to his feet, his back to Jenna and the injured woman she was dragging to safety. Realizing he was going to have to do something extreme to stop this thing, he let his body partially shift, fangs elongating and claws extending. He let out a low growl as the muscles of his shoulders and arms spasmed, twisting as they attempted to gain a drastically different form. The sound rumbled up softly through his chest, but he had no doubt the creature heard it.

The creature took a step back, eyes widening in alarm and confusion. Trevor knew his eyes were blazing yellow gold by now, which undoubtedly made him appear even more intimidating.

After another low growl from Trevor, the creature turned and ran.

"Stay with the woman," Trevor shouted at Jenna, not daring to look over his shoulder at her because he was afraid that she'd see his fangs in the dim light.

Without another word, he took off running, letting his nose lead him as he chased after the creature. Now that he didn't have an audience, Trevor could use his size, strength, and claws to deal with this thing.

The creature was unbelievably fast, leaping over dumpsters and piles of trash, bouncing off walls like some kind of parkour athlete. Whenever its claws hit brick or concrete, they scored long tracks in it, and all Trevor could imagine was what those claws would do to his flesh. Which prompted the question, what the hell was he going to do if he caught the damn thing?

That question was answered for him soon enough. One second, he and the creature were sprinting down a side street, and the next, the thing jumped into a hole in the ground and disappeared. Trevor didn't even slow to consider if following it was a good idea. He simply leaped into the hole and hoped for the best.

He landed in a pile of soggy cardboard and kept going, continuing the pursuit through the pitch-black tunnel. Even down in a sewer filled with stagnant water and worse, his nose could still pick up the creature's scent.

The trail ended at a small, jagged hole in the floor a few hundred feet later. Trevor would have thought someone made it with a jackhammer if it weren't for the claw marks gouged into the floor. Crap. The creature had dug this getaway hole through reinforced concrete. He knelt down and shoved his head through the hole in the floor, not sure how the creature had fit through it. But the strong smell of oily musk coming from the opening confirmed it had.

The passage below the sewer was narrow and roughly hewn out of the stone, concrete, and dirt there. Trevor would have fit but would have had to crawl on his hands and knees the whole time. Not the position he wanted to be in if that creature came at him again.

Knowing it would be stupid beyond measure to keep going after the creature in its own backyard, Trevor retracted his fangs and claws, then turned and headed back the way he'd come.

It took him a lot longer to get back to the alley off Winston Street than he would have liked. He hadn't realized he'd chased the creature for so long, and by the time he picked up Jenna's scent, it was surrounded by several others. Whoever they were, their presence made her heart beat faster. Trevor could almost feel her panic.

Adrenaline surging through his veins, he forced himself to keep his fangs and claws in check as he sprinted the rest of the way.

Four people were arrayed around Jenna as she knelt beside the injured woman. The new arrivals—two men and two women—were dressed like something out of a *Mad Max* movie, right down to the heavy biker boots, leather pants, and black dusters that hung down below their knees. They were hounding Jenna and the woman with endless stupid questions about what they'd seen as one of the men pointed a video camera in their direction. The panic was clear on Jenna's face, and she looked like she might start hyperventilating any minute.

Trevor didn't think. He simply reacted.

Closing the distance between them, he shoved the two men away from Jenna and the injured woman. Even though both men were clearly startled, the guy with the camera got himself together enough to point it at Trevor while the other guy shoved a microphone toward him, getting in his face and asking who he was and what his connection was to the *Skid Row Screamer*.

Deciding he really didn't like either of these guys, Trevor reached out and grabbed the one near him, shoving him and his stupid camera toward the closest dumpster. He would have put him *in* the dumpster but decided at the last second that might be a bit much.

Turning, Trevor knocked the microphone out of his face and got a handful of the second man's duster, ready to toss the jackass across the alley, but then Jenna was by his side, putting a calming hand on his shoulder.

"Trevor, stop," she said softly, her voice immediately penetrating the shroud of anger that had enveloped him. "It's okay. I know them. They can be a nuisance sometimes, but they're harmless."

Trevor didn't release his hold on the man's duster. While he wasn't sure the guy and his friends were as harmless as Jenna claimed, he'd give her the benefit of the doubt. Loosening his grip, Trevor let the jerk go with just the slightest nudge backward. The man immediately lifted the microphone again, but Trevor stopped him with a single uplifted finger.

"Put that thing in my face again—or Jenna's—and I'll shove it up your ass."

The guy apparently got the message, dropping the mic and letting it hang from the strap around his neck. The two women moved over to help the other man off the ground near the dumpster, who was wise enough to turn off his camera before coming toward them.

Trevor turned to check on the injured woman when Microphone Man stepped in front of him.

"I'm Owen Cobb," he said, extending his hand and not really giving Trevor any choice but to shake it. "I run the HOPD team. You've met my cameraman, Isaac Callahan. His sister, Esme, is our lead researcher," he added, gesturing to the blond, then at the dark-haired woman beside her. "And this is Maya Griffin, our main equipment operator."

Trevor stared at the man for a moment, wondering if they were actors or something, because he was pretty sure Owen was wearing makeup. He threw a glance in Jenna's direction, ready to ask her if this guy was for real. Unfortunately, she'd moved over to help the unhoused woman, using the woman's scarf to wrap around the deep scratches on her leg.

"HOPD?" he asked, turning back to Owen, though he wasn't quite sure if he truly wanted to know the answer to the question.

The dark-haired guy looked at Trevor in obvious disbelief. "You've never heard of Hunters of Paranormal Darkness? What, do you live under a rock or something? HOPD is the most recognized and respected team of paranormal investigators in LA. We're famous in a city full of famous people."

Trevor scanned the alleyway, looking for a hidden camera somewhere in the darkness. This guy must be trying to punk him. Right? No one could be that self-absorbed.

"What happened?" Esme asked, motioning toward the woman Jenna was still tending to. "We heard screaming and yelling from this direction. Did the *Skid Row Screamer* attack her?"

The excitement in Esme's dark eyes was downright disturbing. Trevor glanced at the other three members of HOPD to see that they all looked positively giddy at the idea that some kind of paranormal creature had attacked someone.

Trevor was about to ream them a new one for being a bunch of shallow, selfish jerks but was cut off by Jenna clearing her throat.

"We didn't get a good look at the thing, but it definitely wasn't human," Jenna said softly, capturing everyone's attention. "Trevor challenged it and the thing ran off that way," she added, pointing into the darkness deeper along the alley.

Trevor wasn't sure what he expected Jenna to say, but it wasn't all that. Then again, she had said she knew these people. He could only assume that meant she trusted them.

"Isaac, try and find a track. Esme, go with him," Owen said, sending the cameraman and his sister running off into the darkness, then turning to look at Trevor. "That was very brave of you," he said, reaching out to clap Trevor on the shoulder. "But you should never confront an unknown creature of the night. Not without proper training. And never ever chase one down a dark alleyway. That's a good way to get yourself killed—or worse. So while it was brave, it was stupid. It's best to leave this to the professionals."

Before Trevor could say anything, Owen turned and motioned to Maya. "Let's hunt," he said before trotting off down the alley after his HOPD buddies.

Maya hesitated for a second, a guilty expression on her face as she looked back and forth between Trevor, Jenna, and the injured woman sitting on the ground. "I can stay if you need me to help. I know a little first aid."

Trevor supposed he was relieved to see that not all the HOPD contingent were worthless doofuses.

"No, we'll take care of her," Trevor said, moving over to gently scoop the woman off the ground. "You should catch up to your friends before they get too far away."

Maya nodded and started backing away, giving Jenna a wave and saying she'd see her later before turning to run after her friends.

Jenna motioned Trevor toward the entrance to the alley. "Come on. We can take her to the mission on the other side of Winston. They'll make sure she gets the medical help she needs."

Trevor followed as she jogged ahead of him, biting his tongue on the dozens of questions that were spinning through his head right then. What the hell was that thing he'd chased? Had Jenna been looking for the creature when she'd taken him to this part of Skid Row, or was it merely a coincidence? And if she *had* been looking for it, why?

The questions continued to spiral out in his head, one after another, each building on the last, until his head started getting fuzzy. When they got to the Mission and turned the woman in his arms over to several of the people working there, no one asked how the woman had been injured or offered to call the cops. That wasn't too surprising. Unhoused people didn't usually report anything to the police unless they absolutely had to. Unfortunately, their interactions with officers usually tended to be negative more times than not, something he and his teammates back in Dallas were always careful not to do whenever they interacted with anyone.

But since the people helping the woman also didn't ask how she'd gotten hurt, he suspected there might be more to it than that. Yeah, there was definitely something weird going on here.

He and Jenna didn't say anything on the walk back to the rental car. Even as he opened the passenger door for her and then moved around to the driver's side, they both stayed quiet. But when he got behind the wheel and sat staring out the windshield, Trevor knew he had to ask at least one of his questions.

"Do you know what that thing in the alley was?" he asked quietly, turning slowly to look at her. "More importantly, have you seen it before?"

Jenna didn't answer right away, and for many long seconds, he wasn't sure if she would. But then she nodded, almost as if she'd made some kind of decision. "No, I don't know what that thing is. But I have seen it before. It's the same thing that kidnapped my sister ten years ago."

CHAPTER 4

"Hannah and I were walking home from the movies when we first saw it," Jenna said as she and Trevor walked into her apartment and headed toward the guest bedroom. There was something she needed to show him that would make this conversation easier.

Neither of them had spoken since her big reveal about the creature in the alley and its connection to her sister's disappearance. After a lifetime of being told she was insane for saying things like that out loud, Jenna had been ready for the worst from Trevor, too, but he'd simply nodded, then started the rental car and headed for her place. The quiet trip back had been a bit unnerving, but the fact that he hadn't immediately dismissed her claim was a positive in her mind.

"The movie got out late, but Hannah and I had walked home from the theater lots of times, so we didn't give it a second thought," she said over her shoulder. "The streets were well-lit and we were only a few blocks or so from our house."

"How old were you guys?" Trevor asked, stepping into the guest bedroom behind her, his voice much calmer than she expected considering the fact that they'd nearly been attacked by a creature out of a nightmare. Hers to be precise. To be honest, she was stunned at how well he was dealing with this whole thing. Not only did he confront the creature head-on, but then he chased after it. Maybe it was a SWAT thing.

"Hannah was sixteen. I was thirteen." Jenna crossed the room to the sculptures lining the far wall. She smiled a little when she noticed that Trevor had turned some of them around so they wouldn't face the bed. She got that. There was a reason all her art was in this room instead of her own bedroom. No one wants monsters staring at them while they sleep. "Hannah took me to the movies all the time, even the scary ones she hated. She was my big sister and would do anything for me."

Trevor didn't push, but Jenna still had to take a deep breath before continuing. There weren't many people she talked with about this part of her life. When her thirteen-year-old self was repeatedly told she was delusional and that she'd made everything up to get attention, it had a way of forcing her to keep things to herself. It was difficult to be open after that, even with someone like Trevor. Someone she trusted.

"We were walking past an alley when we heard a whimpering sound, like a hurt animal," she finally said, trying to talk loud enough for Trevor to hear but not sure she accomplished that. When he didn't complain, she kept going. "I thought it was a dog or maybe a cat. One look at Hannah and we were both running into the alley. But it wasn't a dog or cat crouched down behind the dumpster. It was the thing we saw tonight. It was this."

With that, she pulled the sheets off the three sculptures at the end of the row, tossing the fabric aside until Trevor could see what she'd been hiding. He moved over until he was standing directly in front of them, leaning in close to see all the details. Admittedly, there were details aplenty. Why wouldn't there be? She'd been working on them off and on for almost ten years.

Each sculpture depicted the creature in a different pose, one standing upright, another leaning forward with a fang-bearing snarl on its face, and the last with the thing dropped down on all fours, like it was running across the ground.

"These are incredible. They're perfect in every detail," Trevor murmured as he moved from side to side, taking in everything before looking up at her. "You did these from memory? How many times have you seen that thing?"

"Before tonight?" she asked. "Just the one time, when I was forced to watch it drag my sister down into the sewers. But I've never forgotten it. The image of that creature, right down to every tiny detail, will be trapped in my head forever. These sculptures are the way I chose to cope with the memories."

She held her breath, waiting for him to say something, fearing the worst. Instead, he simply stepped forward and swept her into a big hug, his strong arms wrapping around her back and shoulders and holding her tightly. She pressed her face to the shirt covering his muscular chest and closed her eyes, focusing on his warmth and comforting scent that seemed to envelop her.

Jenna couldn't remember the last time she'd felt this safe and accepted. A part of her wanted to stay here forever. But knowing there was more she needed to tell him, she forced herself to pull back a little and gaze up at him.

"It happened so fast," she said. "One second, the thing was staring at us, and the next, it was dragging Hannah across the ground the same way that thing was doing with the woman tonight. I tried to stop it, but it was too strong. And then it was gone...and so was my sister."

Images of that night flooded her memory, vivid and horrific. She'd never forget the terrified look on Hannah's face as the creature dragged her away.

"What happened after that?" Trevor asked.

Jenna felt her face heat. "I'm embarrassed to say that I froze. I sat there on the ground behind that dumpster in the alley all night, staring at the last place I saw my sister. Connor found me the next morning, pretty much catatonic."

Trevor seemed to consider that for a moment, his expression thoughtful. "Did you tell Connor about the creature who kidnapped Hannah?"

She nodded. "Connor, my parents, and everyone else. I thought I was helping by telling them exactly what took my sister, but no one believed me. They thought I was either traumatized by what I'd seen or making up wild stories to get attention." Her mouth tightened. "Like I wanted attention for myself when my sister was missing."

"So the police never even looked into the possibility that something had dragged Hannah down into the sewers?"

"No." Jenna was stunned he was approaching this so logically. "As far as I know, the police talked to a few people in the neighborhood and put up a few posters, but within a month or so, they'd already written Hannah off as a runaway and that was the end of it."

Jenna knew she sounded bitter, but she couldn't help it.

"I'm not sure what, if anything, Connor told you about his life growing up in LA, but things sort of fell apart after Hannah disappeared," she said, happy to at least be done with those parts of her memories involving Hannah and the creature. Unfortunately, the rest of it wasn't much better. "I got sent to endless therapy in an attempt to *fix* me, our parents got divorced, and Connor left home to become a cop. Then he ran off to Dallas. Not that it mattered much, I guess. We pretty much stopped being brother and sister the day he refused to believe me. But through it all, I stayed here and searched for my sister."

Trevor turned his attention to the sculptures again, focusing on the one that was leaning forward with its fang showing. She didn't miss the fact that this pose looked exactly like the creature in the alleyway had right before it had come at Trevor.

"How do those idiots from the HOPD play into this?" he asked, glancing at her. "Don't tell me those twits actually found out about that creature's existence on their own?"

She shook her head. "Not exactly. I've been searching for my sister—and the creature that took her—for years on my own and finally came to the conclusion a few months ago that I needed help."

He lifted a brow. "And you thought those four could help you?"

Admittedly, it wasn't one of her smartest decisions, but she'd been desperate.

"It's not like I had a lot of options," she said with a shrug. "In my situation, a paranormal investigator seemed like the best choice, and Hunters of Paranormal Darkness had the best reviews. I didn't realize until after I paid them their initial fee that they're merely a bunch of posers and wannabes. When we went out to the alley where my sister was taken, all they did was screw around and took videos of each other trying to look scared by the *Skid Row Screamer*. That was when I realized I was wasting my time and my money. Esme and Maya chased after me, trying to apologize, but I was too embarrassed—not to mention too furious—to listen. Tonight is the first time I've seen them since."

"Do you think they followed us?" Trevor asked.

"Maybe," she admitted. "Owen can be sort of a jerk that way. But in this case, there was no need to bother, since there have been rumors of a creature running around that part of town for months. Years, maybe."

Trevor's brow furrowed. "Is that why you had us wandering the back alleys of Skid Row? To find this creature?"

Jenna had the presence of mind to feel more than a little chagrined at the realization that her attempts at subtlety with the takeout meals hadn't worked as well as she'd hoped. Trevor had picked up on the way she'd cajoled him into those alleys with her.

"I didn't go in that alley specifically looking for the creature, but I knew there was a chance it might be there," she said. "What I was actually hoping to see was my sister, like I did a couple months ago."

"Wait. What?" Trevor did a double take. "Details.

Now," he nearly growled. Jenna decided he had a nice growl.

Jenna told him that there had been rumors of strange creatures running around the city for years. But recently the stories had started getting more detailed, describing something vaguely baboon-shaped being seen in the Skid Row district.

"The thing they described sounded exactly like the creature that kidnapped Hannah," she added. "I thought that if I could find it, then maybe I could find my sister, too. But instead of running into the creature, I saw Hannah."

"You're sure it was her?"

Jenna nodded. "I'm sure. When I called out her name, she turned to look at me and I got a good look at her face. It was definitely her. I'm certain of it."

"Did she say anything?"

Jenna swallowed hard, tears stinging her eyes. She blinked them away. "No. Hannah looked right at me and I could tell that she recognized me, but then she turned and ran off. Which still doesn't make sense. Anyway, I chased her for blocks and blocks, but just as I got close, she turned down an alley and disappeared through an open manhole and into the sewer."

"Did you go after her?"

Jenna shook her head. "No. I couldn't follow her. Not down there."

She didn't bother to mention the fact that she

was deadly terrified of even the thought of going underground. She had been since the night that creature had dragged Hannah down into the darkness right in front of her. Thinking about it was almost enough to make her hyperventilate.

Jenna took a deep breath. "Even though she ran away from me, I was still thrilled that I finally had confirmation that Hannah really is alive. Unfortunately, I couldn't convince anyone else of that fact. The police took a report but did nothing with it, while my parents only talked to me long enough to call me delusional and suggest I check myself into a psychiatric facility. That's when I went to Dallas to ask Connor for help. He didn't believe me any more than the police or our parents."

She refused to mention the part where her brother had called her *crazy*. Having spent half her life in one form of therapy or another, that wasn't a word she liked.

Trevor was silent for a long time. Jenna held her breath, waiting. To say they had one hell of a night was putting it mildly. She wouldn't be shocked if he packed his bag and walked out right this minute.

But instead, he only continued to regard her thoughtfully. "So what's your next move?"

"I'm going to keep looking for my sister," she said firmly. "And now that I know the creature that took her—or at least the same kind of creature—has made a home in the Skid Row district, that's where I'll focus my search."

Trevor seemed to consider that. Jenna opened her mouth, ready to offer him an easy out. Let him know it was okay if he bailed on her and her long list of complicated issues. But the words got stuck when he took her into his arms and hugged her again. She was so unprepared for the warmth and support that she almost missed what he said. But then the last few words registered, and her heart began to pound.

"...and now that I'm going to help you, I think we need to call for help," he was saying. "If we're going to find your sister and deal with that creature again, we need backup."

Jenna closed her eyes and squeezed him tightly, not trusting herself to speak. Getting someone else to help find Hannah sounded good to her. But who could help with something like this? More importantly, who the hell was going to believe them?

CHAPTER 5

"WHAT CAN I SAY?" TREVOR ASKED WITH A SOFT chuckle as he and Jenna left the guest bedroom and walked into the kitchen. "Chasing after that creature in the alley burned up whatever was left of the burger and doughnuts we had. I'm starving again."

He pretended he didn't see the stunned look on Jenna's face as she opened the cabinet and took out a bag of Oreos. It wasn't her fault that she had no idea how much food an alpha werewolf needed to survive. True, sugary snacks weren't what he was looking for—the partial shift and that short fight with the creature had burned up a ton of calories—but ordering three meat lover's pizzas at this time of night might look weird, so he'd make do with the cookies.

"Speaking of chasing that creature," Jenna said as he tore into the bag of creme-filled goodness. "What happened after you disappeared down that alley? You were gone for so long I was afraid that thing had gotten you."

"Fortunately, the creature didn't try to attack me again. It simply ran—really frigging fast."

He chomped down on two cookies at a time, realizing he felt badly for making Jenna worry. Which was bizarre, since he'd merely done what was necessary. Still, she'd been scared, and it was his fault. It bothered him more than he would have thought possible.

"I chased it about three blocks through the back streets before the thing dove down an open manhole," he continued, deciding he'd ponder his exaggerated reaction to her concern later. "I followed but immediately found a hole in the bottom of the sewer pipe. The creature dug through the concrete with nothing but its claws. I would have kept following it, but the tunnel underneath was way too small for me to fit through. I would have had to crawl on my hands and knees and hope I didn't get stuck."

Trevor was so busy inhaling another cookie he almost missed how pale Jenna's face had gotten. He probably would have if it wasn't for how fast he could hear her heart was racing. He quickly set the bag of cookies on the counter and rested his hands on her shoulders.

"You okay?" he asked softy. "You're pale all of a sudden."

Jenna didn't say anything at first, instead taking slow, deep breaths. After a moment, her heartbeat had returned to normal, and she visibly looked better.

"I'm fine," she said. "I don't like underground spaces, that's all. Especially dark, tight, underground spaces like sewers."

Trevor didn't have to ask to know where Jenna had gotten that phobia. Not after what happened to her sister.

As they stood there eating cookies and drinking the almond milk Jenna poured for them—which he was amazed to realize tasted surprisingly good—they talked some more about what had happened earlier, both of them wondering if there was more than one of those creatures living beneath the city, what it had been planning to do with the unhoused woman it had captured, and whether it lived directly below Skid Row or merely hunted there. The questions Jenna continued to pose made it obvious she'd spent a lot of time thinking about this thing.

Once the bag of Oreos was properly demolished, he pulled out his cell phone, quickly found Hale's number in his contacts, then hit the Call button.

"Dammit, Trevor," his friend grumbled after a few rings. "You'd better have a good reason for calling me at two o'clock in the frigging morning."

"You know I wouldn't be calling if I didn't," Trevor said. "I've got a situation out here and I need some help."

Hale cursed. "Don't tell me that you've screwed up this thing with Jenna already. You've only been out there a day. Even you couldn't have messed up that quickly."

"No," Trevor said. "And if I weren't so focused on what's going on here, I'd be offended by that."

"So what is going on?" Hale asked, fully awake and serious now. "And what can I do to help?"

Trevor breathed a sigh of relief. Unconditional and no-questions-asked support. That was what it meant to be part of a pack. He composed his thoughts, trying to figure out the best way to explain all this, without Jenna hearing something she shouldn't—specifically that the SWAT team was made up of werewolves.

"I've run into a supernatural creature out here in LA—possibly more than one of them—and it's more than I can deal with on my own. Can you talk to Gage and see if he can send some help out?"

Gage Dixon was the commander of the Dallas SWAT team. He was also the alpha of their pack, which made him the alpha of a bunch of other alphas. How he put up with all their crap was anyone's guess, but he did, and that was all that mattered.

"Damn, dude," Hale groaned. "Only you could go out to LA for vacation and stumble across a supernatural creature. At least tell me that Jenna isn't involved. Connor will lose his mind if he finds out."

Trevor hesitated but knew he couldn't hide that particular detail. "Actually, Jenna's right in the middle of it all." He glanced at Jenna to see her eyeing him curiously. "The creature I tangled with is the same kind of thing that grabbed her and Connor's sister a decade ago, and it's almost certainly taken other people since then. We barely stopped it from kidnapping someone tonight."

Rather than play a game of literal telephone, Trevor thumbed the speaker button so Jenna could tell Hale about how the creature had grabbed Hannah in the alley ten years ago. Trevor then told him about chasing the thing underground earlier that evening, going into detail about the creature's impervious skin and the way it could apparently dig through reinforced concrete.

"Jenna did some sculptures of the creature. I'll send you pics after we get done talking so you can show them to Gage. I'm also going to head over to Davina's club tomorrow and see if she knows what we're up against and how to fight it, because going toe-to-toe with the thing definitely didn't work."

"How many of us do you think you'll need as backup?" Hale asked.

"Three should be good. We might need weapons, too," Trevor said, then added, "And it goes without saying that Connor can't know anything about this."

"I figured that," Hale said. "Unfortunately, the more people who know about this, the harder it's going to be to keep your secret from the Pack. But I'll do my best."

"I appreciate it."

Trevor reminded Hale that he'd send him the photos, then hung up.

"Okay, what the heck just happened?" Jenna demanded. "You tell Hale—who seems to be a rational person—that you got into a fight with a supernatural baboon with monstrous fangs and claws, and he didn't even bat an eye. While we're at it, who's Davina, how can she help, and why did Hale refer to your SWAT team as a pack?"

Trevor thought he'd been ready for all Jenna's questions until she asked the one about the Pack. He barely remembered Hale even using the word and was at a complete loss when it came to explaining it. He couldn't very well tell her that he was a werewolf. Not right now anyway. She already had more than enough to process at the moment. He'd tell her soon.

Before the poor excuse was even half finished in his head, Trevor was already berating himself for being a coward. Jenna deserved to know the truth, and it wasn't like he'd ever have a better time than now to bring it up. A little voice in the back of Trevor's head insisted he was withholding the information to protect her, but that was crap and he knew it. After the life she'd been forced to live, the truth was that Jenna was more than strong enough to deal with his little furry secret. Bottom line, he was being a chicken about this, and he couldn't for the life of him understand why.

Okay, that was probably another lie.

If he was being honest with himself, Trevor

would say that his hesitation to come clean with Jenna about this was rooted in fear. Fear that she wouldn't want to have anything to do with him once she knew what he was. He had no idea where this fear of rejection came from, but it was there all the same. It would have been nice if he had time to stand here and explore what his major malfunction on this topic might be, but Jenna was looking at him expectantly, waiting for an answer, so he decided to go with the first—and most simple—explanation that came to mind.

And keep lying to her...and himself.

He pulled up his T-shirt to expose the left side of his chest. He almost laughed when Jenna's eyes widened, preferring to think it was his muscles she was enamored with and not the tattoo there.

"Everyone gets a tat of a wolf's head when we join the SWAT team," he said, glancing down at the image of the wolf on his chest, eyes blazing and fangs exposed. "It shows that we're a part of something bigger than ourselves. Something even more than a team—a pack."

Jenna reached out and lightly ran a finger along the dark lines of the tat. He had to admit he liked the contact and would have gladly let her do what she was doing for the rest of the night. "I guess that makes sense. The artwork of this tattoo is exquisite."

As if just realizing she was caressing his chest,

she quickly took her hand away to reach up and tuck her hair behind her ear.

"What about the other stuff?" she asked. "Why do I get the feeling that describing that monster to Hale wasn't a big deal for him? Now that I think about it, you didn't freak out the way I expected you would, either."

Glad to at least have that slipup about the Pack out of the way, Trevor took another deep breath, trying to figure out how to tell her what she needed to know without revealing any more than he had to.

"Last night wasn't the first time I've encountered a supernatural creature," he said. "There are other things out there that go bump in the night, and because of that, there are people and groups—like my SWAT team—that have experience dealing with them."

Jenna stared at him for a long moment. "You're telling me you've not only seen other creatures like the thing that took my sister but fought them and won?"

He nodded. "Yeah. We've never seen anything quite like this creature, though. That's why I asked Hale to get some of the other guys together and come out here. Because we're going to find this creature and your sister."

She took a deep breath and let it out slowly. "How?"

"I'm not sure yet," he admitted. "But the first

step begins with gathering information on what this creature might be and what its weaknesses are. That's where Davina comes in. She owns a nightclub in LA that caters to clientele of the supernatural variety. This gives her access to a lot of unique information, so I'm hoping she'll know what that thing we fought tonight is and how to deal with it."

Jenna gazed at him for a long time, the expression on her face changing from confusion to doubt to hope and then, finally, curiosity.

"There's a nightclub in LA for supernatural creatures?" she said in amazement. "How has that never shown up on *TMZ*?"

Everything that had happened that evening seemed to catch up with Jenna all at once. One moment, she was brushing her teeth in front of the bathroom mirror, wondering how she was ever going to get to sleep after all the adrenaline being dumped into her system, and the next, she was yawning and trying not to drool toothpaste all over herself.

She'd spent the entire time in the bathroom rehashing everything Trevor had told her, especially about his—and SWAT's—experiences with the supernatural world. While that by itself was a staggering revelation, the bigger takeaway had been the fact that her brother had known about the existence of supernatural creatures for a while now. Yet that hadn't kept him from continuing to reject everything she'd ever said about their sister's kidnapping. Why would he do that if he knew that supernatural beings really existed? Why wouldn't he at least consider the possibility that she was telling the truth? Not understanding that made her even more upset at Connor than she'd ever been. Pushing those painful thoughts aside and finishing up as fast as she could, Jenna walked out of the bathroom, expecting to find Trevor already in the guest room, assuming he'd be as exhausted as she was. But she was surprised when she poked her head in his room and found it empty—except for her sculptures, of course. She glanced down the hallway to see that the lights were off in the rest of the apartment, which meant he probably wasn't in the kitchen getting another snack, which would have been her second guess.

With her bedroom as the only option left in the small apartment, Jenna slowly wandered in to find Trevor standing there studying the various posters and photos on the wall, looking damn good in a pair of shorts and a T-shirt, which were apparently his go-to sleeping gear. She took a moment to appreciate his muscular legs and biceps, wondering how a guy who ate like he did could be so built.

As she walked over to stand beside him, she realized that while he was certainly taking note of the photos of her, he seemed more interested in the ones of her family.

"You probably think it's bizarre to have so many pictures of my family, considering the crappy relationship I have with them," she said softly.

He turned to her with a smile, and she couldn't help but notice that he didn't look tired at all. In fact, he looked ready to keep going for hours. It was probably all those cookies he'd eaten earlier. That much sugar would have anyone pinging off the walls.

"No, it isn't bizarre," he said gently. "I can understand wanting to have pictures of your family around you, even if you're on the outs with them at the moment. It helps remind us that we're really not alone, even if we think we are."

She grimaced. "I'm pretty sure I'm a bit past being *on the outs*." She wasn't sure why she'd admitted that, but for some reason, it felt like she could talk about anything with Trevor and not have to worry about it. Which was wild, considering she'd known him for barely a month, and most of that had been spent doing the long-distance thing. "My parents are almost completely out of the picture, and with the way Connor acted when I saw him last, I don't see us spending much time together in the future, either. So as far as that goes, I guess I truly am alone."

Trevor wrapped his arms around her, holding her close. Jenna rested her face against him, relaxing into his embrace and feeling more at peace than she had in a very long time.

"You're not alone," he murmured, bending down so his mouth was right next to her ear, his warm breath tickling her skin. "You have Madeleine and all your other friends. And you have me. That means you'll never be alone."

Jenna didn't have to look at the photos on the wall to know that Madeleine was in quite a few of them. But while the thought of always having her best friend around was nice, it was the idea of Trevor being there for her all the time that made her melt inside. Since she wasn't quite sure how to put that into words, she simply squeezed him tight. He was so warm and comfortable she could stand there all night.

"How long have you and Madeleine known each other?" Trevor asked.

"We met on my very first movie set three years ago." Smiling at the memory, Jenna pointed at the framed picture on the far right of the wall. She was standing beside a heavily blood-spattered Madeleine, who was smiling ear to ear regardless of the mess. "It was a low-budget apocalyptic thing—all action and no plot—but they needed tons of special effects, gore, and mangled bodies. That's where both Madeleine and I came in. I must have painted her up as twenty different corpses for that movie. We bonded over fake blood and her latex allergies. It was the beginning of a beautiful friendship. I moved in here the day filming wrapped. She got me a discount on my deposit, so I'm legally required to be BFFs with her for life."

Trevor chuckled, the sound making Jenna feel all kinds of goofy inside. Not wanting the moment to end, she told him about the other friends in the rest of the photos. Special effects and movies were a common theme among her closest friends, and she had stories to tell about all of them.

"Madeleine ended up getting a real job as a private chef for the rich and overpaid," Jenna said, pointing at a picture of her best friend in a reptilian costume that everyone fondly referred to as the murder frog. "But she still lets me make her up every now and then, though I think she does it more for me than for the money."

As she and Trevor stood there talking about Madeleine and Jenna's other friends and all the fun times they'd had together, she realized this moment was one of the happiest of her life. She wasn't sure if Trevor knew it or not, but he'd gotten her to realize how many people she still had in her corner. Another point in his favor.

As much as she wanted to hang out and talk, a ridiculous series of yawns gave away her exhaustion.

"I guess it's time to get you to bed," Trevor said softly, his body still pressed warmly to hers. "To say it's been a long day would be an understatement."

As he started to step back, she found herself holding on to him more tightly, not wanting to lose the sense of safety and comfort that came with being in his arms. Normally, she wouldn't even consider being so clingy, but after the day she'd had, she decided she deserved to spoil herself a little.

"I know we've been taking our time with this thing going on between us, but after everything that happened tonight, I'd rather not sleep alone," she said softly. "Do you think you could stay with me, just to sleep?"

He gazed down at her. "Not that I wouldn't love to sleep with you, but are you sure?"

"I'm definitely sure." She grinned. "As long as you're okay with me putting my feet on you, no matter how cold they get."

"I think I can handle that," he said with a chuckle.

Taking her hand, he turned and led her across the room to the bed, then pulled back the blankets and sheets. Jenna climbed in, excitement tingling deep in her stomach. It wasn't like she hadn't slept with guys before—in the literal and biblical sense—but this was different. She wasn't sure exactly how, but it was.

Trevor moved over to the doorway to flick off the overhead light, then walked back across the darkened room. Considering she couldn't see much of anything, she should probably have reached out and turned on the bedside lamp, but from the sound of his steady footsteps, he obviously had no problem avoiding the various obstacles she had lying around the room, including her beloved and cuddly Freddy Krueger plushie, who would probably be in her bed if it wasn't for the much better offer she had right then.

Trevor slipped into the bed, smooth and graceful. Then he wrapped an arm around her waist, pulling her close to his body again, spooning her. Not only was his chest pressing against her, but his crotch and thighs, too. As if it had a mind of its own, her butt wiggled backward, seeking as much contact as possible.

She wasn't disappointed with the results, as her butt found a perfect sleeping spot right there against his shorts, his impressive bulge nestling comfortably against her. Like they were two pieces of the same puzzle, meant to be together.

One of his muscular arms slid under her pillow, while the one around her waist moved up to nestle comfortably beneath her breasts, warming them nicely through her tank top. In fact, he was warming her nicely all over. She was about to tell him as much when he moved slightly, burying his face in her hair, right there at the junction of her neck and shoulder. Then he inhaled deeply—purposefully—letting out an appreciative groan.

It was pretty much the sexiest thing someone had ever done to her, and her heart squeezed a little bit in her chest at the thought that Trevor was possibly the greatest thing since liquid latex.

And considering the affinity she had for using liquid latex in her special effects makeup, that was saying something.

"Good night, Jenna," he whispered against the skin of her neck. "Sleep tight."

"Good night," she whispered back, though she wasn't sure how much sleeping she'd be getting tonight. Not that she was complaining in the slightest.

CHAPTER 6

At first, Trevor thought he was dreaming about some heavenly place that was warm, snuggly, and as fragrant as a garden full of flowers. Honeysuckles to be specific. A few seconds later, the significance of that particular scent finally filtered through his sleep-addled mind, and he woke up to find himself wrapped around Jenna like a vine, one hand under her tank top, fingertips against her middle, and his morning wood pressed firmly against that delectable butt of hers.

Part of him considered pulling back. He didn't want to embarrass himself or Jenna if she woke up and felt his hard-on poking her in the butt. But for the life of him, he couldn't bring himself to move. This seemed like the closest to heaven he would ever get, and his inner wolf refused to let it go.

So Trevor stayed where he was, wrapped around the most incredible woman he'd ever met, concentrating with all his might on memorizing every moment of this miraculous gift. The touch of her skin on his, her scent filling his nose, her warmth seemingly enveloping his soul.

He was on the verge of falling asleep again when a soft sigh from Jenna let him know she was waking up. He moved back a bit so there was a little space between them, letting his right hand slide down to her hip. Then he did his best to think about something else—like how Hale's conversation had gone with Gage—anything so he wouldn't focus on how amazing Jenna's body had felt against his.

She rolled over and pushed herself up on an elbow to gaze down at him sleepily, her silky hair all sleep tousled and sexy as it cascaded around her shoulders.

"Good morning," she murmured, smiling at him as one of her hands came to rest gently on his chest. "I hope you slept well, because I definitely did."

He grinned up at her. "Yeah, best sleep I've had in a long time. I didn't even notice those cold feet you mentioned. It probably goes without saying, but just so you're clear on the matter, anytime you want to share your bed with me, I'm wide open to the idea."

Jenna laughed, the sound musical and bright and the most beautiful thing he'd ever heard. But then she leaned forward and kissed him, and he stopped thinking about anything.

He lifted his hand to weave his fingers in her long hair, deepening the kiss as he teased the tip of his tongue across her lips, tasting more, wanting more. The sexy moans she made sent shivers down his body all the way to his cock, which definitely perked up at the idea of where this might be going.

Getting control of himself before things could get that far, Trevor slowly let his fingers slide out of her hair, nibbling her luscious lips a few more times before pulling away. He wanted this so damn bad but had to take his time. He couldn't screw things up by rushing it.

Jenna must have agreed with his decision to slow things down because she pulled back, too, a sexy smile tugging up the corner of her perfect lips.

"I don't know about you, but I'm feeling a little lazy this morning," she said. "What do you say I get us some coffee and then we lie in bed for a while and maybe figure out what our plan is when it comes to finding Hannah?"

He couldn't think of anything he'd rather do. "Sounds good to me. I don't expect the guys to show up until late afternoon at the earliest, so we have time to come up with a plan. That way, we can hit the ground running when they do get here."

Before he could even get his feet free of the covers, Jenna's hand was on his shoulder, tugging him back. "You stay here and keep the bed warm. I'll get the coffee and be back in a flash. Promise."

Before he could protest, Jenna was climbing across his body, including the exquisite moment when she straddled his hips. That had him completely forgetting anything he might have been about to say. Not grabbing her hips to keep her right where she was turned out to be the hardest thing he'd ever done.

Or not done, he supposed.

Then Jenna was heading for the bedroom door, her butt bouncing delightfully in her shorts. How the hell had he been able to sleep cuddled up close to that ass?

Grinning, Trevor relaxed into the pillows. They still smelled of Jenna's scent. That—along with her taste on his lips—made him wonder about what it would be like to have this for more than merely a week. He knew he was getting ahead of himself, but what was the harm in daydreaming a little bit?

He closed his eyes, listening to the sound of Jenna moving around the kitchen as she ground coffee beans, then scooped them into the machine before getting mugs out of the cabinet. She hummed while she worked, a catchy tune that took a few moments to recognize. When he finally figured it out, he chuckled. It was the theme music to *Halloween*. Because of course it was. What else would Jenna hum?

He started to drift back into sleep, his mind lulled by the bliss of the moment, when the ringing of the doorbell jarred him back to semi-awareness.

"I'll get it," Jenna called out, her bare feet already scurrying across the living room floor. "It's probably Madeleine wanting to know how our date went yesterday."

But even as Trevor settled back against the pillows again, his nose registered a series of familiar scents. Ones that made him shove down the blankets and bound out of bed. He sprinted for the living room with no idea what he was going to do if he got there in time anyway.

Not that he had to worry about that dilemma, since Jenna already had the door open by the time he got there. And yeah, it wasn't Madeleine who'd rung the bell.

Senior Corporal Mike Taylor stood in the doorway. Tall and muscular, he had an intensity about him that Trevor suspected was there even before he became a werewolf. Beside Mike, Hale was casually leaning against the door jamb, a chagrined expression on his face and an apologetic look in his blue eyes as Trevor caught sight of Connor.

To say Jenna's brother wasn't happy would be putting it mildly. Trevor braced himself as Connor's nostrils flared a little. Clearly, he'd picked up Trevor's scent on Jenna and vice versa. Any werewolf with a nose—which meant any werewolf but Hale—would be able to figure out that the two of them hadn't had sex, but obviously, that didn't matter to Connor. The pissed-off glare he was directing at Trevor looked like it could melt steel.

"I didn't expect any of you to show up until later today," Trevor said, slipping an arm casually around Jenna's waist as his pack mates stepped into the apartment. He gave Connor a pointed look. "And some of you, I didn't expect at all."

Connor opened his mouth to say something, but Jenna cut him off, inviting everyone to grab seats in the living room, adding that the coffee would finish brewing soon.

"How did you guys get here so fast?" Trevor asked, taking a seat on the couch beside Jenna and ignoring Connor's glower.

"We have STAT to thank for that," Mike said. "When Gage called to ask if they'd ever dealt with anything like the creature you sent photos of, they got us on the first flight out of Dallas. They've had a run-in or two with the thing you dealt with last night. From what they said, these things are dangerous as hell."

Jenna looked back and forth between Trevor and Mike. "STAT?"

"Remember when I mentioned last night that there are people out there experienced at dealing with supernatural creatures?" Trevor said. "Well, STAT—which stands for Special Threat Assessment Team—is a federal agency that specializes in that. If they've run into this kind of creature before, they're going to be a valuable source of information in tracking the things down."

"Gage also arranged for us to meet with Davina at her club tonight to see if she can help, too," Mike said.

From where he stood by the stuffed chair where Hale was sitting, Connor scowled. "Everyone hold on a damn minute. We don't have any proof that Hannah was kidnapped by a supernatural creature."

Beside Trevor, Jenna's eyes narrowed, a rage-filled flush suffusing her face. He was sure she was about half a second away from screaming at her dumbass brother.

"No proof, huh?" Trevor demanded, glaring at Connor. "Before you open your mouth and say something else stupid, there's something I need to show you."

To head off what was sure to be a knockdown, drag-out argument with his pack mate, Trevor got to his feet, then grabbed Connor's shoulder and dragged him down the hallway toward the guest bedroom. Connor resisted, but Trevor got him there anyway, shoving him until they both ended up in front of the three sculptures of the creatures. Jenna, Hale, and Mike hurried into the room after them.

"I don't know if Hale told you the whole story or showed you the photos I sent to him last night, but this is the creature I fought with," Trevor said. "They're perfect in every detail, right down to the length of the claws and sharpness of the fangs. Your sister sculpted these years ago, Connor. That means she's seen the creature before last night. And if she says it was the thing that kidnapped Hannah in that alley a decade ago, then I believe her. Maybe you should, too."

Connor let out a low growl that was too soft for

Jenna to hear—thankfully. Mike heard it, though, and stepped between them to study the sculptures, though not before throwing Connor a sharp look. The fact that Connor bit his tongue highlighted why Gage had sent Mike on this trip. Mike was one of the team's squad leaders and exceptionally good at keeping the rest of them in line when necessary.

"These are remarkable," Mike said, glancing over his shoulder at Jenna.

"Thanks," she said quietly.

While Connor stood there silently fuming, Trevor and Jenna told Hale and Mike the details of what had happened last night, with Trevor focusing on how dangerous the creature had been.

"It was fast as hell, and its skin was pretty much impenetrable as far as I could tell," he added, describing how the wooden stake had shattered against the thing's chest.

"Do you think a bullet would stop it?" Hale asked.

All Trevor could do was shrug. "I have no idea. Hopefully, that's something Davina will be able to tell us before we go after these things."

His pack mates didn't say anything, and in the silence, a series of soft chimes sounded, making all of them jump a little. Except for Jenna.

"That's the coffee maker," she said softly. "Trevor and I were about to have some when you guys showed up. Anyone else care to join us?"

Hale and Mike immediately nodded, saying they'd love some. Connor didn't say anything one way or the other but simply stared at Trevor, jaw tight. It was clear what his friend wanted.

"Jenna, why don't you and the guys go grab some coffee?" Trevor said casually. "I need a few seconds to talk to your brother. We'll be right out."

Trevor couldn't tell who was more hesitant at that suggestion—Jenna or Mike. Hale looked like he was wondering if he should stay and play referee, too. But after a moment, Jenna and his pack mates left the room. Trevor gave them a few moments to reach the kitchen, then turned to confront Connor. His friend didn't make him wait long before going on the offensive.

"I thought I told you to stay away from my sister," Connor growled, his eyes flaring yellow gold, his hands clenched into fists at his side. At least his claws weren't out yet. Though that could change soon enough. "So why the hell are you in her apartment?"

"Why?" Trevor said calmly. Two pissed-off werewolves would only make the situation that much worse. "Because you don't get to decide who Jenna spends her time with."

"I'm her brother, dammit," Connor growled, taking a step toward him, eyes flashing brighter, hands unclenching as his claws extended a little.

"Yes, you're her brother," Trevor repeated. "Not

her keeper. When you insulted her back in Dallas and she needed a place to stay, she ended up at my place. I listened to what she had to say without judging her, and we ended up developing a connection. We continued to talk after she left to come back here to LA, and when she asked me to come out to visit her, I agreed."

Unfortunately, his calm, reasonable response seemed to have the opposite effect of what he intended. It only enraged Connor even more, and as the muscles in his arms and shoulders began to spasm uncontrollably, Trevor thought his pack mate might shift into a full wolf right there.

Trevor could only imagine how badly Jenna would freak out if she walked into her guest bedroom and found a two-hundred-and-twenty-pound wolf standing there. He needed to calm Connor down before the situation got completely out of control.

"Connor," he began, only to get cut off as his teammate moved within inches of him, bringing them face-to-face and eye-to-eye.

"Jenna suggested you stay in her apartment, so you just naturally assumed that offer comes with the right to sleep with her, you asshole?" Connor snarled, the tips of his upper fangs making an appearance.

Despite his desire not to stir the pot, Trevor couldn't keep his own fangs from extending. "I slept with Jenna last night because she asked me to. And because she's an adult who gets to make those decisions. Maybe you should get over yourself and realize that."

He leaned in close, ready to fight his friend right then and there if that was what the a-hole wanted. But Connor only let out a snort of mocking laughter.

"Maybe you're the one who needs to get over himself," Connor sneered. "Jenna came out to Dallas to try and convince me to come back here and help her find Hannah. When I refused, she moved on to you, sucking you into her delusions."

Trevor stood there in disbelief, stunned at the realization of exactly how little Connor obviously thought of his sister. He knew there were some issues between the two of them, but he'd never thought it was this bad. How had Connor become so blind?

"Delusions, huh?" Trevor said, putting both of his hands on Connor's chest and firmly pushing him away to put some space between the two of them. "You mean like the creature I fought last night in that alley? The one that was attempting to drag a young woman into the sewers? Yeah, that sounds delusional, doesn't it? But it also sounds exactly like the story Jenna told everyone the night Hannah disappeared, doesn't it?"

Connor's eyes glowed brighter than ever, and

Trevor knew a blow was coming his way any second. It was just a matter of whether it would be with a closed fist or extended claws. He'd survive either way, but explaining the wounds and the blood from the claws would be difficult.

Trevor braced himself to block the attack he knew was coming when the sound of footsteps in the hallway had him and Connor quickly moving away from each other. Connor was aware enough to retract his claws and fangs, though it was obvious he was still pissed. Yeah, well, so was Trevor.

Jenna stood in the doorway, looking from him to Connor and back again. There was absolutely no way she could miss the tension filling the room.

"The coffee's getting cold," she said. "And I called to have breakfast delivered. It'll be here in a few minutes."

Trevor caught Jenna looking his way with an expression of concern—when she wasn't glaring at her brother. He smiled and nodded, his muscles releasing some of their tension when she seemed to relax. He started to follow her out of the room when Connor grabbed his arm and yanked him back.

"You hurt my sister and I'll end you," Connor growled in his ear.

Trevor turned to regard Connor. Where the hell had the friend he used to know disappeared to?

Part of Trevor wanted to ignore the jackass and

walk away, but his inner werewolf wouldn't let him. "You don't have to worry about me hurting her. Lately, it seems like you're the only one with a history of doing that. So maybe you should worry about yourself."

Jerking his arm free of Connor's grasp, he strode out of the room and down the hallway to the kitchen, leaving his pack mate to follow—or not. Right then, he really didn't give a damn what Connor did or didn't do.

The sun was low on the horizon as Jenna and Trevor, along with her brother and the other SWAT guys left her apartment to go to the club to meet Davina. By the time they drove across town and found the address they were looking for, it was completely dark out.

"Are you sure this is the right address?" she asked as they entered an alley with buildings on both sides that gave no indication of being home to any kind of nightclub she'd ever seen.

"We're in the right place." Mike pointed at a red neon design in the shape of a cat with its back arched high attached to one of the brick walls directly above a set of nondescript steps that led down below street level. "This is the sign that Davina said to look for."

"Seriously?" Jenna leaned over to look down into the stairwell lit by nothing more than the red glow of the cat sign. There wasn't any name anywhere she could see. Just a really big man standing in the deep shadows by a set of heavy doors at the base of the steps. "What kind of club doesn't even have a name?"

"The kind that's very selective about who they let inside."

Jenna recognized the man's voice before looking up, but she was still a little surprised when Owen and his paranormal investigative team walked toward them from the opposite end of the alley.

"And a huge bouncer at the door who only lets in the right *kind* of people," he added.

She opened her mouth to ask what he meant by that, but she was interrupted by her overprotective brother stepping in front of her.

"Who the hell are you and why were you following us?" Connor demanded.

"Relax, dude," Owen said, holding up his hands in a placating gesture. "We're HOPD."

"Is that supposed to mean something to us?" Hale asked from where he was standing on the other side of Trevor.

Jenna quickly stepped in front of Connor and made the introductions before Owen could say anything, explaining they were paranormal investigators.

"Okay, that answers the question of who you are," Mike said, dark eyes narrowing suspiciously. He was clearly thoroughly unimpressed with the whole HOPD thing. "But not why you were following us."

"Who says we were following you?" Isaac asked, even though he was wearing the guiltiest expression Jenna had ever seen in her life.

"You drive a dark-blue conversion van with a big yellow ghost decal on the side," Mike pointed out, crossing his arms over his chest. "You pulled in behind us the moment we left Jenna's apartment and tailed us all the way here, sticking way too close and running two red lights in the process."

"And then you followed us from the parking garage before slipping around to that end of the alley," Hale added, pointing in the direction Owen and the rest of them had come from. "Where you stood in the shadows, watching us like a bunch of weirdo stalkers."

At least Isaac, Esme, and Maya had the decency to look embarrassed. Owen, on the other hand, snorted.

"We had to follow you," he said. "Especially after we realized that you know a whole lot more about what happened last night down in the Skid Row district than you were telling."

"And what exactly do you think we know?" Trevor asked, his expression almost bordering on amusement as he took in all four members of the paranormal investigation crew before returning his attention to Owen.

Owen shrugged. "I have no idea. But the fact that the first place you decide to visit after leaving your apartment is a club that has a reputation for attracting, well...let's just say...an unusual clientele? You can see why we might be interested in what you're up to."

"Throw in the added muscle you've brought with you, and it's a slam dunk you're up to something," Esme added quietly, motioning toward Connor, Hale, and Mike.

Jenna couldn't help but laugh at the description of her brother as *added muscle*. Given his size and his recent petulant disposition, it was an apt characterization.

"I hate to be the one to disappoint you guys, especially after all the effort you put into following us, but there's nothing mysterious going on tonight," Trevor said. "We're simply here for a private party to celebrate Jenna's brother coming out to visit her."

"Yeah, right," Owen snorted. "You don't expect us to believe that, do you? People don't come to a club like this for a welcome home party."

"Really? We did," Trevor said, his expression bland as he returned Owen's look. "But I guess you'll have to take our word for it because, like I said, it's a private party. And none of you are on the list."

To emphasize his point, Trevor glanced pointedly at the big bouncer at the base of the steps. Owen's mouth tightened angrily. It was clear he wasn't buying Trevor's story, and from the look on their faces, none of the other members of HOPD were either. But with the bouncer guarding the door, there wasn't much they could do about it.

"You may think you've gotten one over on us, but don't think for a minute that we won't figure out what's really going on down in the Skid Row district and how you're involved," Owen said. "You can take this as a promise—we're going to be watching you."

Then he actually did that thing where he pointed two fingers at his eyes before turning them at Trevor. Seriously, he did the *I'm-watching-you* thing.

"Did that just happen?" Mike asked incredulously as Owen and his crew turned and left the alley. "I mean, people out here in LA don't honestly say that, do they?"

"Apparently," Trevor murmured with a shrug. "Come on. We need to get inside. We're already running late for our meeting with Davina."

The big bouncer at the door didn't say a word as they descended the steps and approached him. The muscular blond guy simply reached out and opened one of the metal doors, swinging it wide for them.

"Someone will meet you inside," he murmured, not bothering to even glance their way before turning his attention back to the stairs, obviously dismissing them from his mind already.

They found another set of stairs inside the club, lit by more brightly colored neon cats that flickered and strobed along the walls on either side of them in such a way to make it seem like the felines were actually moving with them as they walked down the steps. It was kind of cool, Jenna thought. Also kind of creepy. But cool at the same time.

When they reached the double doors at the bottom of the stairs, Connor quickly pushed past her and Trevor to reach for the doorknob before either of them could. Like he thought there was a dangerous monster on the other side. Jenna would have laughed if it wasn't so annoying. He was still obsessed with treating her like a fragile porcelain doll, ready to break at the first thing.

The moment Connor opened the door, she wedged her way between him and Trevor, not caring that her shoulders thumped into their arms painfully. She doubted whether the two of them even felt it. She braced herself, expecting her brother to say something stupid, but the moment she saw the inside of the club, she forgot there was anyone else even with her.

Jenna had expected the club to be some kind of rave venue, with one large area, like an underground warehouse. Instead, she found herself in the midst of a scene from that movie *Labyrinth*, with multiple smaller rooms and balconies positioned at all kinds of different levels, each connected with archways, tunnels, stairs, and ramps. It was confusing as hell even with the place fairly well-lit. But when the lights went out—as she imagined they normally were in a place like this—it must be mind-numbing.

It took her a moment to realize that she wasn't the only one rendered speechless. Trevor, Connor, and their teammates were all looking around the eclectic space in awe, paying special attention to the gigantic highly polished bar along one of the back walls. Only it wasn't the bar itself the guys were focused on. It was the man behind the bar who was transferring beer from a plastic crate into a cooler unit. In fact, they weren't merely focused on the guy. They were flat out *staring* at him. Even more bizarre, Trevor, Connor, and Mike were all making faces, noses wrinkling like they'd just smelled something bad.

Jenna was about to ask them what that was about—as covertly as she could, of course—when movement out of the corner of her eye made her look over toward one of the staircases on the other side of the immense dance floor. A tall, lithe woman with blue hair and the most startling lavender eyes

Jenna had ever seen in her life was coming down the steps and heading straight for them.

"I'm Davina DeMirci," she said with a smile as she came to a stop in front of them. "I understand you're here looking for information on short powerful creatures with a habit of dragging people underground. Well, it turns out you're in luck, since I happen to know a thing or two about ghouls."

CHAPTER 7

TREVOR COULDN'T STOP GLANCING BACK AT THE tall, dark-haired bartender as he and everyone else followed Davina up the steps to her office.

"What's wrong?" Jenna asked curiously, glancing back over her shoulder at the man behind the bar as they reached the second-floor landing. "Do you know that guy? Is he a wanted criminal from Dallas or something?"

Trevor exchanged looks with Connor and then Mike. Hale and his broke-ass nose were oblivious, but his other teammates were staring right back at him, obviously realizing the same thing that he had. Of course, it wasn't like he could tell Jenna that the guy behind the bar was a supernatural creature. Because there was no way in hell anything with a scent like that could possibly be human. Given all the other unique and unfamiliar smells in the place, the bartender probably wasn't the only supernatural creature working here, either. Which wasn't surprising, he supposed, considering the club catered to a supernatural clientele.

Behind Jenna, Connor frantically shook his head as if he thought Trevor was dumb enough to tell her anything like that.

"No, nothing like that," Trevor said, giving her a smile. "I thought for a minute that I recognized the guy from the police academy in Dallas. But now, I don't think so."

Jenna didn't look like she entirely believed that, but fortunately Davina opened the door to her office and motioned them inside. That seemed enough to distract Jenna from the questions she'd undoubtedly been about to ask.

Davina's office was large and full of old-world charm, with lots of heavy antique furniture, hand-painted murals covering the walls, and shelves packed with sculptures and lots of ancient-looking books. While the decor seemed out of place in the nightclub, it somehow fit with the woman they were here to talk to. Not only was she a real-life witch who could use spells, she also knew more about the supernatural world than anyone else they'd ever met. Her knowledge and expertise had saved the lives of the Pack more than once.

Thankfully, she hadn't come out and said anything about Trevor or his pack mates being werewolves in front of Jenna. He'd been afraid Davina would bring it up downstairs when she first greeted them, unaware that Jenna didn't know their secret.

But so far, so good.

"Ghouls," Jenna said as Davina moved around behind her big desk. "That's what you called it downstairs. Are you sure that's what it is?"

Davina didn't say anything right away—or sit down. Instead, she grabbed a heavy leather-bound tome from the edge of her desk, sliding it closer. She flipped it open, quickly finding a tasseled bookmark toward the back of the book, then spun the book around.

"After seeing the photos you sent me, it wasn't that difficult to figure out," Davina said. "It didn't hurt that STAT has already run into these things a few times. Though I have to admit, I'm a little shocked to find out that there's a clan of them right here under LA. I feel sort of silly for not knowing that. I'm supposed to be up on this kind of thing."

Trevor stepped closer, leaning over to study the book Davina had put in front of them. The thing was so old that the paper was yellow and tattered along the edges. But the hand-drawn figure on the left side of the page—while crudely rendered—was most definitely the thing he'd fought the other night. He scanned the rest of that page and the one opposite it, hoping it would tell him something helpful. Unfortunately, he couldn't even read it.

"That's definitely the creature," Jenna said, looking at the picture before leaning in closer to study the text, as if a better view would help. "What language is this?

"Early Aramaic," Davina murmured. "Tenth century BC. It's a compendium of supernatural creatures that hounded the regions around Syria during that time. They're mentioned in some of my other books, but this one has the drawing and the most background information on the creatures."

Jenna gazed at the picture of the ghoul, gently running her fingers over the harsh lines of the creature's fangs and claws before glancing up at Davina. "One of them grabbed my sister ten years ago. Could it have traveled here from the Middle East?"

From where he stood beside Jenna, Connor frowned. Trevor hoped he didn't do something stupid like once again insist that the creature hadn't kidnapped Hannah.

"Technically, Syria is actually in the Near East," Davina said. "Possibly, but I've found reference to these creatures all around the world, so it's difficult to be certain. Unfortunately, because these creatures spend nearly their entire lives underground, we don't know much about them. Regardless of how long they've been around."

Jenna took a deep breath and Trevor heard her heart beat faster. He reached out and took her hand, silently letting her know that she wasn't alone in this.

"Okay, so granted, you don't know much about them," Jenna said, giving his hand a squeeze as she looked at Davina. "Is there anything you can tell us that will help?"

Davina spun the book around, her eyes darting back and forth over the spiky-looking letters. "It says that ghouls live in large clans with as many as a hundred members. There's some kind of hierarchy system, with gatherers and workers at the bottom, hunters and artisans in the middle, and a ruling class at the top."

Jenna blinked, stunned. "We could be dealing with a hundred of these things? How is it possible that more people don't know about them?"

"As I said, they spend nearly their entire lives underground," Davina explained. "They've evolved to thrive in that environment. They can live off stuff that would kill any other living thing, such as used oil and biowaste, even radioactive goop. But given a choice, they'd rather dig into graves from the bottom and steal human corpses. They seem to especially like bones more than anything else."

Jenna shuddered and paled at that, and Trevor gave her hand a squeeze.

"If ghouls have adapted so well to living underground, why have they been coming up to the surface lately?" he asked.

"They do come out every once in a while, mostly to protect their clan or to take an odd job here and there, as bizarre as that sounds," Davina said. "They've also been known to occasionally come up to the surface to grab humans, though no one knows for sure why they do that." She gave Jenna a sympathetic look. "I know you don't want to hear this, but it's possible the creatures come to the surface looking for fresher food."

Jenna's heart raced even faster, and Trevor released her hand to wrap his arm around her instead. After a moment, she took a deep breath and shook her head, as if clearing her thoughts.

"If these ghouls are kidnapping people to eat them, then how is it possible my sister is alive a decade after they grabbed her?" Jenna asked. "How could she have lived this long among them?"

Davina gave her a small, sad smile. "I wish I had something definitive to tell you that answered that question. There's mention in one of the books about ghouls kidnapping people to use as labor, but that might be little more than folktale. There's no firsthand account of it ever happening, and even if there was, it wouldn't explain what's going on with your sister. If they're still keeping her against her will and she somehow escaped, why would she run from you?"

Tears welled in Jenna's eyes. "I don't know. None of this makes any sense."

Trevor's heart ached to see Jenna so worried. He wished he could think of something to say to reassure her and make her feel better, but he couldn't. From the looks on Davina's face and those of his pack mates, none of them had anything to say that would help make this situation better, either. The only thing they could do now was rescue Hannah and bring her home. And he was going to do everything in his power to make that happen.

Davina told them a little bit more about ghouls, specifically where they liked to live underground and how to find them. The plan revolved around tracking the ghoul Trevor had fought all the way back through the sewer tunnels and crawling through that rabbit warren of tunnels until they found something.

From where he stood near the far end of her desk, Mike frowned. "Let's put the plan for finding these things on hold for a minute and focus on something equally important—how we take them down. Trevor told us that when he fought that one last night, the wooden stake he tried to stab it with didn't even scratch its skin."

Davina picked up a folder from the other side of the desk and opened it, then flipped through a few pages with a lot of redacted crap all over the place. "I was going to get to that at some point, but now is as good of a time as any. Long, heavily redacted story short, a STAT team recently had a run-in with these creatures in Turkey and then again in New York City. Bottom line, for all intents and purposes, ghouls are bulletproof. I suppose that spending generations chewing through stone has essentially made their flesh as hard as rock. There were several guys like the four of you on the STAT team, including an omega, and it was all they could do to come out of those fights in one piece."

Jenna gave Trevor a curious look. "What does she mean, like the four of you?"

Trevor bit his tongue to keep from cursing as his worst fear was seemingly coming to fruition. Davina had slipped up and outed them as werewolves minutes after Jenna had learned her sister had been kidnapped by creatures that eat people. She'd think he and his pack mates were monsters, too.

"She means that they're SWAT cops like us," Hale said casually, leaning over Davina's desk like he was trying to study the book—upside down. "Omegas are what we call the last guy who enters a room during a breeching operation."

Davina looked at Trevor and his pack mates, obviously confused. But she had nothing on Jenna, who appeared completely baffled. Trevor couldn't believe she was going to buy any of this, even if it did sound pretty good. It was utter BS, of course, because an omega was simply another type of werewolf.

"Um, okay. I guess that makes sense," Jenna said. "So does this mean we can't do anything to stop these creatures, even if we somehow manage to find them?"

Davina flipped through the file again, turning several more pages until reaching the last one. Once there, she skimmed down a few lines to a portion that was more heavily redacted than the rest.

"There was a man who was able to take out one of the ghouls with nothing more than a metal pipe. The details are extremely lacking in the file, but a dead ghoul was confirmed, and the guy"—she swept her lavender gaze over Trevor and his pack mates—" who wasn't one of you SWAT cops—, took credit for it. I'm going to keep digging for information, but if you want a place to start when it comes to stopping these things, I'm guessing that would be it. A metal pipe."

Trevor looked around the office, relieved to see that he wasn't the only one who was worried. While Connor might believe ghouls existed, he was obviously still in denial that the creatures had kidnapped Hannah. Hale and Mike, on the other hand, clearly understood that at some point very soon, the four of them would be coming face-to-face with the creatures. Ones that seemed impervious to any of the weapons Trevor and his teammates would typically use against them—natural or supernatural. But the idea of trusting a cryptic note in some files about a guy killing one with a metal pipe, mentioned only in passing within a STAT report so heavily redacted it was nearly illegible, was a little disconcerting.

But one glance at Jenna and the firm look of conviction on her face suggested she didn't care. She was going to do whatever it took to find her sister, no matter how dangerous it might be. Which meant that Trevor would be, too. Because he'd do anything for her.

Anything.

CHAPTER 8

Jenna didn't say anything as she led the way up the steps to the second floor of her apartment building, then down the hall and into her place. It wasn't difficult for Trevor to imagine why she was so quiet and what she was thinking about. Everything they'd learned tonight was obviously weighing heavily on her. He could understand that. It wasn't that long ago when he'd gone through the same revelation and learned that the world was far scarier than he'd ever imagined and that supernatural creatures really existed. Of course, he'd already been a werewolf at that point, which he supposed had lessened the shock a little bit, but the knowledge that the world was filled with other supernaturals had made his head spin. He had no doubt that it had to be more of a game changer for Jenna.

They'd stopped at In-N-Out Burger for takeout on the way back from the club, so after washing up, he, Jenna, and his pack mates spread out around the living room to eat.

"So there are other monsters out there besides ghouls," Jenna said, pausing with a french fry that she'd dipped in her milkshake halfway to her mouth. "And there are entire books on them and stuff."

"We call them supernaturals instead of monsters," Hale corrected, digging into his second cheeseburger. "Not all of them are bad. Some are just different."

Jenna regarded him curiously. "You've encountered supernaturals who aren't bad then?"

"A few," Hale murmured before taking a big bite of his burger.

Jenna sat there expectantly, like she was waiting for Hale to elaborate. But since it wasn't like he could admit that the entire SWAT team was filled with supernaturals—and that Connor's soul mate was a witch, like Davina—there wasn't much he could tell her.

When it became clear that Hale wasn't going to say anything else, Jenna looked at the rest of them. "Okay, so I guess that brings us back to what we learned tonight about these ghouls. I know Davina said she'd do some digging and try to find more information on the creatures' weaknesses and whether there might be more than one way into their tunnels, but what's our plan? I mean, what are we going to do about these things?"

Trevor opened his mouth to offer his thoughts, only for Connor to cut him off.

"First off, you don't need to know what the plan is," Connor said, his voice firm and clearly on the edge of being angry. "Because you aren't going to be involved in any of this."

Trevor braced himself. When Connor had pulled this same kind of stunt back in Dallas, she'd walked out on her brother, refusing to speak to him for days and ending up in Trevor's apartment. So, he was a little surprised when Jenna simply took a small bite of her cheeseburger and regarded her brother calmly as she chewed.

"You don't get any say in whether I'm involved in this," Jenna said almost casually, pointing at him with a french fry.

"I'm your brother," Connor said with none of the casualness his sister had displayed. "Of course I have a say in whether you risk your life."

"No, you don't," she said, firmer this time. "You gave that up when you turned your back on me all those years ago and then again when I came to you in Dallas asking for your help finding Hannah. In some ways, I suppose I could forgive you for the first time. I was a kid. Who would have believed any kid when she said a monster grabbed her sister and dragged her away? But then I come to Dallas, telling you I've seen Hannah, and you tell me I'm crazy. Now, I find out that you've known that supernatural creatures existed all along. And you want me to care what you think? Don't make me laugh."

Connor's face had gone pale as his sister blasted him, but Jenna either didn't notice or didn't care, because it didn't seem like she was planning to let up.

"I'm going to help find Hannah, no matter what

you say, Connor," she said bluntly. "Because I'm the one who never stopped looking for her while you're the one who gave up and ran away. If you can't handle that, feel free to get back on a plane and go home to Dallas. I'll do it without you, just like I've been doing from the beginning."

Wrapping up her burger, she slid that and the fries closer to where Trevor's extra bag of food was sitting on the table. "You can have the rest of this," she said. "I've lost my appetite." Picking up her milkshake, she looked at Mike. "There's only one guest bedroom, so you guys will have to stay at a hotel. There are some nice ones a few blocks south of here. When you come back in the morning, we can figure out what we're going to do next." She gave Trevor a small smile. "Come to bed when you're ready. I'll leave the bedside lamp on."

The living room was deathly silent after Jenna left and disappeared down the hall toward the back of the apartment. A full minute passed before the shower started, and yet none of his pack mates said a word the entire time. Hale sat there eating while Mike kept glancing back and forth between Trevor and Connor, like he expected a fight to break out any second.

Which, considering the angry expression on Connor's face, was probably a valid concern. He looked like he was ready to explode.

"You're not staying here," Connor growled, his

eyes flaring yellow gold. Even as Trevor watched, the tips of Connor's fangs appeared over his lower lip.

"And you need to calm the hell down," Mike warned. "We can't have you losing control with your sister in the next room."

Mike moved fast, but not fast enough. One minute, Connor was snarling, and the next, he was up and throwing himself in Trevor's direction. Trevor barely made it to his feet before Connor's fist collided with the left side of his jaw, dropping him back onto the couch and nearly throwing him over the back of the thing. He heard the sound of a bone breaking and for a fraction of a second wanted to think it was Connor's hand. Then jarring pain raced through his head, and he realized he was definitely wrong about that. It wasn't his pack mate's hand. It was his own jaw.

Trevor ignored the pain and shoved himself upright, getting an arm raised just in time to block a second punch coming his way, glad it was a fist and not claws. His shove sent Connor sliding back across the floor and into Mike's arms. But Connor merely shook him off and charged at Trevor again, claws whistling through the air this time.

Trevor froze, stunned that his pack mate—his *friend*—was coming at him like this and apparently willing to tear him apart. A few bruises he'd be able to explain to Jenna, but blood and bone-deep lacerations? There'd be no way to hide their secret after that.

He leaped back at the last second, cursing silently as the tips of Connor's claws grazed the front of his shirt. Then Mike and Hale were both grabbing Connor's arms, holding him back as his fangs extended even further, eyes blazing in fury.

"You stay away from my sister!" Connor snarled. "She doesn't need you confusing her when she's trying to deal with this ghoul crap. And she sure as hell doesn't need you trying to sneak into her bed."

"Trevor doesn't have to sneak into my bed," Jenna's angry voice said from the hallway behind them. "Because I invited him in myself!"

Trevor gave a start, shocked he hadn't noticed that the shower had turned off. But the rapid stomp of bare feet told him that not only was Jenna done in the bathroom but that she'd obviously heard them fighting, too. He'd been so wrapped up in the argument with Connor that he hadn't been paying attention to anything else.

And standing there in shorts and a T-shirt, her hair piled loosely atop her head, face flushed, Jenna looked mad as hell.

Trevor glanced at Connor to see that he was still pissed off because his eyes were glowing like a pair of Christmas bulbs and his fangs were fully extended. And from the way he was struggling to get free of Mike and Hale, it would seem he didn't care that his sister was standing right behind him.

Crap.

Trevor surged forward to grab Connor, latching his hands onto his friend's shoulders, then taking a risk by putting his face close to his pack mate's.

"Dammit, Connor," he said in a loud whisper. "What the hell is wrong with you? Is this really how you want your sister to learn about werewolves, right after learning from Davina that monsters are real? She'll be horrified, not to mention terrified of you, her brother."

That seemed to finally get through Connor's thick head, and when Jenna took hold of her brother's arm and yanked him around to face her, the yellow-gold glow disappeared from his eyes and his fangs retracted. Barely in time.

"I already told you," Jenna said, the words coming out in a low growl that would have made any werewolf proud. "You don't get a say in how I live my life, whether it's searching for Hannah or who I decide to spend my time with. You need to get over yourself. And if you can't, you need to get out of my apartment and never come back."

When Connor simply stood there stunned, Jenna brushed past him and looked at Trevor. She frowned at the bruise he had no doubt was already forming along his jaw where Connor had punched him. The discoloration would be gone within the hour, but she didn't know that.

Then Jenna's gaze dropped lower, and her eyes narrowed as she stared at his chest. He glanced down to see four slashes across his T-shirt, thin lines of blood clearly visible through the torn material. The wounds weren't a big deal, but again, she couldn't know that.

"I'll clean those up for you as soon as they leave," she said, throwing a look at her brother that could melt steel. Then, without another word, she turned and went back to her bedroom, slamming the door loudly behind her.

"I better talk to her," Connor said, moving to follow, only for Mike to grab hold of him again.

"I don't think so," Mike said firmly, spinning Connor around. "I'm pretty sure you've done more than enough talking for one night. We're leaving and you're coming with us, whether you want to or not. We still need to see that person STAT arranged for us to meet so we can pick up the weapons they promised us. Even if we don't know how well they'll work, I'd still feel better having a gun if we have to go up against these ghouls."

For a moment, Trevor was sure Connor was going to resist, but then he nodded. Pulling out of Mike's grip, he strode across the living room, not even looking back before walking out the door.

Mike shook his head, then looked at Trevor. "We'll call before we come over in the morning so you can take a shower before we get here. If you don't smell like his sister when we show up, maybe that will keep Connor from losing his mind again."

"I doubt it," Hale murmured before following Mike out of the apartment.

Trevor silently agreed with him. No matter how many showers he took, some of Jenna's scent would still be on him, and that would be all the excuse Connor needed.

Trevor locked the door, then cleaned up the takeout food wrappers and cups before shutting off the lights. By the time he walked down the hallway, Jenna had already come out of her bedroom and was rattling around in the bathroom. A few seconds later, she came out carrying a bottle of peroxide and a box of cotton balls. Trevor couldn't help but smile. He couldn't remember the last time someone had fussed over him.

"That's not really necessary," he said, even as Jenna nudged him into her bedroom and made him sit on the side of the bed. "It's only a few scratches."

The look Jenna gave him was skeptical. "It's more than a few scratches. You're bleeding."

Placing her first aid supplies on the bed beside him, she reached for the bottom of his tee to pull it up over his head, then tossed it aside. Sitting there in nothing but his jeans while Jenna stood there in nothing but a pair of shorts and thin tank top was kind of tough, and it was difficult to resist the urge to pull her close and kiss her.

But the way she stared at the scratches on his chest, her eyes starting to film over with tears, was enough to help him push those urges aside. Now wasn't the time for that.

"My brother is a jerk." She tipped the bottle of peroxide over, soaking a cotton ball, then gently pressed it to one of the scratches. "But at least these don't look as bad as I thought. What the heck did he even cut you with, anyway?"

Trevor looked down. The scratches weren't deep at all and weren't even bleeding now. Not that Jenna seemed to notice as she continued to clean each one carefully. He was only glad the scratches didn't reach his tattoo. He would have been pissed if Connor had messed up his ink. While his skin would heal from a wound, the tattoo probably wouldn't fare so well.

"He must have caught me with his fingernails," Trevor said casually. "He was trying to shove me, and his hand slipped."

Jenna gave him a look as if to say, *do you expect me to believe that?* "His fingernails sliced your T-shirt open?"

He shrugged. "Yeah. I guess he needs to trim them a little."

Jenna didn't say anything, focusing her attention on what she was doing.

"Why is my brother such a jerk?" she asked softly, pulling out another cotton ball, then soaking it in disinfectant and cleaning the next scratch. It was totally unnecessary by now, but something told him that Jenna continued to do it more for her benefit than his.

"I know you don't want to hear this, but I think Connor is only trying to protect you in his own dumb way," Trevor said. "To him, you're still his little sister, and he simply wants to protect you from all the bad things in the world. Which includes me, apparently."

"My brother is a dumbass." Finishing up, she placed her first aid kit on the bedside table. "It's bad enough that he treats me like a child, but if he can't see that you're the best thing that ever happened to me, I feel sorry for him."

Trevor started to smile at the sense of warmth bubbling up in his chest at her words but decided to play it cool. He didn't want to read more into that statement than what Jenna might have intended. Instead, he moved enough so that he could pull the blankets and sheets down on the bed.

"Let's forget about Connor for tonight," he said. "We can worry about him in the morning. If he even comes back."

Jenna sighed but climbed into bed, giving him a view of her butt that was something to behold. Trevor stifled a groan as he grabbed his T-shirt.

"I'm going to change," he said.

He went over to his room long enough to change into a pair of shorts. He considered putting on another tee but figured Jenna had already seen him without it, so why bother now?

Jenna slid close to him the moment he slipped into bed with her and turned off the light on the nightstand. As she rested her head on his chest, Trevor wrapped his arm around her shoulders as if it was the most natural thing in the world. Like this was exactly where she should be all the time.

She placed a hand lightly on his stomach, her fingers almost absently tracing light patterns on his skin. He wondered if she even knew she was doing it. Not that he was planning to stop her. It felt good.

"I'm glad you didn't let Connor chase you off," Jenna said softly, her breathy words warm on his skin, damn near giving him goose bumps. "That would have been worse than anything my brother has ever done."

"I'm not going anywhere," Trevor said firmly, squeezing her shoulders a bit tighter. "There's nothing Connor can do that would get me away from you."

He was so focused on thinking about what he'd just promised—and what it meant for his future with the Pack—that he wasn't aware she pushed herself up off his chest until she bent her head and kissed him.

It was a tame kiss—at least compared to the one they'd shared that morning—but it was tantalizing all the same, and for a moment, Trevor wanted nothing more than to urge Jenna on top of him and kiss her until she fell apart in his arms.

But before things could go that far, Jenna pulled back, smiling down at him in the darkness. "Thanks," she murmured, kissing him gently again. "I can't put into words how much I needed to hear that. I also can't put into words how much you've come to mean to me."

He opened his mouth to respond, but Jenna didn't give him a chance. Instead, she settled back down to his chest, snuggling against him, the hand that had been on his stomach wrapping around him, squeezing him tight. It seemed like it was only a few moments later that he picked up the sounds of her breathing, realizing she had dropped off to sleep.

Trevor lay there in the darkness, smiling up at the ceiling. He wasn't too worried about what came next with him and the Pack, as long as he had this. And as long as he had Jenna in his arms.

CHAPTER 9

"So was it my imagination or did I see three more hunky stud muffins going into your apartment this morning?" Madeleine said as she took a sip of her latte while sitting there trying to act all casual as she gazed at Jenna from across the table at Starbucks. "What, Trevor not enough for you?"

Jenna laughed, so glad she'd made the decision to come out and spend a little time with her best friend this morning instead of going on a ghoul recon with Trevor, Connor, and their teammates. While she wasn't thrilled about Trevor being out there without her, the idea of spending time with her brother—who was still eyeing her with blatant discontent—was more than she was ready for today. Then there was the whole going underground thing. She definitely wasn't up for that. Especially when they didn't even know for sure that Hannah was down there.

"I suppose it was pure coincidence that you were looking through the peephole in your door when the three aforementioned hunky stud muffins arrived this morning?"

Madeleine put on an expression that was probably supposed to convey innocence but failed completely. "It's not my fault those three were making so much noise, with those deep, rumbling voices of theirs. Any woman would have looked in that situation. And what kind of friend would I be if I didn't pay attention when three big muscular men show up at their BFF's apartment out of the blue?"

"Not quite out of the blue," Jenna said, nibbling on the spinach, cheese, and egg whole wheat wrap she'd bought to go with her morning coffee. The combo was her go-to breakfast whenever she came here. "They actually arrived yesterday morning, but I can only guess that you were too busy looking at those big muscular bodies to recognize that my brother was one of them."

Madeleine looked somewhat chastised at that as she put avocado spread on her whole wheat toast, but not much. "I have to admit, I wasn't looking at their faces too much. But I could probably draw those butts from memory. So what's your brother doing in town, who are his friends, and do you know if they're taken?"

Jenna didn't want to think about her best friend staring at her brother's butt so long she'd memorized it, which was why she focused on the questions Madeleine had asked.

"It's a long, complicated story," Jenna said with a smile. "You sure you have enough time to get into it?"

Madeleine looked at her phone where it sat on the table to check the time before nodding. "I have to start getting ready for one of those fancy pop-up dining experiences in Grand Hope Park soon, but I have a little time, so tell me what's going on."

"Okay, this is going to sound a little weird, but Trevor and I saw something the other night while we were down near Skid Row."

"Something concerning Hannah?" Madeleine asked, the piece of avocado toast halfway to her mouth. "Did you see her again?"

Jenna shook her head. Until meeting Trevor, Madeleine was one of very few people she'd ever trusted enough to talk to about her missing sister. She hadn't exactly told her everything. Like the details about which kind of *monster* had grabbed Hannah. Madeleine had assumed it was some kind of psychotic serial killer type, and Jenna had never corrected that assumption. But other than that, she'd been pretty open with her friend. Being able to unload at least some of that trauma had been a lifeline for Jenna, getting her through the past few years.

"No, we didn't see her." Jenna sipped her almond milk latte, not sure how to explain the next part. "But we did see the...guy...who kidnapped her. Trevor fought with him, but the guy got away and disappeared down into the sewers. Trevor decided to call in some backup from his SWAT team in Dallas to help find the guy and look for Hannah. That's where Connor, Hale, and Mike come into it." She made a face. "Though I think my brother only came to try and keep Trevor and me apart. He doesn't seem to think Trevor is good enough for me."

Madeleine blinked. "Okay, there is so much in that whole thing to unpack. But let's start at the beginning. You say you saw the guy who kidnapped your sister? But how do you know for sure it was the same person? It's been a whole decade."

"It was him," Jenna said firmly, though she realized now after talking with Davina that the creature they'd seen probably wasn't the exact same one who'd grabbed Hannah. Just one of many. But the principle was the same. "He was busy trying to drag off another woman when we stumbled across them, and he then disappeared down a manhole in the ground. With an MO like that, I think we can comfortably say it's the same monster."

Madeleine couldn't seem to come up with anything to counter that argument, so after a moment of thought, she moved in another direction. "Did you tell the cops?"

"Why bother?" Jenna snorted. "They've never believed me before, so why would they start now?"

Madeleine looked like she wanted to argue but then must have thought better of it. "So to recap, you and Trevor find the monster that took your sister, your SWAT hunk calls in some of his hunky SWAT buddies from back home to come out to help find this guy—and hopefully Hannah, too—and in the bargain you get your overprotective brother. Does that sound about right?"

"That's pretty much it," Jenna agreed.

"And has he been successful in breaking up you and Trevor?"

"No, but not for lack of trying."

"Does he know you and Trevor are sleeping together?" Madeleine asked.

"We haven't slept together yet, at least not in the way you mean."

Jenna took another long sip of her coffee before looking up to see a blatantly curious expression on her friend's face. She sighed. "Trevor and I have made out, but we haven't had sex yet. I mean, we've slept together in the same bed the past two nights, but that's all we did—sleep. With everything going on down in Skid Row and then my brother showing up and being a dumbass, it didn't seem like the right time."

Madeleine sipped her coffee thoughtfully. "Would you have wanted to do more if all this other stuff wasn't messing up the mood?"

Jenna didn't have to think about that question very long.

"Yeah, I would," she said, realizing how true that was—and how unusual. With the experiences she'd had in her life, trusting people came hard for her. And while she'd slept with a few guys, she'd mostly found it to be...well...less than amazing. She hadn't thought too much about it but simply accepted that connecting with someone sexually required a level of intimacy that was never going to happen for her.

But it wasn't difficult to imagine having that connection with Trevor. Even though they'd just met, in some ways, it seemed like they already had it. It was probably why the idea of sleeping with him already was so appealing.

"Do you believe in love at first sight?" Jenna asked suddenly.

She wasn't sure where she'd found the courage to ask the question that had been bouncing around in the hidden recesses of her mind, but there it was.

On the other side of the table, Madeleine looked shocked for a moment, silently regarding Jenna with eyes full of surprise and maybe a little concern.

"If I'm being completely honest, I'd have to admit that I don't," her friend said softly. "In my experience, it takes time for love to develop and for people to truly get to know each other so they can learn if they're compatible. That way, you can find out if you share the same goals and if your hopes and dreams match up. To know if this other person is going to cherish your heart even above their own. How can all that happen in a moment?"

"Oh," Jenna said, deflating a little in her seat. Madeleine had slammed the door pretty frigging hard on that naive question. "Yeah, I guess that makes sense."

"But hey, that's just me," her friend added quickly, reaching across the table to take Jenna's hand, as if she'd only now realized that maybe she'd been a little too blunt with the complete honesty thing. "I'm not saying it couldn't happen for you. Anything is possible, right? You know me. I like to overanalyze every angle when a man is involved. It could be totally different with you and Trevor." Though Madeleine was smiling, there was still a hint of that same concern on her face that had been there before. Maybe even a little more than earlier. "Do you think that's what's happening between you and Trevor?"

Jenna didn't miss the doubt still being expressed in that question, regardless of what Madeleine had said about anything being possible.

"Trevor is absolutely the most amazing man I've ever met," Jenna said, searching for the right words but knowing she wasn't truly doing him justice. "I don't know how else to say it, other than to tell you that it seems he's perfect for me. Like he's the man I was meant to be with without realizing I was even looking for someone."

Madeleine didn't say anything for a long time but instead sat there regarding her thoughtfully.

Crap. Maybe she'd made a mistake by being so completely open about her feelings.

"I feel bad that my first instinct is to tell you to

be careful," Madeleine finally said with a sigh. "But you're my best friend in the whole world, and I never want to see you get hurt, which is what I'm afraid you're setting yourself up for by falling for Trevor so fast."

Jenna wanted to argue with Madeleine's logic, but there was a part of her that wondered if maybe her friend was right. She had a fleeting thought that falling for a guy this fast couldn't be normal. She could certainly see her therapist saying that she was simply confusing Trevor's friendship and acceptance for something completely different. Jenna felt her heart constrict down to the size of a pea at the thought.

"You don't think there's any chance that what I'm feeling for Trevor could be real?" she asked quietly.

The words felt wrong the moment they were out of her mouth. Like she was lying to herself by even saying something like that.

For a moment, Jenna thought Madeleine would agree with her, but instead, her friend shook her head. "I know it sounds like that's what I was saying, but I'm not. I just don't want to see you get hurt. You're my best friend and I care about you. But at the same time, you deserve happiness in your life more than anyone, so instead of doubting and being the voice of reason, I'm going to be your biggest cheerleader and tell you that if this thing with Trevor feels right, go for it with all your heart."

Jenna couldn't help but laugh, tension she hadn't been aware of slowly slipping off her shoulders like a heavy weight. It was silly. It wasn't like she needed permission to feel the way she felt. But still, it helped somehow having Madeleine in her corner on this.

Her friend squeezed her hand harder, smiling even wider. "Now that we've gotten all that out of the way, have you thought about discussing this same thing with Trevor and telling him how you feel?"

Time seemed to freeze then, Jenna nearly vapor locking at the idea of coming out and telling Trevor everything she'd told Madeleine. It might be how she felt, but could she be that open with him? Allow herself to be so vulnerable in front of him?

"Okay, breathe, hon," Madeleine murmured, squeezing her hand hard enough to pull her out of the tailspin she'd dropped into. "Maybe we can put that idea on hold for now. It probably would be a good idea to have sex with the guy first before you make any declarations. Nothing kills a budding romance like finding out a man sucks in the sack."

Jenna laughed again, even though the idea of Trevor not being beyond amazing in everything he did—even in bed—was too ludicrous to take seriously. Considering how hot she'd gotten simply from kissing him, she had no doubt he'd be scrumptious once the two of them finally made love.

She opened her mouth to tell Madeleine as much when she caught movement out of the corner of her eye of two people slowly coming toward their table, like they were hesitant to intrude. Jenna looked up to see Esme and Maya from HOPD standing there looking guilty as hell.

"Can we help you?" Madeleine asked, giving them a look that suggested she was willing to be polite, but only to a point.

"Hey, Jenna," Esme said slowly, twisting her hands together in front of her anxiously. "Sorry to interrupt, but Maya and I were hoping to talk to you about what's going down in the Skid Row district today."

Jenna wasn't sure about having any kind of conversation with the two women in front of Madeleine, but both Esme and Maya looked pretty worried about something. Knowing that Trevor, Connor, and the other guys were down in the Skid Row district right now was enough to make the conversation worth the risk.

"Have a seat," she murmured, motioning them toward the table.

There was a moment of hesitation, both of the paranormal investigators eyeing Madeleine curiously. But after a moment, they slipped into the two empty chairs.

"This is my friend Madeleine," Jenna introduced her friend. "She's familiar with the situation with my sister and the fact that Trevor and I saw the guy who kidnapped her when we were in the Skid Row area a couple nights ago. Madeleine, this is Esme and Maya. They're with a private investigation firm called the HOPD. I hired them to help find Hannah."

She didn't know whose eyes widened more—Madeleine's or the two women's. Now, she was definitely wishing she'd been a little more honest with her best friend. There was nothing she could do about it right now, but if Esme or Maya let something slip about monsters and the paranormal, Madeleine was going to lose it.

"Wait. You hired a PI firm and didn't tell me?" her friend said, her expression a cross between surprised and pissed off. "When?"

"It was a few months ago," Jenna said. "I didn't bother mentioning it because nothing ever came of it. They were never able to find any leads on the guy who grabbed my sister, and I haven't seen them again until the other night after Trevor and I saw the guy in that alley off Winston Street."

Jenna glanced at Esme and Maya as she said that last part, hoping they understood what she was trying to get across—that they couldn't say anything about being paranormal investigators.

"Okay." Madeleine looked at the two women. "So how did you two end up working in the PI field?"

Crap. Jenna just knew her friend must sense that

something was off about this whole situation. But all she could do was sit there, waiting for either Esme or Maya to say the wrong thing and make a mess of everything.

Maya shrugged. "The way everyone in LA seems to get a job, I suppose. We both came out to be movie stars and ended up falling into something completely different."

Since that story sounded amazingly similar to Madeleine's own career path, her friend seemed to buy it without complaint. But that didn't keep her from opening her mouth to ask another question.

"What was it you wanted to talk to me about, Esme?" Jenna interrupted, cutting off her friend and hopefully getting this conversation going in another direction. "You seemed concerned about something when you walked up to the table."

Esme threw another glance in Madeleine's direction, likely trying to figure out how to say what she wanted to say. But after a second, she turned back to Jenna.

"We ran into your boyfriend while we were doing a recon around the alleys in Skid Row near the place where that woman was attacked the other night," Esme said, obviously choosing her words very carefully. "He had three other big guys with him, and it was clear that they were planning to try and track down that guy you saw."

"Yeah, I know," Jenna said, relieved that it wasn't

anything alarming. "Trevor's plan for this morning was to snoop around a little and get a bead on where the guy might have gone. He wants to see if there was more than one...person...involved in the attack on that woman in the alley."

Esme and Maya both nodded at that, though neither one of them appeared to be any happier.

"That was what Trevor said," Maya murmured. "But were you aware that the plan included going down in the sewers and taking Owen and Isaac with them?"

Even though she knew Trevor would be going underground, it still caused an immediate twinge of panic to settle in Jenna's stomach. She fought it down, trying to stay calm...outwardly at least. "Like I said, Trevor told me he planned to follow the trail left by the attacker. It was kind of a given that he'd have to follow it into the sewers again. Though I have to admit, I'm surprised they took Owen and Isaac with them."

"It's not like Owen gave them a choice," Esme admitted. "He basically threatened to follow them on his own. I think Trevor let the guys go with them simply to keep them from getting into trouble. Owen is really good at that—getting himself and others into trouble."

"Why didn't you and Maya go down into the sewers with them?" Madeleine asked, looking back and forth between the two women.

"Because in addition to being good at getting us into trouble, Owen's also a bit of a jackass when it comes to keeping us *womenfolk* safe." Maya snorted. "He wanted Esme and me to wait topside while he and Isaac did the *manly* thing and went down into the tunnels. We immediately did the smart thing and came to get you, thinking you might want to be there with us in case anything goes wrong."

Jenna sat there, her mind reeling at the mere suggestion of going down into the sewers. She was so lost in her thoughts that it took Madeleine reaching across the table to squeeze her hand again before she could snap out of it even a little.

"You're not seriously thinking about going after them, are you?" her friend asked, clearly alarmed at the thought, knowing what she did about Jenna's particular version of claustrophobia. "That's not a good idea."

Jenna didn't say anything. After all these years, she'd finally found the creature that had kidnapped her sister, and she was apparently too damaged to do anything with that information. The mere thought of going down in those tunnels—even to help Trevor—had her completely tied up in knots and unable to move.

She resisted the comparison, but it was impossible not to think about those moments right after her sister had been taken, when the monster had dragged Hannah away. Jenna had huddled on the ground near that damn dumpster, frozen, too terrified to even try and save her.

Jenna couldn't let that happen to someone else she cared about. Not again.

"I'm going to head over to the Skid Row district with Esme and Maya to have a look around," she said to Madeleine, hurrying on before her friend could say anything. "I know you have to get ready for that pop-up dining experience you're hosting tonight, so don't even try and offer to come with us. Trevor and the others are probably already back above ground as we speak, so it's no big deal."

Madeleine didn't look convinced at all, not even a little. "Jenna…"

"I'm not going down in the sewers," Jenna promised, feeling bad about lying, even if it was for a good cause. "You don't need to worry. Really. I'll call you later and let you know that everything is fine."

Her friend still wasn't thrilled about the idea but finally nodded, if a bit reluctantly. "Okay, I'm going to trust you not to do anything stupid, but only because you promised you wouldn't go down in those tunnels. So don't make me regret this, okay?"

"Okay."

Madeleine grabbed her coffee, and after extracting one more promise not to do anything stupid—and to text her later—her best friend left.

Jenna barely waited for her friend to walk out the door of the coffee shop before turning back to Esme and Maya. "All right, let's get out of here."

Man, she hoped she didn't regret this decision. "But before we go, I need to know how the two of you knew I would be here."

CHAPTER 10

"You put a tracking chip on us?" Trevor demanded. "That's how you knew we were down in Skid Row again?"

He bit back a growl as he led their small group through the sewer tunnels, once again regretting that he'd ever agreed to let Owen and Isaac come with them. None of his pack mates had thought it was a good idea either—especially Connor—but the notion of the two paranormal investigators wandering around the pitch-black tunnels on their own until they got eaten by a ghoul had been enough to let them come along with him and his teammates.

Even though Mike was the senior member of the Pack among the four of them, he'd willingly let Trevor take lead on this operation since he was the reason they were all out here. So after Owen and Isaac had promised to keep their mouths shut and do exactly what they were told, Trevor convinced himself the two paranormal investigators couldn't be that much trouble.

Turns out he'd been wrong.

Owen never shut up, repeatedly asking why he couldn't have a gun like the ones Trevor and his three teammates were carrying. And when he wasn't talking, he was pointing his flashlight in everybody's face, damn near blinding them all.

"You make it sound so illegal when you say it that way," Owen said from his place several spots behind Trevor, flicking his flashlight this way and that, like he was a member of the Scooby Gang looking for a clue. "All we did was attach one of those tiny GPS trackers to the underside of your rental car. You know the ones that helicopter moms clip to their little kid's backpacks? The things are cheap as hell and connect straight to an app on my phone. We put one on Jenna's car, too, so it's not like we were only targeting you or anything."

Trevor bit his lower lip to keep from growling.

"Tagging a person's car with your cheap GPS tracker sounds illegal because it *is* illegal, you dumbass," Connor said from farther back in the tunnel. "It's a misdemeanor in California for anyone but the cops or a licensed PI to do it. And you guys are definitely neither of those things."

"I don't know if anyone has ever told you this, but you come off sounding like a cop when you talk like that," Isaac said.

"That's probably because we are cops," Mike said from directly behind Isaac. "I assumed the fact that we're carrying licensed handguns would be a dead giveaway, but I guess not. Then again, it's not like running around in the sewers looking for supernatural creatures is a normal thing for police to do, so I probably shouldn't hold that against you."

There was silence for a long time as Trevor continued leading them through the tunnels, the dirt and musky scent he'd come to associate with the ghouls incredibly easy to follow. Every once in a while, he or one of his pack mates would use a piece of chalk to mark an arrow on the wall. It wasn't as if they were worried about getting lost down here, but Owen and Isaac were a different matter. If they got separated, hopefully the arrows on the wall would lead them back to the exit.

"Um...I just want to let you know that we never used the trackers on a person before," Isaac finally said, suddenly sounding guilty. "We originally picked them up in case we ever stumbled across a paranormal creature and needed to follow it back to its lair."

Trevor had a sudden vision of Isaac jumping on a vampire's back, trying to clip a GPS tracker on the vamp's belt, even as the bloodsucker tore the rest of his HOPD crew to shreds. These guys were so far out of their league and didn't even know it.

"Have you ever actually run into a real supernatural creature?" Hale asked, clearly thinking the same thing Trevor had.

"Oh yeah. Lots of them," Owen assured them in a tone that suggested it wasn't a big deal at the exact same time that Isaac said, "Not really."

Trevor stopped walking to look back at the two

members of the nerd herd, the beams of their flashlights reflecting off the walls of the tunnel to reveal some seriously embarrassed faces.

"I mean," Owen started slowly, "we've come close to seeing some supernatural creatures. But they always seem to slip away at the last second. They're out there, though. I swear it."

"You don't have to do much to convince us of that," Trevor said, moving out of the way of the flashlights so that they illuminated the hole in the tunnel floor that the creature had disappeared into the other day. "In this case at least, you're right."

Owen hurried over, leaning forward and running his light around the ragged edges of the hole in the concrete, the beam glinting off the pieces of steel rebar the ghoul had sliced clean through. "Where did that come from?"

Trevor dropped to one knee beside the hole. "This is how the creatures we're after are able to move around the city without being seen. It appears these things can claw through concrete and steel like it's tissue paper. I'm guessing that flesh and bone wouldn't present much of a problem, either."

Even in the darkness, it was impossible to miss that Isaac and Owen had become extremely nervous all of a sudden. Their hearts were beating faster and they were sweating a little. Something told Trevor that both men were probably wondering if coming down here had been such a good idea.

"Do you think there are more than one of these creatures?" Owen asked, running his fingers along the edge of the hole like he was trying to understand how any creature could claw through concrete and metal like this. Trevor couldn't blame him. Werewolves had claws, but even they couldn't do anything like this.

"Yeah," Mike said from the back of the group, and Trevor could see him lift his nose to subtly test the air. "There are definitely more than one."

"So..." Isaac said, looking back and forth between the part of the tunnel where Mike was standing and the pitch-black darkness filling the hole in the floor. "Are we going down there to try and follow one of those things?"

"That's the idea," Connor said, mouth curving into a smirk. "Of course, you two are welcome to head back up to the surface and wait for us up there where it's safe."

Isaac seemed like he was ready to accept the offer, but Owen stood straighter and got an obstinate look on his face, like Connor was challenging his manhood or something lame like that.

"Oh, we're going down there all right," Owen said fiercely, taking a step closer to the hole in the floor of the tunnel. "In fact, we're going to go first."

Before he could take a step, Trevor reached out and grabbed his shoulder. "You're not going first and that's the end of it," he said firmly, tugging Owen back.

Trevor looked at each of his pack mates in turn before turning his gaze on Owen and Isaac. "I shouldn't have to repeat this, but I will anyway. We're going down in that hole for one reason, and one reason only—recon. We need to know how extensive these tunnels are and how difficult it will be to navigate them. If we can figure out where these creatures live, we'll consider that gravy at this point. We're going to avoid contact, no matter what. We simply don't know enough about what we're up against to risk a confrontation."

Owen opened his mouth, no doubt to demand they should go running in with guns blazing as if they were in a Hollywood action movie. Fortunately, the man censored himself at the last moment.

"Are you sure we can't have weapons?" he asked instead, peeking down in the hole in the floor again.

"No!" Trevor and his pack mates said in unison.

Jumping into the hole, Trevor immediately began moving forward on his hands and knees. The bottom of this new stretch of tunnel was rougher than the man-made sewer above, with ridges of stones and chunks of rubble that dug into his jean-covered knees and the palms of his hands as he crawled. In some places, the tunnel narrowed, scraping his shoulders and back, while in others, it was big enough to almost walk upright.

As he continued crawling through the tunnel, he

listened for the sound of movement ahead of him. He'd hoped that his nose would clue him in to the presence of any ghouls, but the tunnel they were in reeked of dirt and that musky scent he associated with the creatures, so right now, they could be anywhere.

Sound carried funny through the tunnel, too, and he wondered if creaking in the rock around him was one of those famous California earthquakes or merely a heavy truck passing by on the street overhead.

Unfortunately, hearing anything became difficult soon enough, as Owen began a monologue into his phone about being in the *belly of the beast* and how he was *risking his life to uncover the truth of the Skid Row Screamer*.

Trevor couldn't help but shake his head. Man, the guy was such a total doofus.

Desperate for a distraction from Owen's nonstop talking, Trevor found his mind wandering. His thoughts naturally found their way to Jenna. A big part of that was how amazing it had been to wake up with her in his arms this morning, but the other part was how thrilled he'd been when she'd decided not to come with them on this morning's recon mission. Even if her reasoning had more to do with her fear of going underground and her ongoing spat with Connor. Still, Trevor would have been freaking out if she was down here with them. The mere thought made his heart thump hard and his claws threaten to come out. He never ever wanted to consider Jenna being in danger. Just another sign of how far he was falling for her.

Trevor reached a Y intersection in the tunnel with two passages snaking off into the darkness. He stopped in the open space before the branches, making room for everyone else to gather around in the tight space. Owen and Isaac nervously swept their flashlights all over the place.

"I was hoping this tunnel would lead straight into the center of the creatures' territory, but apparently, we're not going to get that lucky," Trevor said. "So we have a decision to make—stay together and pick one tunnel to follow, or split up."

"We should split up," Connor said firmly before anyone could get another word in. "Mike and I will go left and the rest of you can go right. We can cover more ground that way."

Trevor wasn't surprised Connor wanted to split up or that he refused to be teamed up with him. It had been hard enough getting him to come down into the tunnels in the first place, and Trevor suspected most of that was because his friend couldn't stand the sight of him right now. Then again, maybe he was giving himself too much credit. Maybe the reason Connor hadn't wanted to come was because he believed that if he never saw a ghoul with his own eyes, then he wouldn't have to face the fact that he'd done everything Jenna had accused him of—namely abandoning her and Hannah.

"I don't think splitting up is the best idea," Isaac pointed out. "That's what happens in every sci-fi and horror movie right before people start getting eaten."

Trevor couldn't necessarily disagree with that logic. Splitting up usually did bring scary things out of the woodwork. But in this case, there wasn't much they could do about it. If they stayed together in one large group, the chances of finding anything down here weren't good. For all they knew, they could end up wandering around down here for days. They didn't have that much time to waste, especially because Jenna would almost certainly come looking for him if he was gone too long, and that was flat-out unacceptable.

In the end, Connor did go left with Mike, but they took Isaac with them. Trevor, Hale, and Owen went right. It seemed a concession that everyone could live with.

"We go as far as we can for an hour," Trevor said. "Then, regardless of what either of our teams discover, we turn around and rendezvous back here. No exceptions. If one team comes back here and the other hasn't shown within five minutes, that means something is wrong, and the first team goes into rescue mode at that point."

Trevor hoped that never became necessary, but

it needed to be said. They had to have a plan in case everything went sideways. Mike and Hale nodded as if that made complete sense while Owen and Isaac looked more nervous than before. Like they finally figured out that this was all real. Connor didn't look as if he cared one way or another.

The tunnel Trevor and his small team moved through began descending at a steady slant, becoming wider and wider the farther they went. Within a few hundred feet, they were all able to stand up and walk, even if he and Hale still had to lean over to keep from hitting their heads on the ceiling.

"Why does a creature that's barely three feet tall need to dig a tunnel that's six feet high?" Hale asked softly as he made another chalk mark on the rough wall. "That doesn't make a whole lot of sense."

"Wait a minute," Owen said, turning to shine his light in Hale's direction. "You've seen one of the Screamers, too? When?"

"Screamers?" Hale said curiously, looking back and forth between Owen and Trevor.

"That's what the locals call these things, no doubt thanks to Owen, I'm sure," Trevor said, turning to focus his attention on the passage ahead of them. "And no, Owen, Hale has never seen one of them. But he has seen the life-size sculptures that Jenna did. They're perfect in every detail."

"Jenna sculpted life-size models of these things?" Owen said, his voice rising a little. "And she never bothered to show them to me or my crew? Why not?"

"You might want to keep your voice down," Trevor said calmly, glancing over his shoulder at him. "Unless you want to come face-to-face with the creatures much sooner than you want."

Owen looked ready to argue for a moment but then finally nodded and lowered his voice. "I just don't understand why she didn't show us right from the beginning."

"Maybe it was because you seemed to make a joke out of everything when she took you to the alley where her sister got kidnapped," Trevor said, biting back a growl at the memory of Jenna telling him that story. "She thought you were nothing but a bunch of jerks with no intention of ever actually helping her, so why would she bother to show you anything?"

Owen had the grace to look ashamed at that.

They continued moving along the tunnel in silence for a while. Trevor kept an eye on his watch as they passed several smaller passages to the left and right of their pathway. Without comment, they all decided to stay with the main tunnel. It seemed clear it was obviously heading somewhere important.

"Have you noticed these holes in the walls?" Owen said a little while later, stopping to shine his light into one that was about twenty inches in diameter and positioned about waist height. "You think they're air holes or something like that? If they are, they don't smell very fresh at all." He made a face. "Actually, they smell like a skunk."

Trevor and Hale both leaned in close. Considering the fact that they were at least three or four hundred feet underground, the hole could be home to skunks, he supposed. But from the strong musky scent coming out of the small opening, it was obvious that one or more ghouls regularly moved through it.

"They might dig these for air movement," Trevor said. "But I also think they use them to travel through as well."

"We'd better be careful then," Hale murmured, sticking his head completely in the hole to look around. "If the creatures realize we're here, these holes will let them surround us damn quick."

"Which is a good reason to make sure they never realize we're here," Trevor pointed out before turning to keep leading the way through the tunnel.

Another dozen side passages later, the tunnel leveled out, opening onto what could only be described as a main concourse, over seven feet in height and wide enough to drive a small car through it. Trevor looked around, expecting to see Mike and his team waiting for them, but there was no sign of them. He couldn't even get a whiff of their scents. Then again, who knew how expansive these tunnels were? Mike and the others could be miles away by now along that other passage they'd taken. Hell, they could be back on the surface already for all anyone knew.

Trevor was trying to figure out if he should go left or right when he smelled smoke. A second later, he noticed a flicking orange glow softly highlighting the tunnel to the left. There was obviously some kind of fire or torch burning down there. Without thinking twice, he spun around to motion for Owen to turn off his flashlight.

The paranormal investigator fumbled with the light so much he almost dropped the damn thing, but he ended up getting it together enough to flip the switch before splashing the beam all over the tunnel.

"What is it?" Owen whispered loudly. "I can't see a thing."

Trevor grabbed his shoulder and turned him in the direction he'd seen the fire, leaning in close to the man's ear. "Keep looking in that direction until your eyes adjust to the darkness."

Not twenty seconds later, he felt Owen tense.

"Crap, is that a fire?" Owen asked softly. "These frigging creatures know how to use fire? How the hell is that possible? They're monsters."

Trevor wanted to point out that there was probably something prejudicial about that but decided not to bother. Something told him that Owen wouldn't get anything he tried to tell him. It was better to save himself a wasted effort.

"I know it's dark as hell in here for you," Trevor said instead. "If you want to keep going, I'll have to guide you with a hand on your shoulder. That's probably going to be tough for you, so if you want to stay right here, that's not a problem. Hale and I will go check out whatever is up ahead, then come back and get you."

"No. I want to keep going," Owen said, barely hesitating before giving his answer in a voice a lot stronger than it probably had any right to be given the situation.

At a nod from Trevor, Hale drew his handgun and moved across the tunnel, reaching the far wall, then motioned back for them to follow. Trevor started forward, holding his weapon with one hand and keeping the other on Owen's shoulder to steer him in the right direction. Owen moved with slow, careful steps, feeling out in front of him with his toes, obviously afraid of falling flat on his face.

Once they reached the wall, Trevor turned Owen to the left, then slowly started edging them closer to the soft glow of the fire ahead of them. Hale crept silently as a wraith across the stone floor toward the next curve in the tunnel. Trevor could tell the moment his pack mate was able to see around it because Hale froze before dropping to one knee, motioning Trevor and Owen toward him. When he got there, Trevor slowly poked his head around the round corner, stunned at what he saw.

The tunnel ahead opened into a broad cavern that was easily fifty feet across and twenty feet tall, with three small fires burning in pits in the center of the space. Earthenware pots hung over the pits, smoke curling up and around them before heading for vent holes in the ceiling.

There were at least twenty ghouls that Trevor could see, some of them female—at least that was what he had to guess from the toga-like wraps they wore across their left shoulders. But more surprising than that were the three humans moving around the cavern. Two women and a man, they all wore filthy rags. The man was hauling pieces of wood for the fire pits, while the two women tended the earthenware pots.

Damn. Davina was right. The ghouls did keep humans as property.

"What the hell are we going to do?" Owen asked softly after they'd moved back down the tunnel a bit. "There are way more of those things than I thought there'd be."

Trevor wished he had a good answer. He hadn't seen any obvious weapons anywhere in the cavern. Not that it mattered. With the claws the ghouls had—along with their impervious skin—there was no way he, Hale, and an unarmed Owen could hope to deal with twenty of the creatures.

Not without getting the three captives killed—and outing their own supernatural identities to the last person on earth they'd want to share it with.

Trevor glanced at his watch to see that it was getting close to time for them to head back anyway. "We'll go back to the rendezvous point and meet up with the others, then come up with a plan to get those people out of there."

"Should we tell the police?" Owen asked, looking back and forth between him and Hale.

That was the plan most people would go with, so he couldn't fault Owen for it. But in this situation, that wasn't going to help.

"You want to take a guess how cops would respond to something like this—assuming we could get them to believe us with anything less than a psychiatric evaluation?" Hale asked softly. "They'd send a couple dozen heavily armored cops into the tunnels above us, making more noise than a herd of elephants, and the ghouls would be long gone before the police ever saw them—along with their captives. Then where would we be? Back in the hospital for round two of that psychiatric evaluation. That's where."

In the darkness, Trevor could see Owen consider that idea. Finally, the logic of it must have seeped in, because the man nodded.

"Okay, you're right," Owen said. "We get out of here and come up with a plan. Then we'll come back and get those people out."

Trevor breathed a sigh of relief. He'd thought for a second that Owen might give them some trouble. But the guy merely turned in the general direction of the tunnel they'd descended down, waiting for Trevor to guide him out.

Before he could, the clanging of metal on metal filled the tunnels, seemingly coming from everywhere at once. Okay, that couldn't be good. A fraction of a second later, Trevor heard snarls and the slap of unshod feet on stone coming their way from the cavern. He had no idea what had happened, but yup, they were screwed.

"What's that?" Owen asked nervously.

"Trouble."

Trevor barely got the word out before a handful of ghouls ran around the corner, fangs and claws reflecting the dim light coming from the fires behind them. Owen's flashlight flickered to life, illuminating the area of the tunnel around them—and all the creatures coming to kill them.

Hale started shooting first, Trevor pulling Owen behind him before firing the 9mm that STAT had given them to use. It wasn't the caliber he preferred, but it was better than nothing. Unfortunately, in this case, the rounds simply bounced right off the creatures' skin, not even leaving a dent.

"Davina was right!" Hale shouted. "Bullets are worthless against these things."

"Get to the tunnel!" Trevor yelled, giving Owen

a shove in the right direction. "We'll try to hold them off long enough for you to get a head start."

Owen didn't even think about protesting. He simply started running toward the way out, the beam of his flashlight bouncing in every direction, strobing off the floor, walls, and ceiling. Trevor got his attention back around to face the threat just in time as a three-foot ball of clawed fury came flying his way. He put three bullets right in the creature's face. It was enough to knock it aside but not damage it.

"Move!" Trevor shouted in Hale's direction, shoving the 9mm in the holster at his back and letting his claws extend to their full length. "It will be easier to keep them off us once we're in the tunnel!"

He and Hale covered each other as they continued to fall back toward the sloping tunnel. Then they started moving up it, one slow step at a time. The creatures threw themselves at him and Hale with wild fury, claws whistling through the air like knife blades. It was more luck than skill that kept him and Hale from being sliced to shreds.

They made surprisingly good time retreating up the sloping tunnel, punching, kicking, and slashing to keep the creatures at bay, but it still seemed to take forever. It was exhausting, but knowing that every step took them closer to daylight and safety, Trevor kept fighting. The ghouls were coming at them hard as hell, like they were desperate to keep him and Hale from getting away. In between snarling and growling, the creatures let out an endless series of chirps and grunts. Trevor was pretty sure they were talking to each other.

He glanced at Hale to see his friend fighting right there with him, claws and fangs fully extended, smashing creatures into the wall over and over again. It still didn't hurt them, but at least it slowed them down a little.

Trevor thought this might actually work out. By his guess, they only had four or five hundred feet to go to reach the intersection where they'd split from Mike, Connor, and Isaac. If everything went according to plan, the guys would be waiting for them. Their increased numbers would hopefully scare the creatures off their pursuit.

Then he heard the thud of running footsteps.

At first, he thought it was his pack mates coming to the rescue. Then he picked up an incredibly familiar scent, and suddenly every scrap of hope he had for a good outcome to this situation blew up in his face.

Trevor barely had time to force his fangs and claws to retract before Jenna ran up to him, a hiker's light strapped to her forehead and an aluminum softball bat in her hands. She immediately started swinging it at the closest ghoul, looking about as freaked out as Trevor was.

Esme and Maya were right behind Jenna, each

carrying their own bats, with lights on their heads. Owen raced after them, flashlight bobbing like wild as he tried to run forward and look backward at the same time.

"They've gotten behind us!" he shouted, a frigging rock clutched in his free hand for a weapon. "They popped out of those little holes in the walls and are coming this way. We're cut off from the rendezvous point with the others!"

Well, crap.

CHAPTER 11

"So what's with the softball bats?" Esme asked curiously as she and Maya led Jenna through the alleys toward the manhole cover Trevor and the others had disappeared through well over an hour ago. With all the twists and turns, Jenna was surprised they'd remembered the way.

They'd gotten the bats Esme was referring to a few blocks from their present location at a sporting goods shop on Maple Avenue. Along with three sets of those fancy LED lights that you can wear on your head so you can keep your hands free. Jenna wasn't sure if she would look cool—or stupid—in the thing. But if she was going underground—as terrifying as that idea might be—she was bringing the brightest light she could find.

"I have it on good authority that these creatures have a problem with metal," she answered. Stopping in front of the open manhole cover positioned in the middle of the alley, she pulled the aluminum bats out of the duffel bag she'd bought in the same sporting goods shop. "I hope we never have to find out one way or another, but if it comes down to it, I'd like us to be able to protect ourselves if we run into one of those things."

It was like the air temperature dropped as Esme and Maya suddenly froze right in front of her. Maybe they'd come to the unsettling conclusion that this was for real and that they were going to climb down into the same hole that an extremely dangerous creature had disappeared into a few days ago. And while the idea of coming to the rescue of their friends might have seemed like a good one at the time, she got the feeling they were scared right now.

"Maybe they've already come out," Esme said softly, almost hopefully. "You know, while we were going to get you."

"I think they would have closed the manhole cover if that was the case," Jenna pointed out, even though she was sure the other women already knew that.

Esme took a deep breath. "So we're really going to do this?" She looked down at the aluminum bat Jenna handed her with wide-eyed intensity, then at the inky blackness that filled the hole in the asphalt. "We're really going to go down there looking for them?"

Nobody said a word, but then again, an answer wasn't necessary.

Jenna gazed down into the hole, barely able to see farther than the first rung of the ladder stuck in the side of the concrete wall. But that was all it took to make her heart beat faster.

"Okay," she started, taking a step closer to the opening. "In the interest of full disclosure, I should probably mention that I'm deathly afraid of tight, dark places, and the thought of going down in the sewer makes me want to pass out—or throw up—or both."

Esme blinked. "Then why are you doing this?"

"Because Trevor is down there and so are my brother and two of their friends," she said. "They could be in trouble, so I have to go after them."

"I understand what you're saying," Esme answered. "I feel the same way about Isaac and Owen. It's just that I can't help but wonder what the three of us are supposed to do down there that the four of them can't?"

Taking another deep breath, Jenna leaned down to slip her foot through the sewer entrance, one toe searching for the ladder rung on the curving wall of the tunnel beneath her. "I guess we're about to find out," she whispered, breathing getting harder and faster the deeper she descended into the darkness, like she was slipping into freezing cold water.

Jenna almost forgot to turn on her headlamp, only remembering it when she was completely below street level and the darkness threatened to overwhelm her. She felt silly wearing the thing but was glad to have it all the same. The bright light from the multiple LED bulbs filled the space around her, revealing filthy walls and sludge-covered ladder rungs.

When she reached the bottom of the tunnel, Jenna forced herself to take a few steps to the side to make room for Esme and Maya. The already-tight walls began to close in on her and her legs refused to listen to her any longer. Then her lungs started to pump like two bellows and the dark space began to get even darker.

Okay, coming down here had been a really bad idea.

Esme and Maya joined her a few moments later, neither one of them noticing that she was in distress.

"Look, there's the chalk mark they told us they'd be using," Maya said, aiming her headlamp at a blue powder marking on the left side of the tunnel wall. "All we have to do is follow the marks and we should be able to easily find them."

Esme and Maya started to move down the tunnel, only to stop when they realized Jenna wasn't following. They hurried back, apparently picking up on the fact that there was something wrong with her.

"Hey, are you okay?" Esme asked softly, gently placing a hand on her shoulder.

At least Jenna thought there was a hand on her shoulder. Her head was spinning so much from lack of oxygen that she wasn't sure of anything.

"She's hyperventilating," Maya said a moment later. "I think she's having a panic attack from being down here."

Both women moved closer—which didn't help at all—and started trying to help her, providing suggestions such as "try to slow your breathing," "focus on a happy thought," and "calm down."

Unfortunately, their advice only made her more anxious.

Ignoring the well-intentioned but ultimately worthless guidance, Jenna fell back on the techniques her therapist had taught her for dealing with an anxiety attack.

Three things you can see, she whispered in the recesses of her mind. *Blue chalk mark, the concrete wall of the tunnel, and mud.*

Three sounds you can hear, she said to herself next. *Esme and Maya's voices, the hum of vehicles moving on the streets nearby, and the trickle of water running across the floor of the tunnel.*

Three parts of your body you can move, Jenna thought last as fresh air finally started finding its way into her lungs. *Toes, fingers, and tongue.*

Jenna had to run through the whole 333 rule a second time before she felt enough control to lift her head and look at Esme and Maya, letting them know she was okay.

"Sorry about that," she whispered. "Coming down here hit me harder than I thought it would."

Esme exchanged looks with Maya. "Maybe your panic attack is a sign that we should go back up topside and wait for the guys there."

Jenna only had to think of Trevor being in trouble somewhere down in the sewer for a few seconds before shaking her head. "No, we should keep going. I just need you guys to talk to me and help keep me out of my own head."

She expected the standard response to her request—what should we talk about? But instead, Maya nodded and moved up close so she was walking right beside her, Esme on their heels.

"I saw a mermaid when I was fourteen," Esme said suddenly, the announcement so unexpected that it definitely had the desired effect. Because Jenna certainly wasn't thinking about being underground anymore. "It changed my life and is why I ended up becoming part of HOPD."

Jenna kept walking but slowed a little as she glanced at Esme. "You're not just making that up to get me talking, are you?"

"No, I'm not making it up—promise," Esme said with a shake of her head. "My family went to Catalina on vacation that summer. Isaac and I were out walking along the pier at Avalon Harbor when I heard a splash in the water, then a giggle. I thought it was somebody diving off one of the boats in the harbor. Maybe even skinny-dipping."

"Let me guess." Maya let out a soft laugh. "You immediately went running to see so you could get a free show?"

"I was very mature for my age—and curious."

Esme shrugged. "Regardless, I ran ahead, and when I reached the end of the pier, there was a girl in the water about my age with really long, platinum-blond hair. She giggled and waved at me, then surged out of the water, doing a complete flip in the air. That's when I saw her tail—as in her mermaid tail, scales and all."

"Are you sure it wasn't someone wearing a fake mermaid tail?" Jenna asked curiously. "You know, like the ones they use in those mermaid shows in Vegas."

Esme shook her head. "I've seen those shows and her tail wasn't like the costumes they wear. She surged ten feet out of the water, then slapped the water so hard with her tail that she soaked me where I stood twenty feet away on the pier. That was no fake tail."

"What happened then?" Maya asked eagerly. "Did Isaac see her, too?"

"He ran up seconds after I got splashed," Esme said, checking the wall to find the next chalk mark. "But all he was able to catch was the mermaid's tail and part of her back."

"Did he realize what she was?" Maya asked, practically bouncing up and down now as she walked. "Did he know she was a mermaid?"

"No." Esme smiled a little, like she was replaying the memory. "He didn't realize it was a mermaid until I told him."

"Did he believe you'd really seen a mermaid?" Jenna asked, suddenly feeling out of breath again, but for a completely different reason this time.

"Yeah, of course," Esme said, giving her a confused look. "He's my brother. Why wouldn't he believe me? In fact, Isaac was so sure I was right, he's the one who insisted we start looking for other supernatural creatures. It's why he stayed here in LA with me, so we could look for them together. He's the real reason we joined up with Owen and Maya."

Jenna felt like she'd been punched in the gut. She told herself that what had happened between Esme and her brother was completely different from the situation with Connor, but in the end, she knew it wasn't. Esme's brother had believed her totally and without hesitation when she'd claimed to see something strange and impossible. Jenna's brother had called her insane—and then abandoned her. Jenna was glad the tunnels were so dark, so Esme and Maya couldn't see the tears welling up in her eyes.

Fortunately, the hole in the floor of the tunnel they almost fell through a few minutes later served to get Jenna's head back in the game, distracting her enough so that she stopped thinking about trading brothers with Esme.

"There's a chalk mark right beside the hole," Maya said. She looked kind of pale, even in the bright light from their headlamps. "This is definitely the way they went."

Jenna leaned over to peek into the hole, her light illuminating the tight confines of the passage underneath. The idea of crawling through that tunnel on her hands and knees made her want to hyperventilate all over again.

Until Maya jumped down in the hole without warning, quickly disappearing from sight. Jenna followed before she could chicken out.

The passage under the sewer tunnel was as bad as she'd thought it would be and more than a little hard on her jean-clad knees. But Esme and Maya kept up a nonstop dialogue of their life here in LA, their jobs, things they'd gotten into with HOPD, and guys—lots and lots about guys. Esme and Maya seemed to follow the maxim that *when in doubt, ask him out.*

But the endless conversation served its purpose. Before Jenna even realized it, the tunnel was large enough for them to stand up and walk. Admittedly, there was another moment of panic when they reached a Y intersection in the tunnel, two passages leading off into the darkness, both with chalk marks scratched on the walls.

"Which way should we go?" Jenna whispered, looking from the blue mark on the rightmost passage to the white mark on the left. It was obvious the guys had split up, but she had no idea which direction Trevor would have gone. It struck her then that almost the entirety of her concern was for Trevor. She still loved her brother, regardless of him being a dumbass, but her first thought was still for the man she'd just met. She knew that meant something monumental, though she wasn't sure what.

"I can't believe they split up," Esme whispered. "It's like they're begging to get eaten. Isaac, at least, should know better."

Jenna went back and forth with Esme and Maya about which way they should go, but in the end, they decided that all they could do was pick a passage at random and hope for the best.

"You're the reason we're down here, Jenna, so you should pick," Maya said, Esme nodding her agreement. "We go with whatever your instincts decide."

Jenna took a deep breath. "Then we go right," she said, refusing to second-guess her choice. She was going to find Trevor, and he would be completely fine.

"Do either of you hear something?" Esme asked a few dozen feet later, holding up a hand and slowing them. "Maybe it's just background noise from being so deep underground, but it sounds like someone banging on pots."

Jenna listened and thought that maybe she heard...something. But she couldn't determine what it might be.

Esme shook her head. "It's probably nothing. Let's keep going. The sooner we find them, the sooner we can get out of this creepy place."

The tunnel floor began to slope immediately, which actually made traveling easier, though Jenna wasn't thrilled at the idea of how much more difficult it would be to walk back up the hill. But the thought of doing it with Trevor helped.

Small openings began to appear here and there in the side walls of the tunnel, like wormholes in an apple core, and Jenna had the unsettling sensation that there were *things* in those openings...watching them.

The uncomfortable feeling continued to build until Jenna could practically feel it on her skin. A second later, she almost screamed out loud as a figure came running up on them from lower down in the tunnel, flashlight flailing around wildly. She jerked her bat above her shoulder, ready to pummel whatever it might be, even as a little voice in the back of her head pointed out that a ghoul probably wouldn't be using a flashlight.

Jenna realized it was Owen barely a second before she hit him with her bat. He pulled up short, a hand coming up to block the glare of light coming from her headlamp.

"What are you guys doing down here?" he demanded, swinging his flashlight around to point at Esme and Maya. "Forget it. We don't have time to talk. We have to get out of here...now!"

Jenna immediately felt a tremor of panic as every instinct screamed that Trevor was in trouble. Esme and Maya must have picked up on the tension because they started peppering Owen with one question after another.

"What's wrong?" Jenna asked, cutting the other two women off and taking a step closer to Owen so he was forced to look only at her. "Is Trevor in trouble?"

For a second, she thought Owen was going to lie, but then he sighed. "The ghouls know we're here. Trevor and Hale are farther down the tunnel, trying to hold them off. We need to leave while we still can."

Jenna turned before the man had even finished, ready to take off running in Trevor's direction. But then Maya screamed. Jenna spun around to see her staring back the way they'd come, her headlamp illuminating the tunnel behind them—and the three ghouls crawling out of those small holes in the walls she'd seen minutes earlier.

She stilled at the sight of the creatures oozing out of the wall, their big eyes reflecting the light of Maya's headlamp, mouths spread wide to display fangs dripping with saliva. This was now the third time Jenna had seen these things, but the sight of them still had the power to terrify her into complete immobility.

Then the first of the creatures dropped to the

floor and began to advance toward them, claw-tipped hands reaching for them.

Jenna's insides froze solid.

Then Maya stepped forward and swung her bat at the thing. The creature let out a horrible shriek as the aluminum weapon bounced off its head. The ghoul didn't seem hurt exactly, but it was definitely surprised—and pissed.

A split second later, it got to its feet and charged at them.

Jenna found herself moving. Before her head could catch up and tell her how stupid this was, she was already swinging her bat with all her might.

She would never in a million years describe herself as an athlete, but she ended up landing a surprisingly solid strike on the ghoul's shoulder. It didn't appear like she'd hurt the thing, but the creature stumbled sideways a couple feet. But at the same time, the bat vibrated violently in her hands, numbing her fingers. It was like she'd hit a brick wall.

Still, the thing fell back, and the other two ghouls hesitated, clearly not sure how to handle this kind of attack. That was good enough for Jenna.

"Head down the tunnel!" she yelled, turning that direction to give Owen and Esme a shove. "We'll never make it around these three ghouls on our own. We need help."

As one, she and her new friends ran down the

tunnel, nearly tumbling out of control on the inclined floor. But no matter how fast they ran, the ghouls were right there behind them, their claws scrabbling on the rough stone of the tunnel floor.

When they didn't run into Trevor and Hale after a few hundred feet, Jenna worried that they'd accidentally turned down a side tunnel in the darkness without realizing it. But then she heard snarling and growling from up ahead of them. The next thing she knew, Trevor and Hale were in front of her and the others, going toe-to-toe with a handful of raging ghouls, fighting them off with nothing but their bare hands.

Jenna didn't slow down to think but simply surged past a stunned Trevor to swing at one of the equally surprised ghouls with her aluminum bat. While she didn't hurt it, she sure as hell freaked it out so badly it stopped attacking, instead quickly backpedaling and staring at her in confusion.

"The ghouls are behind us!" Owen yelled to Trevor and Hale. "They came out of the holes in the walls and cut us off from the rendezvous point."

Jenna wasn't sure what Owen meant about a rendezvous point, but getting cut off from it didn't sound good.

She didn't have long to think about it before Trevor appeared at her side, swinging an aluminum bat that he must have gotten from Esme or Maya. He used it to much greater effect than Jenna ever could, that was for sure. When he hit the ghouls, it still didn't seem to injure them, but they definitely flew through the air.

"Go with Hale," Trevor said without looking at her. "Help him clear a path back up the tunnel."

"What about you?" she asked.

"I'll be right behind you," he said. "Go!"

Jenna hated the idea of leaving Trevor even for a minute but did as he asked, scrambling up the passage. Hale had a bat now, too, while Esme and Maya stuck close behind him for protection. Trevor's friend was going after the three creatures who'd chased them down from higher in the tunnel, swinging the bat hard. As she watched, he caught one of the ghouls in the ribs, sending the creature bouncing off the nearest wall. The sound of impact was stunningly loud, even above all the shrieking and yelling going on.

Running up the tunnel was like something out of one of the horror movies Jenna worked on. Strobing lights combined with screams of panic and fear that were punctuated by thuds as she, Trevor, and Hale took their bats to the ghouls again and again. Even scarier were the occasional grunts of pain Trevor and Hale let out. It sounded to her like they were being clawed by the ghouls, but in the darkness, she couldn't see enough to know for sure. Even with the stupid headlamp she was wearing.

Jenna hadn't realized they'd made it to the Y intersection where the tunnel had split into two passages until she heard shouting, and then her brother was in her face, looking pissed off as hell.

"What the hell are you doing down here?" he demanded, yanking the aluminum bat out of her hand, shoving her behind him, slamming the metal weapon straight down onto the head of the nearest ghoul. The thing fell down but was back up again less than a second later.

"You guys were gone too long," Jenna shouted over the noise. "Esme and Maya started getting worried, so they came to get me to help."

As he swung the bat again, her brother grumbled something about stubborn sisters who refused to do as they're told and trying their damnedest to get themselves killed.

"Well, if that's the way you're going to be about it, give me my damn softball bat back, and I'll take care of this myself!" she yelled back.

Connor ignored her as they continued to make their way through the passage, which was starting to get smaller as they approached the entry to the man-made sewer tunnels. Even Jenna had to walk hunched over now. The fact that Trevor, her brother, and their teammates didn't have flashlights completely boggled the mind. Why the hell had they come down here without them? She could understand if one or two of them had dropped their lights during the struggle, but certainly not all four of them. Had they dropped them?

It was in the middle of this conundrum that everything suddenly went quiet. One second, it was pure bedlam, and the next, complete silence. It was creepy beyond belief.

"Where did they all go?" Mike questioned suspiciously. "There were easily a dozen of those things surrounding us a few seconds ago, and now they decide to give up and run?"

The silence continued, broken only by the sounds of heavy breathing. But as Jenna glanced around, her headlamp taking everyone in, she realized she and the HOPD peeps were the ones gasping for air. Trevor, Connor, and their SWAT teammates didn't even look winded, even though they'd borne the brunt of the burden when it came to fighting off the ghouls.

Jenna was still regarding Trevor, trying to make sense of that when she saw the blood. His shirt had been torn along one shoulder and was soaked through with something dark that glittered in the beam of light. There was even more along both forearms. Crap, he'd been hurt by one of those creatures and hadn't said a word.

She'd taken a single step in his direction, heart pounding out of control, when the rumbling started. It was like thunder rolling in the distance. A split second later, pebbles and dust drifted down from the ceiling of the tunnel around them.

"I don't like this," Isaac murmured.

Jenna didn't like it, either.

But the rumbling started to fade and she allowed herself to breathe again. Then a large boulder fell from the ceiling, missing Esme's shoulder by an inch. Esme screamed and jumped back even as the rumbling resumed and more pieces of the ceiling fell.

"They're collapsing the tunnel!" Trevor yelled. "Everyone move—fast! We have to get back to the sewer entrance before they drop the whole thing on our heads."

The scramble through the tunnel was a nightmare, especially as it got smaller and tighter until all of them were shuffling forward on their hands and knees. The stone around them shook and heaved, large chunks of rock falling all over them, the air filling with so much dust that breathing was nearly impossible.

As the tunnel walls closed in around Jenna, another panic attack hovered at the edges of her consciousness, waiting for the right moment to strike. Trevor had somehow gotten himself directly behind her in the mad rush to escape, and it was his hand reassuringly finding its way onto her back that kept her from losing it completely. He was right there and would keep her safe. She felt that down to her very soul.

She was so terrified that at any second they could all be crushed to death, she barely realized they'd reached the rough opening into the sewer system until Trevor shoved her through so hard she practically popped out of the hole like a whack-a-mole. Within moments, everyone else climbed through the opening, all of them ending up in a haphazard pile of arms and legs there on the wet, dirty floor, gasping for air as the world around them continued to shake.

"Everyone okay?" Mike asked.

Jenna pushed herself up to a sitting position, looking around to see Trevor, Connor, and everyone else doing the same. Dust and pieces of rock clung to their hair and clothes. She was pretty sure she was just as dirty. But they were alive. That was what was important.

Hale leaned over the opening they'd escaped out of moments earlier. "The tunnels below us are completely collapsed."

Panic gripped Jenna. They might have lost their only way to reach Hannah. "How are we going to get back in there then?"

Hale shook his head. "I don't know. But I think it's safe to say we sure as hell won't be going back in there from this direction."

Trevor reached out to take Jenna's hand, holding on to it tightly. She could feel her brother's glare on them, but she refused to acknowledge his existence.

"Maybe now would be a good time for you guys to explain exactly what the hell happened down there," Owen said. His usual bravado was gone and in its place was what looked like doubt and confusion. "Because I can't imagine why anyone would ever want to go back down into that hell again."

Jenna looked at Trevor, waiting for him to answer, but then her headlamp illuminated his bloody shoulder and arms. That was when she remembered that he'd been injured.

Crap.

She glanced around to see that Trevor wasn't the only one who was bleeding. Connor, Hale, and Mike were injured as well.

"That's going to have to wait until we get Trevor and everyone else to the hospital," she announced firmly.

CHAPTER 12

"Nope, nothing happened," Jenna said casually into her phone as she moved around her kitchen, wondering if she should put the pizza in the oven or the fridge, not sure when Trevor would get back from the hospital he'd gone to in order to have his and everyone else's injuries taken care of. "The whole thing was kind of boring, actually."

"Hold on. You're telling me that all you did was stand in that alley and wait for Trevor and everyone else to come out of that hole?" Madeleine asked in surprise, her voice barely audible over the din of hundreds of people talking in the background and enjoying her pop-up dining experience.

"Pretty much," Jenna answered.

She was glad she was talking to Madeleine over the phone instead of in person. One look at her face and her friend would have known she was lying. She was a terrible liar.

Jenna felt like crap for fibbing to her friend, but it was sort of late in the game to even think about being honest. Madeleine had no idea there was anything supernatural going on down on Skid Row, so bringing up the subject of carnivorous subterranean creatures now might be a problem.

"I know you mentioned Trevor was out doing something with his SWAT teammates, but have you given any thought to my earlier suggestion about having a conversation with Trevor about how you feel about him?" Madeleine asked. "Or were you planning to jump straight to the sex part and spring the serious stuff on him afterward?"

"I'd be okay with either of those options," Jenna said with a snort of laughter. "But unfortunately, I'm not sure it's going to happen, at least not tonight. I haven't even gotten a text from him."

Madeleine must have picked up on the tension in her voice, because her friend started making those worried tutting sounds like a mother hen. "What happened? Why hasn't he texted you? Did something else happen today that you haven't told me about?"

Jenna hesitated, not sure how to say what had been bothering her for the past few hours since she'd left Trevor, Connor, and their teammates in the alley.

"When Trevor was down in those tunnels, he ended up getting injured," she said.

She didn't mention that Connor, Hale, and Mike had also been bleeding. There'd be no way to explain away that many injuries.

"Oh my gosh! Is he okay?" Madeleine asked in alarm. "More importantly, if he's hurt, why aren't you with him?"

"Trevor insisted it wasn't a big deal and that he was barely scratched," Jenna said softly, hoping her friend would be able to hear her over the background noise. "And I'm not with him because he didn't want me to go to the hospital with him. He insisted I come home and that he'd meet me here later."

Of course, Trevor hadn't put it quite that bluntly. Instead, he'd tried to convince her that she should make sure the HOPD peeps got home safely—without running out to blab about what they'd seen down in those tunnels. But Jenna recognized when she was being dismissed and shuffled off to the side. It had happened to her enough times over the last decade to know the signs. The fact that Trevor hadn't even bothered to text her essentially confirmed it. And if the complete silence on the other end of the phone was any indication, Madeleine understood what she was getting at as well.

"Why wouldn't Trevor want you to go to the hospital with him?" her friend asked.

"I don't know," Jenna said. "I honestly thought there was something between us, but now I'm not so sure. The way he was pushing me away, I can't shake the feeling that he's hiding something from me."

"Like what? Are you worried that he's injured worse than he was letting on, or is it something else completely?"

While Jenna had been thinking about that same

issue nonstop since leaving Skid Row, she hadn't been able to come up with an answer. Part of that was probably because she was hurting so much. It was ridiculous, but there was almost this sense of betrayal when she thought about Trevor keeping something important from her. The pain was making it hard to look at the situation objectively.

"I wish I knew," she said with a sigh. "I don't think this is about him getting hurt, though. Somehow, it feels bigger than that. Don't ask me how I know, but I can feel that there's something going on that he's keeping to himself."

She didn't add her next thought. That it was something Connor and the other members of the SWAT team were almost assuredly aware of.

"You're going to talk to him about all this when he finally gets back, right?" Madeleine asked. "I really think you should."

"And what am I supposed to say to him?" Jenna let out a snort. "Oh, hey, Trevor, I want to let you know that you really hurt my feelings when you wouldn't let me come to the hospital with you earlier. And while we're on the topic of *feelings*, why do I *feel* like you're keeping something from me?"

Jenna could practically hear Madeleine wince over the phone. "You're right. That might be a bit awkward. I guess you could always wait until you have sex, then hit him up with your questions while he's in a postorgasmic haze."

"Postorgasmic haze?" Jenna almost laughed. "Seriously?"

"Seriously. Girl, after a good romp, men's brains turn to mush and they'll tell you pretty much anything you want to know. Well, at least until they fall asleep."

Jenna did laugh at that. Then spent the next few minutes talking about Madeleine's pop-up dining event. Setting up a high-class restaurant in the middle of a park, complete with linen napkins, china plates, and fancy silverware sounded like an enormous amount of work to Jenna, but from the sounds of it, Madeleine was having a wonderful time.

"I have to run. They're almost ready for dessert," her friend said. "Talk to Trevor, huh? If you want this thing between you and him to have any chance, you need to know where you stand."

Jenna murmured something she expected sounded somewhat conciliatory before hanging up. She checked her messages, trying not to be disappointed when she saw that Trevor still hadn't texted her.

Sighing, she picked up the pizza box the delivery person had brought a few minutes earlier and put it in the fridge. It was almost five o'clock, nearly three hours since she'd seen Trevor. If he hadn't made it back to the apartment by now, it was probably because he was doing something more than going to the hospital to get some *scratches* cleaned up.

Something he hadn't felt Jenna needed to know about.

A horrible thought popped into her head of Trevor and Connor finding a way to go back down into those tunnels, along with Hale and Mike. Jenna tried to tell herself that he wouldn't do something like that, not after everything that had happened earlier today. But then again, she'd told Madeleine that Trevor was keeping something from her. If she was being honest with herself, she supposed she needed to accept that she had no idea what he was doing at the moment.

Not in the mood for TV—and refusing to be the one who texted first—Jenna headed for the guest bedroom, stopping in front of one of the worktables. A few minutes later, she had a wire armature set up, bending and twisting the metal into the basic shape she was envisioning in her head. Then she pulled out a huge block of plastic-covered clay, cutting off big chunks and slapping them onto the armature.

Her hands worked without conscious thought, pushing and shaping the dense clay into one of the horrifying images seared forever in her head. It was the moment she'd found Trevor down in those tunnels, all those ghouls coming at him with their fang-filled mouths spread wide, claw-tipped fingers reaching. It was this most violent memory that her fingers teased out of the clay.

Jenna lost herself in the flow of her favorite medium, letting the work drain the stress from her mind. It was probably strange, but it was when she was sculpting the most hideous creatures from her nightmares that she felt the most at peace.

She wasn't sure how much time had passed, but one moment, she was using the tip of her pinkie finger to shape a ghoul fang, and the next, Trevor was standing beside her, watching her work. Jenna jumped a little, a myriad of confusing and nearly overwhelming emotions washing through her at the sight of him. She was concerned, for sure, but she was also more than a little angry, too. Hadn't he known she'd be worried about him, dammit?

Jenna couldn't miss the gauze wrapped around both of Trevor's forearms, spiraling up from his wrists all the way to his elbows. She glanced up at his shoulder, where blood had soaked through his shirt earlier. But there was nothing to see because he was wearing a new shirt now. There wasn't even an outline to make her think he was wearing a bandage under it. She wanted to ask if he was okay, but the words simply wouldn't come.

"You're back," she finally said, turning to focus on the sculpture again. It hurt not to look at him, but if she didn't do something to occupy herself, she was going to start crying.

"Yeah," he said.

Trevor stood there, like he was waiting for her to say something else, but she couldn't.

"Jenna, is something wrong?" he asked softly, his voice so filled with confusion that she wanted to scream.

Of course, he didn't realize anything was wrong. In fact, he probably hadn't given her a second thought after leaving that alley hours ago.

"Wrong?" she murmured, refusing to look at anything but the sculpture of the ghoul, its maw spread so wide open, it could have easily swallowed her entire hand. "I don't know. You tell me."

Trevor would be the first to admit he didn't really understand women. But as uninformed on the subject as he was, he still recognized that Jenna was upset. And okay, maybe even a little mad. Considering the fact that she refused to look his way, he could only guess she was mad at him. Though for the life of him, he wasn't sure why.

Passive-aggressive was definitely not Jenna's style. At least it hadn't been until now.

He replayed the earlier part of the day through his mind, searching for anything that might explain the anger he was picking up on. Since he hadn't wanted Jenna to see how fast their wounds healed, Trevor had asked her to make sure Owen and the other members of the HOPD got home okay and to remind them not to talk about anything they'd seen. He couldn't see how any of that would have upset her.

He silently watched Jenna as she stood there in a pair of shorts and a T-shirt, fingers working the clay like a magician. He had no idea how long Jenna had been crafting the piece, but it couldn't have been that long. Yet she'd already sculpted the face, shoulders, and chest of the ghoul in exquisite detail. He would probably never understand how she found comfort in the act of creating these images, but it seemed clear that was why she did it.

Right now, though, Trevor needed her attention on whatever was bothering her.

"Jenna, would you please stop working on that sculpture for a second and look at me?" he said gently, reaching out to touch her shoulder. "It's clear that you're upset, and I'd like to understand why, especially since it seems to be my fault."

She stopped sliding her fingers through the clay but still didn't look his way. Instead, she stood there, staring at her creation, her heart beating faster, a gleam of tears in her eyes.

Trevor still wasn't sure what he'd done, but it was obviously bad. *Very* bad. Realizing that he'd somehow hurt Jenna made his heart constrict in his chest in a way that convinced him more than ever that Jenna was *The One* for him. Because he couldn't imagine feeling pain like this for any other reason.

"Where have you been?" Jenna asked, finally turning to face him as she cleaned the clay off her hands with a towel. The tears weren't quite as evident now, but he could tell from the tension in her shoulders that she was still angry. "I assume from the new shirt that you ended up somewhere other than the hospital."

Trevor frowned, his head swimming as he tried to understand what she was upset about. "Um... yeah. We went over to Davina's club. We wanted to tell her about the tunnel network we found. She had us draw out as much of it as we could remember in the hopes that she might be able to use that to find another way into the ghouls' caverns. I got this shirt out of the club's lost-and-found box. Apparently, a lot of clothing gets left behind in the place. Which is something I probably don't want to ponder too deeply now that I'm thinking about it."

Jenna's expression darkened. "You had time to draw maps of underground tunnel networks and dig through a lost-and-found box at a nightclub for a new shirt, but you didn't have time to text me and let me know everything had gone okay at the hospital? That you were even *alive*?"

Trevor felt a stab of panic as he got his first sense of what he'd done wrong. "But I told you it wasn't anything more than a few scratches."

"*Scratches*?" Jenna said, her pretty hazel eyes going wide. "You were bleeding all over the place. Those creatures must have sliced you down to the bone. I thought you were going to die!"

She was hyperventilating by the time she'd finished speaking, her heart pounding so fast and hard that Trevor could see the blood pulsing under the pale skin of her throat. And the tears that she'd been fighting to hold back earlier were now cascading down her cheeks in endless streams that damn near tore his heart out to see.

Trevor wrapped his arms around her, holding her close, unable to speak.

"I thought you were going to die," she said again, the words nearly incomprehensible through her sobs. "I wanted to go to the hospital with you and you wouldn't let me. You never called to tell me you were okay."

Trevor stood there holding Jenna as she cried, feeling like a complete and utter jackass. He wasn't sure which of his offenses made him feel worse. Was it the fact that he'd never even considered that Jenna—who was almost certainly his soul mate—might have been worried about him? Or because he hadn't given a single thought to texting or calling her to let her know he was okay after tending to his wounds?

Of course, part of that was because he and his pack mates had never gone to the hospital. Instead, they'd gone straight to Davina's club and cleaned up in one of her bathrooms. Since the worst of the ghouls' slashes closed up within minutes of coming out of the tunnels, there was no reason for a hospital. In fact, the cleanup had come down to little more than washing the blood off and wrapping his arms in gauze so Jenna wouldn't realize how quickly the wounds had healed.

Still, that was no excuse. He should have known Jenna would be worried about him. If the situations had been reversed, Trevor would have been losing his mind.

"I'm sorry," he said hoarsely, squeezing her tighter and rocking her back and forth. She curled the fingers of one hand around the fabric of his shirt, clenching it like she never intended to let him go. "I should have thought of you. I should have called."

"Why didn't you?" Jenna murmured, the words hard to hear as she kept her face pressed to his chest, sniffles and sobs still making her shoulders shake.

Trevor paused before saying anything, accepting that Jenna was looking for a real answer and not some meaningless platitude. And after the way he'd blown her off, she certainly deserved a little introspection on his part. Unfortunately, even after a few moments of thoughts, he still wasn't entirely sure what to say. It struck him painfully hard that he had no conscious excuse on why he hadn't called her, much less considered that she'd be worried.

Part of him thought it might be easiest if he simply admitted to being a werewolf. But that was out of the question, for obvious reasons. Worse, he didn't think his furry problem had anything to do with his inability to operate a phone.

"I know this is going to come out as the lamest excuse in the history of the world," he said after a few moments of thought, his chin resting on the top of her head, his hand making slow, soothing circles on her back. "But the reason I didn't think to call you is because I haven't had anyone waiting at home to be worried about me. So I don't think I immediately connected with the possibility that you would be one of those people."

Jenna's shoulders stopped shaking in his embrace, her sobs quieting. Then, after a few seconds, she slowly pulled back to gaze up at him with eyes all red and puffy. Trevor would rather be kicked in the balls by a Clydesdale than see her like that.

"So you're telling me that the reason you didn't call is because you seriously had no idea I cared?" she asked incredulously.

He wanted to tell her that it was far more complicated than that. He wanted to explain that it had been so long since he'd worried about the consequences of getting injured because, well...werewolf...and that the thought that anyone would care about a few slashes and a couple pints of blood simply didn't register.

"Um...it sounds so much worse when you say it that way," he murmured. "And more than a bit pathetic. But basically, yeah. Since I became an adult and moved out on my own, the only person who worried about me was me. Sure, in the army and on my SWAT team, we look out for each other, but that's completely different from having someone at home worry about you." He sighed. "I know it's a horrible excuse. I'm genuinely sorry for not thinking to have you there when my injuries were being looked at. And for not texting or calling you, too. I can only promise to never do that to you again. I promise that if I ever get hurt in the future, I'll make sure to keep you informed. No matter what."

She regarded him silently for a moment. Her expression clearly said she was still upset, but at least she didn't seem angry anymore. And thank goodness she wasn't crying. He'd decided that seeing Jenna cry was the most painful thing in the world.

"Okay," she whispered, her voice rough with emotion. "At some later date, we're going to sit down and have a long conversation about you thinking there's nobody around to worry about you, but for now, maybe you could simply promise to make sure you're never in a position to get hurt again?"

Trevor wanted to nod and go with that, relieved Jenna seemed to be at least willing to accept his apology, but he knew he couldn't do that.

"I wish I could tell you that I'm never going to get hurt again," he started slowly. "But given that we'll probably be going back down into those tunnels again as soon as we find a way back in, that's not anything I can promise."

When Jenna didn't say anything, Trevor was sure he'd screwed up again, but then she nodded her acceptance.

"I never got a chance to ask, but what happened down there?" she wondered. "Did you see Hannah?"

Trevor shook his head, then told her what had happened down in the tunnels, including the details he'd gotten from Mike and Connor. "We didn't see anyone who looked like Hannah, but there are definitely more than a few people being held captive down there. There's a chance we could have found her if we could have kept looking, but one of the ghouls spotted Isaac, and the creatures sent up an alarm that roused the whole place."

Jenna seemed to consider all that for a moment before nodding once again. "Do you really think Davina will be able to find another way into the tunnels?"

"If anyone can, it's Davina," Trevor said confidently, thinking of all the ancient-looking books and maps she'd had spread across her office when he and his pack mates had stopped in to talk to her that afternoon. "We're going to check in with her tomorrow morning to see what she's come up with. I'm hoping for the best."

"Okay, but what are we going to do even if she does find another way down there?" Jenna asked. "We didn't exactly come off too well in our first run-in with those creatures."

"I can't say you're wrong about that," Trevor admitted, enveloping Jenna in his arms again and resting his chin on the top of her head. She pressed herself to him and wrapped her arms around him, squeezing tight. "But we need to get those people out of there—your sister included—so we're going to have to come up with some way to make it work. I don't know how yet. I just know that we will."

"I can't ask you to do that," Jenna said, her words soft as she kept her face pressed to his chest. "It was one thing to go down into those tunnels to look around, but it's something completely different to go back now that we know what we're up against. I can't ask you to risk your life like that."

"You aren't asking. I'm offering," Trevor murmured, pressing his lips to her hair, losing himself for a few seconds in her incredible scent. "There's nothing I wouldn't do for you—and your sister."

Jenna pulled back again, eyes gleaming with fresh tears. "How in the world did I get so lucky to find you? If I'd never gone to Dallas to try and talk Connor into helping me, I would never have met you and you would never have come out to LA, and we would never have…this."

Trevor could hear Jenna's heart thump a little faster at the idea that something could have come between them meeting. It made him wish he could tell her about this whole soul mate thing. It must be confusing and overwhelming for her to be feeling all these emotions and not have a clue where it was all coming from.

"I don't think you need to worry about that," he said softly, resting his forehead against hers. "Something tells me that we were destined to meet. Fate would have found a way to bring us together, no matter what."

"You know, for a big, brawny SWAT cop, you say the most romantic things," she said with a smile, tipping her head back a little to kiss him.

Trevor kissed her back, assuming this would be the same, almost sweet but still hot kind of thing they'd been doing since he'd gotten here. But when Jenna's hands found their way up to the back of his neck, fingers tugging at the short hair growing there, he realized that this time was going to be different.

And he sure as hell wasn't going to complain.

Jenna let out a soft moan as he teased the tip of her tongue with his, her mouth opening to invite him in. The kiss deepened and he tugged her closer until their bodies were pressed so tightly together that it was hard to tell where one of them stopped and the other started.

Trevor groaned as Jenna's fingernails found their way into his hair and massaged his scalp, her touch sending electrical sensations zipping down his spine. Moving of their own accord, his hands slid down her back, coming to rest on the curve of her butt. As he slid his hands down to cup her bottom, she surprised him by jumping up a little, gracefully wrapping her legs around his waist and locking her ankles behind his back. Then she pulled back to gaze at him intensely.

"Will you take me to bed?" she asked demurely, her hazel eyes full of hunger. "And before you ask, yes, I'm sure. We've had one hell of a bizarre day, and I need to be with you right now. *Really* with you."

Trevor leaned his head down and kissed her again, softly but with all the desire he felt in his body. Then he turned and headed out of the room and into Jenna's, her legs still wrapped around his waist.

CHAPTER 13

When Trevor had first walked into her workshop/guest bedroom, the thought that she might end up sleeping with him tonight had never entered her mind. In fact, in those moments when she'd been sobbing against his chest, wondering how a man could be so completely clueless, she'd been much closer to smacking him than kissing him.

But after hearing Trevor explain why he'd forgotten to call her, she had to admit to being in a completely different mood. Who knew she was a sucker for a guy who'd never had anyone care about him before?

And while those kisses certainly hadn't hurt, truthfully it was what Trevor said about the two of them being destined to meet. That fate would have found a way to bring them together, no matter what. That had done her in. Period. End of sentence.

When they reached her room, Jenna expected a mad dash straight to the bed, but instead, Trevor paused, pressing her against the wall right inside the door. With her legs around his waist the way they were, the position allowed him to grind nicely between her thighs. She moaned out loud at how good it felt.

The position also let Jenna know exactly how excited Trevor was, too. The obvious bulge in his jeans told her he wanted this as much as she did.

"I never realized how comfortable a wall could be," Jenna murmured as Trevor continued to grind against the cleft between her legs, making her wetter and wetter as his mouth came down to nibble on the delicate skin of her neck at the same time. "I think I wouldn't mind trying this position later after we get all these clothes out of the way."

Trevor chuckled against her neck, sending shivers all over her body as she wiggled back and forth a little to settle her bottom a bit more into his large, oh-so-strong hands.

"I think that's something we can arrange," he said, his low, husky voice connecting directly with that warm place between her legs.

Trevor moved his mouth from Jenna's neck to her jawline, tracing kisses and nips from there to her ear and then to her lips. The sensations of his warm mouth and his hard-on rocking against her core made her almost dizzy as she wondered how long he could keep this teasing up. Something told her that he'd happily do this for hours.

She was good with that.

She felt a tingling between her legs by the time Trevor pulled her away from the wall and moved across her bedroom. Jenna naturally assumed he was heading for the bed this time, but instead he stopped at the dresser, dropping his hands away and gently sitting her butt on the edge of the waist-high piece of furniture, leaving her balanced there. Her legs—which were still wrapped around his hips—were the only thing keeping her upright.

"You enjoyed the wall so much, I thought you might like to try out a few other places around the room," he murmured with another one of those soft, sexy laughs, his hands sliding up the bare skin of her thighs.

As his fingers drifted under the hem of her T-shirt, nudging it up until he urged it over her head, she decided to let him run the show. He certainly hadn't steered her wrong yet. So she lifted her arms and let him yank her shirt off and toss it aside. Her bra soon followed, leaving her topless under his heated gaze. His dark eyes seemingly blazed almost yellow gold in the reflected glow from the overhead light as he took in the sight of her breasts laid bare to him.

She didn't pause to think as she reached out, lacing her fingers behind his neck and dragging his mouth where she wanted it. Trevor's warm mouth immediately found one of her breasts, teasing and nipping exactly the way she liked it.

"Yes, just like that," she whispered, yanking his hair fiercely as he sucked at her sensitive nipple, moaning loudly as one of his hands came up to cup her other breast, tweaking that nipple between his thumb and forefinger.

Jenna was so lost in the glorious sensations cascading through her body that she completely missed the moment Trevor popped the buttons on her shorts until he was working them over her hips. Then he stepped back from between her legs, lifting her bottom enough to slide both her shorts and panties down her thighs.

Shoes, shorts, and panties all went flying. Within seconds, Jenna was left there perched on her dresser completely naked. Trevor eyed her like he was ready to devour her. And if the throbbing between her legs was any indication, there were parts of her that were completely wide open to that idea.

Trevor positioned himself in front of her again, draping her bare ankles casually over his hips. Being totally naked there in front of him with her legs spread wide was luridly sexual. Against all possible explanation, Jenna found the situation incredibly arousing.

Before she could say anything, Trevor's mouth was on hers. One strong hand trailed up the inside of her thigh, his touch pure electricity. When he reached the juncture between her thighs, fingers slipping through her wet folds, she jerked so hard she would have fallen off the dresser if it wasn't for his other hand in her hair, holding her firm.

His kisses were hard, almost hypnotizing, distracting her for a moment. But only until two of Trevor's long fingers slipped inside her, the tips caressing that perfect place she'd rarely ever been able to reach. The tingles deep in her core quickly turned into shivers, and she was forced to drop her hands down to the top of the dresser, clenching the edge tightly to keep herself steady.

She reluctantly dragged her mouth away from Trevor's, gasping for breath, kissing impossible. But even then, he kept his hand in her hair, holding her still and gazing deep into her eyes as his fingers continued to move quickly inside her.

Her orgasm hit hard and fast.

Instead of the slow, graceful buildup Jenna was used to, this one felt like she was being shot out of a cannon. One moment, she was holding her breath waiting for the wave to hit her, and the next, she was screaming so hard it hurt. But man, was the pain worth it. She couldn't remember coming so hard in forever.

Jenna only had a vague sense of how long her orgasm lasted, but it seemed like an exceedingly long time. At least that was what she assumed, based on how limp and wrung out all her muscles felt after the fact. When she finally gained some sense of awareness, it was to find herself still sitting atop her dresser, leaning back against the wall behind it, Trevor nowhere in sight in her rather small bedroom.

She pushed herself upright, trying not to slide off the dresser in her postorgasmic haze, when

Trevor came walking back into the room, a handful of familiar foil packets in his hand.

"I don't want to make any assumptions," he said softly as he held the condoms out to her. "But I thought we might need these."

Seeing the hunger in his eyes, all Jenna could do was smile and nod as she took the packets from his hand. Carefully tearing one open, she tossed the others onto the dresser beside her. But she found herself pausing as Trevor began to strip off his clothes, his boots thumping to the floor first, soon followed by his jeans and shirt. Until there was nothing left but the bandages around his forearms.

Trevor's shoulders were broad, his chest thick with the perfect number of muscles. His abs weren't outlandishly ripped like some guy who'd never eaten a slice of cheesecake in his life, but they were definitely well-defined and begging to be sculpted.

The wolf tattoo on his chest stood out vividly in the light of her room, the eyes seemingly gazing straight at her. And while the beast was snarling and showing its fangs, it didn't seem intimidating in the least. If anything, it seemed inviting to her.

The hunky SWAT cop's happy trail led her eyes downward toward a cock that was so thick and mouth-watering that Jenna could only stare. It was probably rude, but she couldn't help it. Trevor was simply so gorgeous that all she wanted to do for the rest of the night was gaze at him. Okay, maybe that last part wasn't true. She also wanted to touch him. Lots and lots of touching. And maybe some licking. Yeah, definitely some licking.

Trevor took a step closer, which prompted Jenna to notice his nice muscular legs. But truthfully, she'd been so distracted by his other glorious parts that she'd forgotten to check them out.

He stepped between her legs, letting her ankles rest on his hips again. The proximity to his thick erection had her core pulsing all over again with anticipation. Giving in to temptation, Jenna reached out to wrap her hands around his shaft, exhilarating at the feeling of him pulsing under her fingers.

The urge to simply sit there and caress his cock was rivaled only by the need to slide off the dresser so she could drop to her knees and lick him. But when Trevor took the condom packet from her hands, Jenna knew he had something else in mind.

Working together, the two of them rolled the condom down over his erection. It seemed like a shame to cover up something so perfect—like putting the wrapping paper back on a great present during your birthday party. But knowing what would be coming next helped settle her disappointment. But she still promised herself that she'd spend some quality time tasting his cock as soon as possible.

As soon as he was ready, Trevor reached down and grabbed her ankles, tilting her back on the dresser as he lifted them to his shoulders, putting her exactly where he wanted her.

"So dresser sex, huh?" she murmured, watching as he wrapped one of his hands around his shaft and began running the head of his cock up and down her very wet folds. "You know, there's a perfectly good bed a few feet behind you."

"Oh, don't worry," Trevor murmured with a low, rumbling chuckle. "We'll get to the bed soon enough. And the wall again. But this dresser is at the perfect height for this, and I wouldn't want to waste that."

Jenna couldn't argue with that logic, especially not when Trevor began to slide inside her, eliciting one long, continuous moan from her throat and making her see sparkles as he filled her completely.

He didn't stop until he was fully seated inside her, nudging places previously left untouched. It was wildly spectacular and all she could do was wrap her legs around his waist and hold on tight. He kissed her then, slow and lazy, one hand coming down to steady her hip while the other laced itself into her hair again.

Trevor clearly liked tugging her hair.

Apparently, she liked it, too.

She rested her hands on his shoulders as he began to thrust, her fingers grazing over all that warm skin. A distracted part of her mind noted some scratches marring the perfection of his left shoulder. Looking down, she casually realized that this must have been where the ghoul had gotten Trevor with its claws. But it didn't look bad at all, nothing more than a half dozen well-healed scratch marks. She was sure they would have been worse, especially considering all the blood she'd seen soaking through his shirt. But she supposed Trevor had been right. They truly had been nothing but some scratches.

Jenna stopped worrying about anything as inconsequential as scratches, focusing on the fact that Trevor was thrusting harder now. And she was already seeing stars. She lowered her legs down to the edge of the dresser top again, lifting her butt up some so she could push back, meeting him halfway.

It was Trevor who broke the kiss this time, his head falling back as he groaned low and long, damn near growling as he picked up the intensity of his movements, his thrusts making her dresser bounce back against the wall behind it. The pounding made her melt and spasm at the same time. She couldn't remember ever having sex feel so good. She wasn't sure if it was the position responsible for all these overwhelming sensations or Trevor himself. Either way, she would never be able to look at this dresser the same way again.

In fact, she might need to mount a plaque over it and declare it a national treasure.

Trevor slid his hand out of her hair so he could

get a firm grip on her bottom, thrusting even harder. Not needing to steady herself as much now that he had both his hands on her, Jenna slipped one of her hands down between her thighs, fingers twirling little circles right over her clit.

Her second orgasm came on as fast and violent as the first, except this time, Trevor was right there with her, his hoarse groans rumbling up through his chest as she felt his whole body tense. His head came up, his eyes locking with hers, and she swore they gleamed yellow gold again, even though there should have been no way from the overhead light to reflect off them at this angle.

But she forgot about that conundrum as her orgasm continued to spiral higher and higher until the pleasure was almost more than she could bear, and her vision started going dim. Then Trevor slammed deep inside her one last time, holding himself there as heat suffused her core. Even though she knew he was wearing a condom, it still felt amazing, adding to the pleasure she was feeling.

If Jenna had been limp before, she was an overcooked pasta noodle now. If Trevor hadn't been holding on to her so tightly, she likely would have slid right onto the floor. Instead, he picked her up and carried her to the bed, setting her down gently before sliding out to head to the bathroom. Jenna missed the sensation of him inside her immediately and almost got up to follow.

He was back moments later, moving toward the bed with a grace and strength that could only be described as predatory. But it was as he was stopping by the dresser to pick up another condom packet that Jenna realized he was still hard and hungry looking.

"Now," he said softly as he tore open the foil package. "What was that you mentioned earlier about sex up against the wall?"

Jenna should have been too exhausted to even move, but as Trevor walked toward her, she had to admit, if wall sex was half as good as dresser sex, she might just pass out.

Jenna was beyond exhausted by the time they fell into bed…three hours later. They'd showered off a little while ago, which probably would have meant more sleep for them both if Trevor hadn't taken her against the wall of the bathroom only seconds after they'd stepped out of the water. To say the sex had been good was an understatement. Kind of like suggesting that pizza was better the second day out of the fridge than straight from the oven.

Well…duh.

Snuggling up with her pillow, Jenna let out a happy sigh as Trevor turned out the lights. The glow of the city coming through the windows still lit up the room well enough for her to see him cross the room and slip under the covers with her. His arm immediately came up to wrap around her waist, tugging her close. Even as tired as she was, having him against her like that was enough to quicken her pulse again. Not enough to make her want to do anything about it, because...seriously...she was done for the day. But it was still amazing the way her body responded to his touch.

"Hope I didn't tire you out too much," Trevor murmured, his breath deliciously warm against her neck as he kissed her there. "That meeting at Davina's club is pretty early tomorrow, so if you want to skip it, that's not a problem. I can fill you in on everything when I get back."

Jenna groaned at the thought of crawling out of bed early in the morning. But there was no way she wanted to miss this conversation with Davina. "Well, you definitely tired me out, but in the best way possible. So let me sleep an extra ten minutes in the morning and we'll call it even."

"Deal."

Kissing her neck again, he snuggled her even closer, the arm he had around her waist hugging her against him. It felt so good being in his arms like this, and for the life of her, she couldn't imagine how this thing between them could get any better.

Sliding her right hand up, she weaved her fingers through Trevor's, clutching his arm to her body even more tightly, never wanting to let it go. Tipping her head down, she kissed his knuckles, once again wondering how the hell she'd gotten so lucky.

Just as her eyes were getting heavy with sleep, something caught her gaze and she looked over at the arm Trevor had shoved under her pillow. Part of his arm was sticking out from underneath it, including most of the section covered with gauze. The bandage had moved at some point, though whether it was during one of their many rounds of sex, during the shower, or from sliding it under her pillow, she had no idea. All she knew for sure was that it had almost come completely undone, revealing a good portion of his forearm, including two of the gashes from the ghoul's attack.

Half asleep as she was, her head couldn't comprehend what she was seeing. Instead of the heavily stitched slashes she'd been expecting, all she saw were two thin lines of scarring, both well-healed and nearly impossible to make out in the dim light coming from the window. In fact, they weren't much worse than the scratches she'd seen on his shoulder. Part of her wanted to lift her head and get a closer look, maybe even turn his arm toward the light a bit. Anything to get a better look. Anything to help her understand how any of this was possible.

But before she could move, her heavy eyes drifted closed, and sleep started to shut her logic functions down for the night. The mystery would have to wait until tomorrow.

CHAPTER 14

As Trevor walked into Davina's club, he noticed that the entryway looked completely different now that the strobing neon cats weren't illuminated like they had been during his previous visits. Moving farther inside, he realized that the place sounded almost completely empty. That wasn't shocking, he guessed. It was barely past eight o'clock in the morning. Even the bars in LA had to shut down at some point.

It felt a little weird walking through the club now that it was brightly lit with industrial fluorescent bulbs instead of the usual neon. But even more than that was how empty it was. Sure, he could smell and hear a couple people moving about the place, but still, it felt almost lifeless compared to the energy that filled the place last night. It made him wonder if there was some kind of supernatural element to that. Davina was a witch. Maybe she used magic to make her club more *alive* when necessary.

When he stepped out of the long entryway corridor, he immediately caught sight of Hale and Mike standing over by the main bar, chatting with a blue-haired woman who looked like a younger version of Davina and the bartender they'd seen the first time they'd come here—the one who smelled so unusual. Trevor looked around for Connor but didn't see him. He didn't smell him, either, so that meant he probably wasn't here.

"Connor was in the mood for doughnuts this morning," Mike said as Trevor approached them, having apparently seen him glancing around. "He knows a place on West Manchester Boulevard that he said is amazing, so he went to pick some up for us."

Trevor grunted but didn't say anything. There was a better chance Connor had gone on the food run simply to put off talking to him for as long as possible. Trevor had to admit that he wasn't looking forward to it, either.

"Speaking of people being late," Hale said. "Where's Jenna? I thought she'd be here for this for sure."

"She got called into the studio on some kind of special effects crisis, if you can believe it," Trevor said.

He watched as the bartender moved a full-sized beer keg around like it weighed nothing at all before helping Davina's daughter restock the coolers behind the bar, filling them with rack after rack of beer, wine coolers, and all kinds of fancy drinks Trevor didn't recognize.

"Apparently her coworkers were making some kind of huge dinosaur costume and the mold got stuck together," Trevor added. "They asked her to come in to help break the thing open. I guess she's some kind of mold whisperer or something. She promised it wouldn't take too long and that she'd come over as soon as she was done."

Trevor wasn't quite sure how molds worked or the ins and outs of how to get them open, but that seemed enough to satisfy Hale because he turned and pointed to the couple behind the bar.

"You've probably already figured this out, but this is Davina's daughter, Lydia. And this is Kamden Lang, one of the club's bartenders."

Trevor gave the man a nod in greeting, unable to stop himself from leaning across the bar a little bit and inhaling the guy's scent. It was just so... different. He tried to do it as nonchalantly as he could, but Kamden must have caught him doing it, because he threw a frown Trevor's way.

"Before you ask, no, I'm not human," he said, gray eyes full of annoyance, his tone a cross between defensive and plain pissed off. "But you're not either, so don't get all judgy on me."

Trevor held up his hands in surrender. "I wouldn't dream of it. I'm curious is all."

"Kamden is a skin walker," Lydia said casually as she continued stacking beer bottles in the closest fridge. "But don't worry. He's an ethically sourcing skin walker, which means he only assumes the bodies of the recently deceased."

Mike lifted a brow. "If that's considered ethical

sourcing, what would you consider the unethical alternative?"

"Killing a person so I can assume their body," Kamden said flatly. "Doing it my way means the body won't stay stable and viable for as long, and my fine motor skills can be adversely affected sometimes, but if I eat right and exercise, it works out okay. It's easier on my conscience too."

Trevor had no idea what to say to that. The implications of an entire race of creatures *assuming* other people's bodies was a bit much to wrap his head around. He suddenly remembered Davina saying something in passing conversation several weeks ago—when she was helping them with another case—about Lydia and Kamden being involved with one another. And the issues they'd have to face when it came time for him to change bodies. Trevor didn't even want to consider how the hell that was going to work out.

He was still thinking about their imminent predicament when Mike spoke.

"So now that you've slept with Jenna, have you figured out if she's actually *The One* for you?" he asked as casually as if he was talking about the weather. "Or are you merely having a good time with Connor's sister to piss him off?"

"What? No! Of course I didn't sleep with Jenna to piss off her dumbass brother," Trevor barked, ignoring the glances Lydia and Kamden gave him.

He sniffed the T-shirt he was wearing as subtly as he could. He'd taken a shower this morning—a long one. But apparently, it hadn't been long enough. Then again, he and Jenna had made love quite a few times last night. Definitely more than a single shower could erase.

"So that means she's *The One* then, right?" Hale prompted. "Have you said anything to her about it yet? Let her know how you feel?"

Trevor's mind flashed back to last night and their lovemaking, then what it had been like to slip into bed and sleep with her afterward. But as amazing as all that had been, it was waking up with Jenna in his arms this morning that really did it for him. He'd known he was hooked and that he couldn't imagine not having her with him every day for the rest of his life. Even if he had no idea how he was going to make it happen.

"Yeah, I'm pretty sure she is. My soul mate, I mean," Trevor said softly. "No, actually, check that. I *know* Jenna is my soul mate. But no, I haven't even tried telling her how I feel about her yet. I was going to talk to her this morning on the way over here, but then she got that call from work, and it messed up my plan, so I'll have to find another time to tell her. Soon."

"Have you thought about what you're going to say to her?" Mike asked, turning to lean back against the bar. "I mean, are you going with the soul-mate thing first or straight to the claws and fangs, then use that to explain how soul mates are possible?"

Trevor ran a hand through his hair. "Truthfully, I don't have a frigging clue. I kinda think telling her about the whole werewolf thing is off the table. Not just now, but maybe forever."

"What the hell does that mean?" Hale asked, clearly confused.

Mike looked just as baffled. "Why wouldn't you want to tell her you're a werewolf?"

Trevor dropped onto the nearest barstool. He wasn't sure how it was possible, but he was physically exhausted from going round and round in his head about the subject.

"Jenna has had her entire life turned upside down by monsters," he said quietly. "I completely hate that I have to hide that part of my life from her, but how can I tell her the truth? What am I going to do if she doesn't want to have anything to do with a werewolf? I can't take that risk."

"O-kay," Mike said slowly, his tone suggesting he clearly disagreed with him. "But if you don't tell her, how do you see this all working out? You can try and hide what you are, but you have to know that it will come out sooner or later. I mean, seriously, how many times have we watched this same thing blow up in our pack mates' faces. Usually in spectacular fashion and at the worst possible time."

Trevor couldn't argue with that assessment. For

some reason, all his pack mates had run into some serious drama when it came to revealing to their soul mates that they were werewolves. It usually involved lots of shouting, misunderstandings, and tears.

It wasn't a pretty picture.

"I know all that." Getting to his feet, Trevor paced back and forth for a minute. The more he tried to figure out what to do, the more frustrated he got. "But what the hell am I supposed to do? Tell her and risk losing her right off the bat, or keep it from her and risk everything blowing up in my face at some point in the future?"

"That's a choice you're going to have to make on your own," Mike murmured. "But I can tell you from experience that when you're lucky enough to find the person you're supposed to be with for the rest of your life, you do whatever you have to do to be with them. You don't waste time and you don't take chances, because you never know when it could all be taken away from you."

Trevor resisted the urge to ask questions, even though he wanted to. Everyone on the Dallas SWAT team knew that Mike had been in a serious relationship and that something bad had happened to his fiancée, but none of them knew the details.

Trevor looked at Hale. "You were all for the idea of me pursuing Jenna when I first got here, so what do you think I should do? Tell her or not?"

Trevor expected Hale to immediately launch into some romantic plan to throw himself at Jenna's mercy in an effort to help her understand what it meant to be a soul mate. But instead, Hale frowned, looking uncomfortable.

"I was all about you and Jenna at first," Hale admitted. "When it was merely an idea. And when I wasn't sure she was your soul mate. Now that's it's getting serious, I'm not so sure it's a good idea anymore."

Trevor did a double take. "What? Why the hell not?"

Hale sighed. "Because you're basically putting yourself between a brother and sister. Connor will never accept your relationship with Jenna, so for her to be with you, she'll have to choose you over her family. Do you honestly want to put her in that position? Do *you* want to be in that position? And then there's the whole pack thing."

"The Pack?" Trevor echoed, baffled as hell. "What do they have to do with this?"

Hale threw up his hands in exasperation. "Dude, if Connor is dead set against you being with his sister, how is that going to work out when the two of you are pack mates? What, are the two of you just going to fight all the time? Or will you leave the Pack?"

"Leave the Pack?" Trevor repeated softly.

"Yeah," Hale said. "Because that's what you

might have to do. Are you really willing to leave the Pack to be with Jenna?"

Trevor stared at his friend. His brother. His *pack mate*. He'd vowed to himself the other night to do anything for Jenna, and while leaving the Pack would hurt like hell, he'd do it in a heartbeat to be with her.

Before he could say anything, Connor walked in, two boxes of amazing-smelling doughnuts balanced in one hand and a cardboard carrier with four large cups of coffee in the other. He didn't say anything as he set everything on top of the bar. Ignoring Trevor like he wasn't even there, he opened one of the boxes of doughnuts, revealing a variety of glazed, cinnamon crumb, chocolate, and Boston cream.

Connor reached for one, then suddenly stopped cold, his head snapping around and his nose coming up to sniff the air. A split second later, his hazel eyes blazed with a yellow-gold glow so vivid it was like they were electric.

From the corner of his eye, Trevor saw Kamden take Lydia's hand and urge her toward the far end of the bar.

"Davina doesn't like fighting in here," Kamden said firmly, giving them a stern look. "If you break anything, you're buying it."

Lydia stopped, her gaze going from Trevor to Connor to the boxes of doughnuts, indecision clear on her face. After a moment, she hurried over to grab both boxes, then ran back over to Kamden where they—and the doughnuts—would be safe from the brawl they seemed convinced was about to happen.

"We're not getting into a fight," Trevor assured them.

The words were barely out of his mouth when Connor flipped one of the barstools across the dance floor and took a threatening step toward him, his face suffused with anger.

Okay, maybe there would be a fight.

"You asshole," Connor snarled, the tips of his fangs showing over his lower lip and his claws springing out. "You slept with my sister, even after I told you to stay away from her!"

Trevor felt his own anger surging. He was so damn tired of dealing with Connor and his misplaced, over-the-top protective streak.

"Yeah, you told me to stay away from Jenna," he growled, barely keeping his own inner wolf at bay. "Right around the same time she pointed out that you have no say in how she lives her life or who she spends her time with. That includes who she decides to sleep with. And she decided to sleep with me. So you need to get the hell over it!"

One moment, Connor was standing a few steps away, looking angry as hell, and the next, he was grabbing Trevor and slinging him across the room.

Trevor crashed into a table piled high with

upside down chairs. The things broke and splintered under him. A piece of wood pierced his hip, but he ignored it even as he tumbled across the dance floor. He pushed himself upright as Connor came at him again.

Trevor shifted out of pure instinct, his inner wolf knowing his pack mate intended to hurt him this time. Muscles twisted and bunched along his back and shoulders while claws and fangs elongated as a growl rumbled up from his chest. Spinning, he barely braced himself before Connor was coming through the air in his direction, clawed hands swinging and face twisted with rage.

Trevor threw up an arm, blocking the slash coming toward his face, refusing to let his pack mate rip him apart because he was having a temper tantrum brought on by his sister deciding to have sex with someone he didn't like. Not that Connor would probably consider anyone good enough to sleep with Jenna.

Trevor was so done with this shit.

He launched himself forward, slamming one of his shoulders into Connor's chest. There were a few cracking and crunching sounds as bones broke—both his collarbone as well as Connor's ribs. Then his friend was flying across the room to bounce off the bar hard enough to leave a dent in the metal foot rail.

Connor was up and coming his way again in the blink of an eye, moving so fast he was nearly a blur. Halfway across the room, he leaned down and picked up the remnants of one of the broken chairs, flinging it in Trevor's direction.

Trevor ducked, avoiding the piece of wood but not Connor's claws. They tore through Trevor's forearm, drawing blood. Trevor was tempted to slash him in return, but at the last second, he retracted his claws, refusing to scar his pack mate and his friend—even if that pack mate and friend was being a complete asshole right now.

Instead, he punched Connor, his closed fist coming up to connect with the underside of his jaw. The sound of fangs smashing together was almost as enjoyable as the sight of his pack mate flying backward to land on his ass.

Almost.

But Connor refused to give up, coming at him over and over, willing to inflict a level of damage that shocked Trevor. But one look at Connor's face revealed that his pack mate—and still his friend regardless—was so enraged, Trevor doubted he was even aware of what he was doing.

Their fight went back and forth across the entire room, from the seating area in front of the bar filled with tables and chairs, then out onto the main dance floor. Not only were they making a mess of the club, but they were making a mess of each other, too. Trevor had already been slashed half a dozen times, and he suspected Connor likely had at least that many broken bones. And yet his pack mate seemed nowhere close to stopping. If anything, it seemed like Connor was losing control by the second. Considering how far his jawline and face were starting to jut out, Trevor expected him to shift into a full wolf before long.

If that happened, Trevor would have to do the same simply to protect himself.

That was when the real damage would start.

Out of the corner of his eye, Trevor saw Davina leaning over one of the upper floor railings, gazing down with clear disapproval. Lydia and Kamden were nowhere in sight.

Hale and Mike finally inserted themselves into the fight, trying to drag Trevor and Connor apart. It didn't go so well as the four of them ended up in a cluster in the center of the dance floor, punching and clawing at each other, with Hale and Mike attempting to limit the damage while trying to keep themselves from getting hit at the same time.

Trevor was kneeling in the middle of the floor, his hands wrapped around each of Connor's wrists, just trying to keep those claws at bay, when a simple gasp froze everything. A second later, an overwhelmingly familiar scent hit his nose, followed by several others that were not nearly as precious to him but still familiar.

Connor jerked his head up, his glowing eyes locked on something directly over Trevor's right shoulder.

Trevor turned slowly, already knowing what he'd see.

Jenna was standing on the stairs at the top of the entryway, eyes wide, her mouth hanging open in shock. Behind her, Owen and the rest of the HOPD crew stood staring, varying degrees of disbelief on their faces.

Jenna's gaze moved back and forth between Trevor and Connor before locking solely on Trevor. He saw a myriad of emotions playing there, changing so quickly it was impossible to read them all. But he definitely recognized confusion, quickly followed by understanding, anger, and then finally something that could only be described as heart-rending pain.

Then Jenna turned and ran back up the steps, and Trevor swore it felt like she was ripping out his heart and carrying it away with her as she went.

He immediately moved to follow, but a firm hand on his shoulder stopped him. He whirled around, assuming it was Connor, ready to keep fighting. But he was surprised when he found Davina gazing up at him with a sad expression in her lavender eyes, like she knew exactly how bad the whole messed-up situation had become.

"I think you should wait and give her some space so she can calm down," Davina said softly, her hand still resting on Trevor's shoulder. "She's confused and hurt right now, and if you chase after her, she'll run for sure. And something tells me that in her condition, she may never stop."

Though it was the hardest thing he'd ever done, Trevor knew he needed to follow her advice and let Jenna go for now if he ever hoped to have a chance to get her back at all. That didn't mean he couldn't send her a text. But as the club's heavy door slammed closed and echoed in his ears, something inside him felt like it died, and all he could do was wonder if that was the last time he'd ever see his soul mate.

CHAPTER 15

Jenna's head was spinning so much that it wasn't until she was standing at the door of her apartment that she realized she'd gone straight home after leaving the club. She didn't remember anything beyond starting her car and speeding out of the parking lot. She wasn't sure if she'd even stopped for any traffic lights between here and there.

Reaching into the front right pocket of her jeans for her keys, Jenna was confused when she didn't find them. She always put her keys in the front right pocket of her pants. It was kind of her thing. One of the many routines that had developed into an obsessive behavior during her years of therapy.

She checked her other pockets almost frantically, only to discover that she didn't have her keys anywhere on her. Since her apartment keys were on the same ring as her car keys, she began to question if she'd actually driven herself home at all. Had she taken an Uber and left her keys on the seat of some stranger's Prius? Or maybe she'd actually walked home and her keys were lying on a sidewalk somewhere? Or maybe her keys were simply still in the ignition of her car, down in the parking lot?

Jenna knew she should probably go back down to the parking lot and check, but suddenly it all just seemed too much to deal with, and she found herself sliding down the door until she was sitting on the floor in front of her apartment. Tears she wasn't sure how she'd held at bay until now ran down her face.

Images spun through her head as she sat there sniffling softly. Walking into Davina's club. Hearing the fight long before she saw it. Then the scene of Trevor and Connor throwing each other around the dance floor like some kind of wild animals.

Jenna had felt anxious, remembered looking around the club as she tried to understand what was happening. But then she'd seen her brother's glowing yellow eyes and fangs so long that his entire jawline reshaped to make room for them. She thought she might have let out a gasp when she saw Connor's claws.

Claws that were shockingly similar to the ones the ghouls had.

Her anxiety descended into a full-on panic attack at that point. But it wasn't until Trevor had turned around and she saw the gold eyes and the fangs and the blood that she fell apart. She usually froze in situations like that—the way she had when the ghoul grabbed her sister—but for some reason, this time, she ran.

The details from that point on were kind of

fuzzy. Maybe because she might have been disassociating a bit from the trauma of what she'd seen. Normally she'd berate herself for being weak, especially since she'd worked so hard to overcome that, but this time, she was in a forgiving mood. After all, she'd just learned that both her brother and the man she'd been falling in love with were monsters.

She was still sitting on the floor of the hallway, crying softly as she pondered that rather mind-numbing fact, when the door directly across from her opened. Then Madeleine was suddenly at her side, gently urging her up to her feet and into her own apartment.

"Jenna, honey. What happened?" Madeleine asked as she parked Jenna in one of the chairs at the kitchen table, hovering frantically. "Are you hurt? Do you need me to call someone—like the police maybe?"

Jenna got herself together enough to shake her head. "No, it's nothing like that. I just learned something…alarming…and it shook me up a bit. Then I left my keys in my car—I think—and decided to have a moment. On the floor. In the hallway."

Madeleine regarded her thoughtfully, her eyes filled with concern. "Wait here."

Turning, Madeleine hurried out of the kitchen. The apartment was the same layout as Jenna's, so she knew her friend was heading for the bathroom.

A few moments later, she came back with a box of tissues, handing it to Jenna. Then she opened one of the overhead cabinets, coming out with a familiar box of fancy, gourmet hot chocolate.

"I think this calls for some cocoa, don't you?" Madeleine said, shaking the box in Jenna's direction and giving her a small smile.

Jenna used one of the tissues to wipe away the worst of the tears. "Depends. Do you have any of those organic little marshmallows?"

Madeleine turned back to the same cabinet the hot chocolate had been in, dug around for a few seconds before coming out with a plastic bag, brow arched. "Did you ever have any doubt?"

Her friend didn't say anything while she got the cocoa ready, and Jenna didn't either. Instead, she simply sat there at the kitchen table, wondering what the hell she was supposed to say. Madeleine wasn't going to accept some generic series of excuses to explain why she'd been crying out in the hallway. Especially after she'd already admitted to learning something alarming.

Jenna wished she was witty and clever enough to come up with some lies and half-truths that would rationally explain this bizarre situation. But that simply wasn't her. Even if it had been, there was a part of her that wanted to finally open up and tell her best friend the truth. Because she desperately needed to talk to someone. But how the hell was she supposed to dump all this on Madeleine out of the blue after lying to her all this time?

A mug of hot chocolate suddenly appeared in front of her, a dozen marshmallows floating on the top. It smelled delicious and was exactly what she needed right then.

Along with her best friend.

"I've been keeping something from you for a while," Jenna finally said after taking a long sip of perfectly sweetened cocoa and letting the heat of the mug absorb into her hands. "I want to apologize for that first. I should have told you before now, but I need you to understand that I simply didn't think I could."

On the other side of the table, Madeleine got a worried look on her face. "What kind of things?"

"Things that are going to sound...well...unbelievable." Jenna blew on her cocoa before taking another sip. "And coming from me, I know that's pretty serious. But I'm telling you right now, everything I'm going to tell you is true. No matter how impossible it sounds."

Now, Madeleine looked downright alarmed. But she didn't say anything. Instead, she sat there regarding Jenna expectantly, her own cocoa sitting forgotten in front of her.

"First off, the guy who kidnapped my sister ten years ago—the one Trevor and I saw a couple of nights ago—well...the truth is...he's not actually a guy at all," Jenna said, not looking at her friend while she spoke. She paused to take a deep breath before continuing. "He's a member of a supernatural species known as ghouls. They're underground dwellers who live in small clans, digging tunnels through solid rock with their claws and occasionally kidnapping humans from the surface to use for manual labor but also possibly as a source of food."

Jenna kept her focus on the mug of hot chocolate in front of her, afraid to see Madeleine looking at her with that all-too-familiar expression of pity. Jenna wouldn't be able to handle it if she got that from her best friend. Like she'd gotten it from everyone else.

Maybe this had been a really bad idea.

"Your sister was kidnapped by creatures living under the city that eat people," Madeleine said slowly. "And you're just getting around to telling me now?"

Jenna lifted her head to look at her friend. She hadn't expected that kind of response. But Madeleine was sitting there calmly as she waited for an answer to her question.

"Honestly, I didn't become aware of exactly what kind of creatures they were until the other day," Jenna admitted with a sigh. "I wanted to tell you, but considering the fact that I've been lying to you since I told you about what happened to my sister, it wasn't like I could come out and suddenly spring the truth on you now."

"Why didn't you tell me the truth from the beginning then?" Madeleine asked, obviously hurt Jenna had kept something like this from her. "I've known for years that you weren't telling me everything."

Jenna blinked. "You have?"

Madeleine nodded.

Jenna sipped her cocoa with a shrug. "Can you blame me? I had no reason to think you'd believe me. No one else ever has—not even my family. I didn't want to lose the only real friend I'd had in a long time, so I took the easy way out and lied to you."

It was Madeleine's turn to sigh. "Okay, I guess I can understand that. I'd like to think that you could have talked to me about anything, even back when we first met, but if we're being honest, I'm not sure I would have handled the whole supernatural species thing very well."

Jenna studied her friend. "But you're willing to buy it now?"

"What choice do I have?" Madeleine took a sip of cocoa. "It's not like I'd ever call my best friend a liar. Besides, if *TMZ* came out with evidence that half the people in LA were actually extraterrestrials or cannibalistic humanoid underground dwellers, I wouldn't be all that surprised. So if my best friend tells me that her sister was kidnapped by a clan of ghouls, I suppose I have no choice but to go along with it."

It wasn't exactly the same thing as Madeleine saying she believed her, but right now, Jenna would take it.

"Have you seen any of these ghoul creatures besides the one time in Skid Row with Trevor?" her friend asked, taking another sip of cocoa. "Except the first time you saw one. You know...back then."

Jenna nodded, understanding what Madeleine was trying to say. "Um, since I'm being honest, then I should probably tell you that we ran into a bunch of them yesterday after I left you at the coffee shop. That's actually how Trevor, my brother, and their teammates got hurt."

"What?" Madeleine said in alarm. "You said Trevor got a scratch while down in those tunnels! Are you saying they were attacked by these ghouls...and that you were there?"

Jenna told Madeleine the whole story of how she, Esme, and Maya had gone looking for the guys and ended up getting involved in a pitched battle down in the darkness of the sewers and how they'd barely made it out before the tunnel had collapsed.

On the other side of the table, her friend stared at her incredulously. "So is that why you were outside in the hallway crying? Because Trevor is hurt worse than he let on?"

Jenna shook her head. "No, thank goodness it's nothing like that. I got a look at his injuries last night when we slept together, and as impossible as it is to believe, they really were nothing more than scratches."

Madeleine seemed ready to ask another question, but then her eyes sharpened suddenly. "Wait a second. You looked at his injuries while you were sleeping together? Is that sleeping together or *sleeping* together?"

"Is there a difference?" Jenna asked, arching a brow.

"You know damn well there is," Madeleine said, leaning across the kitchen table to pin her with a look. "Did you have sex with Trevor or not? And is that why you're all upset? Did he say something to you this morning about it? Oh, crap! Is he married? Is that the *alarming* thing you learned this morning?"

Jenna almost spit out her now tepid cocoa at that. How the heck had her friend gone so far off the rails in such an amazingly short period of time?

And people call me crazy.

She set down her mug and held up her hand. "Okay, just stop. Yes, Trevor and I made love last night. And before you ask, yes, it was amazing. No, he didn't say anything to me this morning that was alarming. And no, he's not married."

"Then what the heck is going on?" Madeleine groaned, setting her mug down, but only so she could throw her hands in the air. "Because I'm at my wit's end here."

"Trevor has fangs!" Jenna practically shouted, the words coming out so fast they were nearly incomprehensible. She ran both hands through her hair. "I was supposed to meet up with Trevor, my brother, and their friends at a club across town this morning," she said, her voice much lower now. "We were meeting with a person who might have information on another way to get into the sewer tunnels so we can go back down there to look for Hannah. But the moment I stepped inside, I heard fighting. I knew without a doubt that it was Trevor and my dumbass brother going at it again."

"Fangs?" Madeleine whispered, eyes wide but still sort of dubious.

She nodded. "When I saw them, they were throwing each other around the room like rag dolls. I thought they were trying to kill each other."

"Oh my gosh!"

"Then I saw the fangs. Connor's first, then Trevor's. Both of their eyes were glowing this vivid yellow gold and they had..."

"They had what?" Madeleine prompted when Jenna sputtered to a stop. "What else did you see?"

"Claws." Jenna took a deep breath. "Trevor and my brother both had claws. They were long, at least an inch, and sharp looking as hell. Connor must have used his on Trevor a few times because there was blood everywhere. Hale and Mike—their teammates—were trying to separate them, but it wasn't working too well."

Madeleine continued to sit there, blinking her eyes slowly, like a deer in the headlights. Finally, her friend shook her head. "Um...what did they say? After they saw you standing there, I mean."

That was probably an intelligent question, given the situation. Unfortunately, Jenna didn't have an answer for her.

"I have no idea," she said softly. "The moment I saw...what I saw...I turned and ran as fast as I could. I don't remember much after that. I sort of got lost in the sauce, you know? The next thing I knew, I was sitting on the floor crying, and you were helping me up."

Madeleine was quiet for a long time. "So the guy you slept with last night has claws and fangs like a ghoul. Do you think maybe getting scratched by the creatures means that Trevor and your brother are turning into ghouls?"

She lowered her voice as she spoke, looking left and right, like she thought there might be someone around to overhear. In her own kitchen.

Jenna allowed herself to seriously entertain the possibility that Trevor and Connor had somehow been infected by the earlier ghoul attack. But it didn't take long to dismiss the idea.

"I don't think so," she murmured. "From the way Hale and Mike were dealing with the situation like it wasn't that big of a deal, I get the feeling they weren't shocked by the claws and fangs. I don't know why, but I think both Trevor and my brother are different. I think they're some other kind of supernatural creature."

Madeleine's eyes widened even more. "You had sex with a monster?"

Jenna sagged back in her chair, letting out a long, tired sigh. "I tell you an incredible story straight out of a Hollywood horror movie, and the first thing you jump on is the fact that I slept with a guy who has claws and fangs? That's the important part you glean from my entire confession? And I never said Trevor's a monster." But she *had* thought it, she was ashamed to admit. "He might have fangs, claws, glowing eyes—and apparently, supernatural strength—but that doesn't make him a monster. It just makes him different."

Madeleine stared at her for a bit, probably trying to figure out if she was being serious or not. "Okay, I thought I was onto something, but you don't seem torn up over the fact that you slept with a guy who's *different*. Which brings me back to my previous question. Why were you crying on my doorstep?"

Jenna flushed, more than a little embarrassed about that. "I wasn't crying on your doorstep," she corrected. "It was mine."

"Oh, that does make all the difference, I suppose," her friend said dryly. "Come on, I'm serious, Jenna. You were obviously upset by what you saw this morning, but if you're not bothered by him being some kind of supernatural, and you're not upset about sleeping with him, then I'm a little baffled about what's bothering you."

"Honestly, I guess I am, too." Jenna said softly, realizing she wasn't sure what had gotten her so spun up. "I mean, sure, I freaked when I saw the claws and fangs, but I think that's to be expected. Now that I'm thinking about it, I don't think I genuinely care that Trevor and my brother are different. And I'm certainly not upset that I decided to sleep with Trevor. Like I said, it was amazing."

Across from her, it was obvious that Madeleine was trying to understand what was going on with her. But she didn't push the issue. Instead, she sat there quietly, waiting patiently for Jenna to work through it on her own.

It took a while to get there—and another mug of hot chocolate—before Jenna had an idea about what was nagging at her so much. At least it felt like the right answer.

"I think the thing that bothered me the most is that I trusted Trevor," she said. "It's probably stupid, but I thought we had this connection. I told him everything about me—every secret I have—and I thought he would be completely open with me, too. I guess I was wrong, though. Now, I can't get past this feeling that's he's somehow betrayed me. Like I said, it's stupid."

"I don't think it's stupid," Madeleine said. "You

said you kept getting the feeling he was hiding something from you. You think maybe this is that something?"

Jenna hadn't even thought of that, but it certainly made sense. All she could do was shrug. "I guess so."

There was a long stretch of silence as Jenna nursed her second mug of hot chocolate, replaying the moment she'd seen Trevor's transformed face. It had been drastically different from the one she'd spent so much time kissing last night, but it had still been him. Her fingers itched with a sudden need to sculpt what she'd seen. The fangs, the shifted jaw line, everything.

"I'm not defending him," Madeleine said, interrupting Jenna's thoughts. "But I gotta think that it's difficult for Trevor to trust people enough to tell them about the whole claw-and-fang thing. You kept secrets from me, too, remember? Like you, he probably had his reasons. Maybe, now that you've already seen him...different...he'll be able to talk about it."

"Maybe." Jenna stood and walked over to the sink to rinse out her mug. She knew from experience how much of a pain it was to get hot chocolate out once it dried.

"What are you going to do?" Madeleine asked as Jenna put the mug on the counter, then dried her hands on a paper towel.

Jenna leaned back against the counter as she considered the question for a few moments. "First, I guess I'll head downstairs to search my car and hopefully find my keys. Then I'll come back up here and start working the clay. I need to clear my head, and sculpting what's trapped in there is the only way I know to do that."

"Then what?"

"Then I have no idea."

CHAPTER 16

"I told you to stay away from her," Connor mumbled softly, his words a bit slurred from the broken jaw that was still in the process of healing. "Now look what you've done. Jenna has run off to who knows where, and it's all your fault."

Trevor bit his tongue to keep from saying something that would start another brawl, concentrating instead on wrapping a bandage around his left forearm, the one he'd used to block most of Connor's strikes. While he might not be keen on fighting with Connor again, his pack mate sure as hell sounded like he was.

From the corner of his eye, Trevor saw Hale and Mike perk up a little from where they stood on the far side of the huge room, along with Davina and the four members of HOPD. Mike had shoved him and Connor over to this table shortly after Jenna had left, telling them to stay there until they worked their issues out. Trevor felt like a kid on time-out.

He turned his attention back to Connor, bracing himself in case his friend was looking to throw hands again. But Connor looked too worn out and defeated. Maybe all the fight had drained out of him the second his sister had run out of the club.

Trevor could understand that. His insides were a churned-up mess, too. Sure, some of that had to do with fighting one of his best friends, but mostly it was the image of Jenna and the expression on her face before she'd left. He wanted to believe that Davina had been right about letting her have some space, but within minutes, he was already questioning his decision. What if she wasn't okay with this? What if she ran and never came back? What if he never saw her again?

The thought had Trevor breathing hard and his fingertips tingling as his inner wolf fought to come out, needing to do something to fix this.

"I'm sure that seeing her brother losing his mind and trying to kill her soul mate had nothing to do with Jenna running away," Trevor murmured, twisting his left arm this way and that, checking to see if there was any blood seeping through the gauze. "No, it's definitely my fault, because I had the audacity to fall in love with my friend's sister."

"She's not your soul mate," Connor growled, though there wasn't much—if any—fire left in his tone.

"Actually, she is," Trevor replied, surprised at how calmly the statement had come out. He supposed a good bit of his own fire had gone out with Jenna's departure, too. "I think I've known since I first met her that day in your apartment in Dallas and smelled her amazing honeysuckle scent. The connection has only gotten stronger since I came out here to LA. Now, the mere thought of not being with her makes me feel sick."

He expected more resistance, but Connor simply went back to staring at the table, his eyes tracing along one of the large scratches across its surface. Trevor absently wondered how many of the tables scattered around the dance floor Davina would be able to save. Most of them had been damaged to some degree during the fight, and he couldn't help but grimace at the thought of paying for all of them, even if he and Connor split the cost.

"Have you told her yet?" Connor asked suddenly, still not looking up from the table, his voice sounding practically subdued now. "About how you feel about her, I mean. I think it's obvious to everyone you never got around to mentioning the whole werewolf-soul-mate thing."

"I haven't been able to find the right time to tell her," Trevor admitted. "But that's mostly because I've had to focus so much of my attention on dealing with her pain-in-the-ass brother. If you can believe it, all he wants to do is keep us apart. Without once ever asking his friend—or his sister—what they wanted."

"I was only trying to protect her," Connor said, but there wasn't a whole lot of conviction in his words. "It's what a brother is supposed to do."

Trevor really wanted to push back against that and tell Connor he was full of crap. But at the last second, he stopped himself, deciding to give his pack mate the benefit of the doubt. He was talking instead of throwing punches. That had to count for something.

"And what exactly were you protecting Jenna from?" Trevor wondered, asking the question that had been bothering him from the beginning. "Is this really about me not being good enough for your sister? I mean, did you honestly think I was going to hurt her?"

Connor didn't say anything right away. Instead, he sat there, staring at the table again.

"I don't think it was ever about you," he finally said, the words coming out so softly that Trevor could barely hear them, even with his werewolf-enhanced hearing.

Connor fell silent again and Trevor had to resist the urge to push. He waited, tense and unsure of where this was going next.

"I didn't believe her," Connor whispered. "When Jenna told me that Hannah had been being taken by a monster. I never believed her." There was another long stretch of silence, the pain on his friend's face agonizing to see. "I somehow convinced myself that if Jenna was wrong, that if she'd made everything up, then it wouldn't be my fault that I did absolutely nothing to help find Hannah. It's a shitty thing to do, but once I let myself believe the lie—even for a second—I couldn't stop."

"So you painted Jenna as the bad guy in order for you to be able to live without the guilt of doing nothing?" Trevor asked slowly.

He should be angry, but he wasn't. Just disappointed. Really frigging disappointed. He guessed there were no lies so great as the ones we tell ourselves.

Connor nodded, almost imperceptibly. "By the time Jenna showed up in Dallas, saying she'd seen Hannah, I'd become so invested in the lie, it had become my truth. And if my sister was wrong about what had happened to Hannah, then in my mind, she was wrong about you, too. So I did everything I could to keep you two apart because there was no way you could be right for one another. Jenna had to be wrong. She had to be."

Trevor shook his head at the way Connor had been forced to twist himself—and reality—into knots in his effort to keep the lie going. He would have felt sorry for his friend if it wasn't for the fact that Jenna was the one who'd been the victim here. She was the one who'd borne all the pain for her brother's stupidity.

"Not that I really care or anything, because seriously, you're a complete a-hole," Trevor finally said, trying—and failing—to keep the anger out of his voice. "But how's your world going now that reality has intruded and proven Jenna right and you wrong?"

Connor's eyes flashed yellow gold, and for a second, Trevor thought he was about to lose control again. Then it seemed like the air—and the fight—went out of his friend all of a sudden, and his shoulders visibly slumped.

"How am I supposed to live with knowing that I abandoned Jenna when she needed me the most?" Connor said, his words thick with emotion he was clearly working hard to suppress. "That I said all those horrible things to my sister? That Hannah has been a prisoner of these ghouls for a decade without me ever doing a damn thing about it? How am I supposed to live with that kind of guilt? How do I fix this?"

"I have no idea how you deal with it," Trevor admitted. "That's between you and your conscience, I suppose. But when it comes to fixing it, first, we need to focus on finding Hannah and getting her back. Once we've done that, you'll need to sit down and tell Jenna exactly what you just told me. There's a chance she may never forgive you, but you have to start there."

Connor didn't say anything for a long time, but then he finally nodded. "Okay, we focus on Hannah first. And afterward, I'll try and talk to Jenna. Do you think that maybe you could help with that?"

To say Trevor was shocked that Connor would ask for his help was an understatement. Truthfully, he wasn't too sure he wanted to be put in that kind of position. Even if Connor was a pack mate and a friend, Trevor was still firmly on Team Jenna when it came to this issue. But in the end, he murmured something that sounded appropriately positive, simply to end the conversation.

Connor seemed to accept that, because he stood without comment and headed over to join everyone else at the bar. Trevor followed, catching sight of Hale lifting a brow and mouthing the words *everything okay?* in his direction. Trevor had no doubt that Hale had been eavesdropping on their conversation and had heard everything they said, but he nodded at his friend all the same.

Hale and Mike—along with Davina and all four of the investigators from HOPD—were pouring over a large piece of paper, easily as wide as the bar and at least four feet long. It didn't take Trevor long to figure out what it was.

"What's going on with the old street map?" Connor asked, turning his head this way and that to get a look at the thing. "Have you found another way into the ghoul caverns?"

Everyone exchanged looks with each other for a second, leaving Trevor to wonder what they'd missed. He'd been too focused on the conversation with Connor to pay attention to anything they'd been discussing over here.

"Davina found the map for us," Mike said. "It shows pretty much everything that's underground here in LA, from the old tunnels that serviced the speakeasies during the Prohibition era of the twenties and thirties to the small subway system that was shut down in the fifties. It also includes all the major sewer lines and utility corridors plus those parts of the LA aqueduct system that run underground. If there's another way into the ghoul caverns, it should be on here."

Trevor leaned over and looked at all the crisscrossing, colored lines, some heavy, most much thinner, a few of them nothing but faint penciled-in marks. "That's a lot of tunnels to search. Especially when we're not quite certain what we're even looking for."

"That's an understatement," Davina assured him. "There are over eleven miles of Prohibition tunnels alone. Throw in everything else and you're easily talking a couple hundred miles of underground lines to contend with."

"And unfortunately, we don't have that kind of time to waste," Mike said firmly. "We have to find a way into those caverns, and we need to do it fast."

Trevor glanced at Connor to see his concern mirrored on his friend's face.

"What's wrong?" Trevor asked slowly. "Did something happen?"

"The ghouls grabbed five unhoused people out of an alley on the western edge of the Skid Row area late last night," Owen said grimly. "Two of them are friends of Jenna's. Ada and Nicole. The cops came and took a report, but as you can imagine, they're not putting much emphasis on this one since witnesses told them the *Skid Row Screamer* did it."

"Five people all at once?" Connor questioned, looking around at them. "Has that ever happened before?"

The HOPD peeps and Davina all shook their heads.

"I have some old books that I'm digging through," Davina said. "I'm hoping they might tell me something, but even without that, I can't imagine a move this aggressive by the ghouls meaning anything good."

Trevor silently agreed as he joined the rest of them in pouring over the map and trying to narrow down where they should start.

"It looks like some of the old Prohibition tunnels run close to the Skid Row district," Mike said, running his finger along some of the heavier black lines on the map, stopping at an intersection near the Hall of Records on Temple Street. "This entrance into the tunnels is only about a mile to the east of the alley where those people were taken last night. I think we should focus our attention on those tunnels first and see if we can pick up their scent so we can hopefully track them from there."

They continued to go back and forth for a while, but ultimately, nobody had a better suggestion than Mike's.

"Have you thought about what you're going to do if you do run into the ghouls again?" Owen asked. "I know you said that werewolves are damn near indestructible, but even you guys could barely keep those things at bay. And you definitely couldn't stop them. How do you expect us to go into the middle of their territory to rescue all these captives—assuming we can find them—and make it out alive? I mean, don't we need a better way to fight these things?"

Trevor threw Hale a questioning look. "You told them all about us?"

He wasn't necessarily surprised. Once Owen and his HOPD crew had seen the claws and fangs, there was no going back.

Hale nodded absently, only half paying attention as he listened to Davina mention that she was trying to get in contact with the guy from STAT who'd supposedly killed one of the ghouls with a metal pipe.

"Unfortunately, he's been very difficult to reach," she added. "But I'm hoping that he'll be able to give me more details on how he handled that ghoul. Until we have something solid to go on, it's critical that you all avoid a direct confrontation with the ghouls."

Connor frowned. "I agree we need to avoid a direct confrontation, but that doesn't mean we can't still do a careful recon to see if we can pick up a scent trail."

Trevor would have liked to help out with the plan for the scouting mission, but he had something more important that he needed to do right now.

"I'm going to go talk to Jenna," he announced. "She'll want to know about Ada and Nicole. It's also time for me to come clean about a few things with her. I'll get back as soon as I can."

Connor gave him a nod but didn't say anything as he went back to the map he'd been studying earlier. That was about as close as he was ever going to get to giving his blessing, Trevor supposed.

He could live with that.

CHAPTER 17

This time, Jenna heard the door of her apartment open even though she was deeply entranced in the sculpture she was busy working on. Since there were only two people who had keys to her place—Madeleine and Trevor—she had a pretty good idea who it was. Part of her wanted to storm into the living room and confront him immediately, to keep him out of her workshop... her sanctuary. But in the end, her fingers just kept working the clay, seeking to recreate the vivid image that was trapped inside her head.

Jenna felt his presence at the door of her home studio space long before catching a glimpse of him out of the corner of her eye. She didn't pause her work, instead putting all her focus on getting the jawline right. Achieving the width necessary for the fangs while retaining the inherent beauty and perfection of the form was tricky.

Trevor didn't seem interested in pushing her. He simply stood there in the doorway with his shoulder leaning on the jamb, watching her work. It probably should have irritated her, but for some reason, it didn't. There was a bizarre comfort in knowing he was close by.

She found herself wondering about that feeling of comfort. She had every reason to be upset with Trevor. Furious even. But for some reason, that wasn't the emotion she was experiencing at the moment.

"Remember when I told you that I got out of the army because I was injured during a deployment?" Trevor said, the sudden words not startling Jenna as much as she might have expected. "You asked if it was bad, and I sort of made it out to be no big deal."

Jenna nodded but didn't answer, her heart racing a little faster at the direction of this one-sided conversation. The jawline on the sculpture was good now, but she couldn't get the shape of the mouth quite right. In the mental snapshot locked forever in her head, Trevor's lips had been pulled back, revealing his long, glistening fangs. But somehow his humanity had still been evident and clear. That dichotomy was difficult to capture in clay.

"Well, it turns out that it was definitely a big deal," Trevor added, coming closer, watching her work. "It was the night my entire life changed and I became a werewolf."

The word grabbed her attention and she stopped working to look his way. That was probably a mistake because the pain and torment in his soulful brown eyes nearly took her breath away. She was supposed to be mad at him, but it was difficult to remember that when he was gazing at her like someone lost and alone.

"Werewolf?" Jenna questioned softly, breaking eye contact to focus on the sculpture again in an attempt to regain control of her flailing emotions. "That's what you are? The fangs and everything else?"

Jenna saw him nod a little from the corner of her eye, his own attention now focused on her hands and the clay being shaped under them.

"Yes, I'm a werewolf. Though not in the sense you're probably imagining. I wasn't bitten or scratched by another werewolf or anything like that. That's not how it works."

She looked over at him again, not trying to hide her confusion. "Then how does it work? How did you become what you are?"

"A traumatic event," he said simply.

"I don't understand," she murmured even as her heart began to beat faster and her chest tightened, making it hard to breathe. There was something visceral and instinctive about the words that she didn't like.

"Some people are born with a unique piece of genetic material in their DNA that turns them into werewolves," Trevor explained.

"Okay," Jenna said, not really understanding what that meant. "Where does the traumatic part come in? Or do I even want to know?"

"The gene requires a specific combination of chemicals—namely adrenaline and cortisol—to turn on, and that only happens in the levels necessary during an extremely stressful fight-or-flight situation that comes with a life-or-death kind of thing."

"And that's what happened when you were injured on that deployment?" she asked, heart thudding even faster now as she turned to face him.

He nodded. "I was in Afghanistan as part of a NATO-led support mission. It was supposed to be a noncombat deployment—we were only there to do vehicle maintenance for the locals—but it didn't work out that way. Our small forward-operating base outside Kandahar was hit in the middle of the night. The perimeter was overwhelmed in minutes, and I spent the rest of the night fighting building to building and tent to tent." He paused, swallowing hard. "The battle was out of control and my fellow soldiers—friends—went down one after another. I was shot multiple times, but somehow, I kept going, trying to help as many people as I could. Getting the injured somewhere safe became more and more difficult as the night wore on, since the fighting was everywhere. I vaguely remember thinking that if we could hold on until morning and see the sun come up, we'd be okay." He shook his head. "I never did see it come up, though, because I lost consciousness way before that."

Jenna didn't realize she was crying until she felt silent tears rolling down her face. She would have wiped them away, but there was too much clay staining her fingers to try it. So she simply let them fall, not wanting to interrupt Trevor's story.

"When I finally woke up hours later in the field hospital, I found myself on a stretcher with an empty IV bag in my arm, surrounded by a whole lot of dead people." Trevor's gaze was distant, as if lost in the memories. "It seems that during the initial triage, I'd been deemed a category four non-salvageable, and the doctors were forced to set me aside so they could focus on those soldiers who had a better chance of survival. To say I surprised them when I stumbled out of that mortuary tent would be an understatement."

Jenna stared at him. She couldn't imagine experiencing that kind of horror. She was still envisioning the terrifying realization of waking up surrounded by dead bodies when Trevor continued.

"I don't blame the doctors," he added as an aside, almost as if it wasn't even important. "I have no doubt that at some point during the night, I probably died. But what the doctors didn't know—what they couldn't possibly have known—is that my injuries tripped that little segment of genetic material and that I had changed and become a werewolf."

"Being a werewolf helps you heal from injuries?" she whispered, remembering the smooth scars she'd seen on his shoulder and the faint lines on his forearms.

Trevor didn't answer. Instead, he simply unwrapped the bandage around his left arm, the one that had been bleeding so badly only a few hours ago. After the gauze was off, he held it up, letting her see the scars across his skin. She leaned forward, her clay-covered fingers coming up of their own accord, tracing the lines. She could make out two sets of cuts, one more healed than the other. But even the fresh ones from that morning looked days old.

"I'm guessing that my brother is a werewolf like you," she said.

"Yeah, he's a werewolf like me."

"What happened to turn him?"

Trevor hesitated. "Something just as traumatic as what happened to me, but I think he should be the one to tell you details."

"Okay." She nodded, not wanting to speculate what had happened to him, much less think about it. Connor might be a stubborn, irritating, pain in the ass lately, but he was also her brother and she loved him. The idea of him being in that kind of pain was difficult to bear. "But why did he do this to you?"

Trevor let out a sigh. "Let's just say that your brother realized we slept together, and he wasn't very happy about that."

Jenna wanted to ask how her brother could possibly have known about them sleeping together, but right now, there was something else she needed to know.

"This is what you were hiding from me all along, isn't it?" she asked, shaking the other thoughts out of her head and refocusing on the issues that had brought them to this point. "That you're a werewolf."

"Hiding?" Trevor asked, confusion clear on his face. "What do you mean?"

"I can't explain it really," she said with a shrug. "But I've felt for a while that you were keeping something from me. I had no idea what it was, but I knew it was something important. I guess being a werewolf counts as important."

Trevor didn't say anything for a moment. "You understand why I couldn't come out and tell you, right? It's not the kind of secret I could tell and hope you'd handle it well. I had to worry about the repercussions not only for me but for the other members of my pack, too."

"Pack?" she whispered, knowing she'd heard him use that word before but not sure exactly where or when. "Like a wolf pack?"

"Yeah," he murmured hesitantly, like he'd just realized what he'd said. "It's how my SWAT teammates and I refer to our team."

Jenna thought for a minute, connections forming quickly in her mind.

"The wolf tattoo on your chest," she murmured, more to herself than him as the significance of the exquisite ink work became clear. "The whole SWAT team...Mike and Hale...they're all...?"

Trevor didn't answer, but given the look on his face, he didn't need to say anything. It made complete sense now. The entire SWAT team was a pack of werewolves. It seemed impossible but obvious at the same time. She had even more questions now. How had they found each other? How had they kept their secret hidden? Were there people outside the pack who knew about them like Jenna now did? But before any of those questions could slip out, something else popped into her head. Something much more important.

"So where do we go from here?" Jenna asked slowly, picking up her work towel and cleaning off her fingers as she slowly took a step closer to him, looking up into his eyes and preparing herself for the worst. "With us, I mean."

"I suppose that depends on you," he said softly, dark eyes curious. "I know we haven't had a chance to talk about this, but where would you have wanted things to go between us if you'd never found out I was a werewolf? And could you see yourself still wanting that now that you do know?"

Jenna forced herself to take a breath. What did she want her future with Trevor to look like? Sure, she'd told Madeleine that he was perfect for her.

That he was the man she was meant to be with. But what the heck did that truly mean?

"I don't know where I would have wanted things to go between us." she finally said. "But that's because I've been so focused on enjoying what we have right now that I haven't let myself think about the future too much. I mean, you've only been out here for a few days, and we've slept together a grand total of once. And while that one time was absolutely amazing, I haven't even let myself worry about *defining the relationship* at this point. I didn't want to mess up what we have overthinking what might happen."

He nodded. "Okay, that's completely fair."

Trevor moved a little bit closer until she could feel the heat coming off his muscular body in waves. Were all those perfect muscles—all that heat—because he was a werewolf?

"But if you *were* going to *define the relationship* without fear getting in the way," he added, tilting his head slightly to the side as he smiled down at her. "What would it look like?"

Jenna took a deep breath and said the words out loud before she had a chance to sensor herself. "I would say that I don't really care what it looks like, as long as we're together. I know this is going to sound wild, but there's something in me that wants to stay with you forever, no matter what. But that's bizarre. Right?"

He grinned a little wider and shook his head. "Probably not. But I don't think it matters what I think. What does matter is if you could still feel that way—could still want that with me—knowing what I am."

She gazed up at him for a moment before answering. "Yes. I'm not scared of you. I mean, when I first saw you and Connor fighting at the club, I'll admit I was caught off guard. And confused and also hurt that there was something this big that you were keeping from me. But I was never scared of you. Never."

One second, Trevor was standing there in front of her, his expression doubtful, and the next, his face was changing, jaw widening, fang tips appearing over his lower lip, eyes glowing yellow gold. He wasn't nearly as wolflike as he'd looked during the fight with her brother, but it was enough to remind her that he was indeed more unique than anyone she'd ever known.

"Are you sure about that?" he asked softly.

Jenna didn't even pause to think but went up on her toes and threw her arms around Trevor's neck, then pulled his head down for a kiss. She quickly discovered that it was...different...kissing a man with fangs.

Not bad.

Definitely not bad.

Just different.

Wanting to make sure he understood she was completely comfortable with this part of him, Jenna took her time exploring his extra-long fangs, tracing them with the tip of her tongue, feeling their texture, the sharpness of their tips.

Trevor stood statue still for several long moments before finally giving in with a groan and sliding his arms around her and tugging her in close. Then those fangs started nibbling at her lips, and Jenna couldn't help but moan herself. That felt so good! It shouldn't have, but somehow it did.

She wasn't sure when it happened, but at some point, Jenna found her hands cupping his widened jaw, feeling the muscles moving under her fingertips as he kissed her. And then, just like that, she felt the muscles twitching under her touch as his fangs began to retract and his jawline shifted back to its familiar form.

Trevor was smiling when Jenna finally broke the kiss and dropped back down off her toes. For a moment, they stood there, gazing at each other warmly. Jenna probably would have stayed there like that for the rest of the day, but after a minute, he turned and motioned toward the sculpture she'd been working on.

"I can't believe you captured this much detail," he said, his eyes locked on the work in progress. "You barely had a chance to look at me for more than a few seconds before you left the club."

She almost laughed at the way he studied the piece, his tongue subconsciously sliding across his teeth as if he was wondering if that was really the way his fangs made him look.

"I have a good memory, I guess," she murmured, not really wanting to think about the fact that the image of Trevor's werewolf appearance was trapped in her head now right alongside the ghoul that took Hannah. But he and the ghoul weren't the same at all. She wasn't frightened of Trevor. "Speaking of the club, what did I miss after I left?" she asked, wanting to move the conversation toward any way that didn't have to do with the scenes in her head. "You stayed for a while, so I assume something good came up."

Jenna couldn't miss the way Trevor's shoulders tensed up almost immediately, and she suddenly knew that her brother must have done something even dumber than usual. Or maybe it was one of the HOPD peeps? Had Owen gone running to the internet with his newfound knowledge of werewolves?

"Davina found a series of tunnels she thinks might lead us back down into the caverns we saw before everything collapsed," Trevor said, his words coming out a bit more positive than she'd expected. "We're going to head down there as soon as I get back to sniff around a bit."

Jenna definitely didn't like the sound of that, but something in his face had her even more concerned.

"Why do I think there's something else that you're not telling me?" she asked, immediately starting to worry even more when Trevor reached out to take her hands, squeezing them gently and getting that look on his face. The one people get right before they give someone crappy news. "What's wrong?"

"There's no easy way to put this, so I'll just come out and say it," he said with a long sigh. "The ghouls showed up in the Skid Row district late last night. A lot of them apparently. They grabbed five people, including your friends, Ada and Nicole."

CHAPTER 18

"So Jenna knows we're all werewolves?" Connor asked as he looked down a well-lit side tunnel before sticking his head in there to take a long, deep sniff. He mustn't have smelled anything interesting, because he immediately pulled back and continued down the main corridor with Trevor. "How'd she take it?"

Trevor glanced at his pack mate, surprised at how calm Connor seemed right then. At least compared to earlier when his friend had tried to kill him for sleeping with his sister. A peek out of the corner of his eye revealed that Hale and Mike—walking along the far side of the very broad section of tunnel with Owen and Maya—were clearly eavesdropping on the conversation and seemed as surprised as Trevor was by Connor's behavior.

"Way better than I thought she would," Trevor said. "I told her how I'd become a werewolf after what happened in Afghanistan. She was upset I hadn't told her before this but seemed to understand why I hadn't mentioned it earlier."

Trevor took a sniff down another side passage, not surprised when all he smelled was old cardboard and stale paper. It turned out that many of the spaces down in these old tunnels had been turned into long-term storage for the city, becoming a final resting place for decades of paperwork that no one would ever set eyes on again.

The directions Davina had provided led them to the entrance of the old Prohibition tunnels easily enough. It was an old service elevator on the back side of the Hall of Records. Unfortunately, their plan of going down into the tunnels right away had been shot to hell when they realized the public space had been crawling with people. As a result, they'd been forced to wait until dark for the hordes of nine-to-five office workers to thin out enough for them to slip into the elevator and down into the tunnels without being seen.

The tunnels—at least the section near the elevator—were nothing like Trevor had envisioned. Instead of the dank, nasty sewer lines he'd expected, they'd found a series of large, brightly lit, clean passages. Like those utilidors under Disney World. The idea that ghouls could be wandering around down here seemed ludicrous. But they'd only been down here for a few minutes. Maybe the tunnels would look different once they'd traveled a bit farther.

"And Jenna wasn't freaked out with the whole... monster...thing?" Connor asked, his whispered words echoing in the large expanse of tunnel.

Trevor shook his head. "Once again, I think you

underestimate your sister. Jenna is stronger than you want to give her credit for. She's not the type to be freaked by some fangs and claws. She didn't run out of the club because she was scared. She ran out because she was furious that someone was keeping yet another secret from her."

Connor winced. "I guess I never thought about it that way. She was furious enough when she figured out that we knew about the existence of monsters and never told her. But I'm never going to be able to live down the fact that I called her crazy for claiming there were monsters in the world when it turns out that I happen to be one. At least in some respects."

"I'm pretty sure your sister doesn't think you're a monster," Trevor said. "A complete and utter dumbass, but not a monster."

"How can you be sure?" Connor replied. "Not about the dumbass part—I'm sure you're right about that. I mean, how can you know she doesn't see us both as monsters?"

Trevor was tempted to tell him about Jenna kissing his fangs as she nibbled on his lips but at the last moment thought better of it. Connor wasn't trying to tear him to shreds at the moment, but there was no reason to tempt fate.

"Because Jenna looked me directly in the eye and told me she didn't think that," Trevor said simply. "And I believe her."

Connor seemed to consider that a moment before nodding. "It's hard to admit, but I guess I'm simply going to have to accept that you probably have a better read on how my sister feels about things right now than I do. Maybe better than I ever did."

There wasn't much Trevor could say about that, so he didn't even try.

"Do you think she'll ever forgive me?" Connor asked after a minute or so as Hale, Mike, and the others moved ahead of them and turned out of sight at the next corner. "For not believing in her like a brother should, I mean?"

Trevor's first thought was to point out that it was none of his business whether Jenna ever talked to Connor again, but one look at his pack mate's slumped shoulders and broken expression, and he knew he couldn't do that to his friend. But at the same time, he wouldn't lie to him, either.

"I don't honestly know," Trevor said, his voice low. "I wish I could say it's going to be fine, but I know that if it was me, I don't think I'd ever forgive you. That said—and Jenna being the wonderful and warm person that she is—I think that you and she will get past this at some point. Just remember, you spent years digging this hole you're currently in. It might take years to dig yourself back out."

That obviously wasn't the answer Connor had been hoping for, but he didn't say anything as they made their way down the corridor and around the corner, only to discover that they'd reached the end of the Disney-like part of the tunnels.

"This is going to be messy," Connor murmured as they stepped into a few inches of slimy-looking water leading toward the three branching passageways ahead of them. "Good thing Jenna decided to help Davina. She would hate trudging through this slop."

Trevor doubted that. Jenna had agreed to hang at Davina's club with Isaac and Esme to help find a way to defeat the ghouls. She'd wanted to come with Trevor and Connor but had gone to the club because she thought that was where she could be the most helpful. To suggest that a little dirty water would have mattered to her was silly. Then again, Connor had admitted that he didn't know his sister very well. Trevor supposed that was simply another example of it.

"Do we split up again?" Owen asked, looking down each of the three dimly lit passageways one after the other. "Like we did last time."

"No!" was the firm answer from Trevor and everyone else in the tunnel, including Maya.

Trevor almost laughed out loud at how close she stuck to Owen, blatantly refusing to be separated from him for even a moment. It was obvious that she had a thing for Owen, but the guy was simply too dim to notice.

"We take the passage on the right," Trevor said. "If my sense of direction is still intact down here, it should lead to the southeast and toward Skid Row. That should hopefully get us close to the cavern entrance we're looking for—if it exists."

Mike and Hale took point as they headed that way. Owen and Maya—and their flashlights—followed. Trevor and Connor brought up the rear. They walked slowly and as quietly as they could through the ankle-deep water, not wanting to make any more noise than necessary. They had no idea if the ghouls had extra good hearing, but they didn't want to risk it. Before coming down here, the one thing they'd all agreed on was that they had to avoid another confrontation with the creatures. Until they came up with a better way to fight them, they couldn't take the chance.

"So Jenna is fine with you being a werewolf, but what did she say about the whole soul mate thing?" Connor asked softly, slowing to put a little more distance between them and everyone else.

Trevor winced. "Um...we didn't exactly have a chance to talk about that yet."

"Seriously?" Connor said, splashing to a stop in the water. "Wasn't that one of the key things you went over there to talk about? How could you leave without telling her that she's *The One* for you? She needs to know why she's experiencing all the weird things she's almost certainly feeling right now."

Trevor bit back a curse. "I know all that," he said

in exasperation. "But I had to pick my battles, and getting her to accept the whole fang-and-claw thing without a meltdown was my first priority. I plan to ease into the soul mate stuff a little more gracefully so she doesn't come off thinking I've taken away her free will."

Connor looked prone to argue but then let out a long sigh. "Okay, I guess I see your point, but you really need to tell her soon. She deserves the truth from you."

With that, he started walking again, leaving Trevor no choice but to follow.

Trevor agreed with everything Connor said but couldn't imagine how he was going to bring up the subject without freaking her out.

Hey, I know you feel this really intense connection to me that makes you want to stay with me forever. Well, it turns out we have this werewolf soul bond. We're fated to be together. Who knew?

That sounded cringey, and he hadn't even said it out loud.

They'd just caught up with the others when Trevor picked up that familiar dirt and musky scent. Mike and Connor must have caught it at the exact same moment, because their claws and fangs came out. Trevor did the same.

"What's wrong?" Owen asked, gripping the aluminum bat in his hand even tighter. "Should we run? Try to hide?"

Before Trevor or anyone else could answer, four ghouls rounded the corner. Trevor leaned forward, ready to attack even as his teammates did the same. It would buy Owen and Maya some time and give them a chance to escape at least.

Trevor started forward, only to freeze when a woman pushed her way through the crowd of creatures, who'd come to a dead standstill in the middle of the tunnel. To say he was shocked to see her moving comfortably through the midst of the ghouls was an understatement. She was in her early twenties, he guessed, wearing heavy boots, dirty jeans, and a sweatshirt emblazoned with an *I Love Hollywood!* slogan. Her long, blond hair was held back in a ponytail tied with a bandanna, revealing sharp hazel eyes that regarded them calmly as one of her hands casually rested on the hilt of an old fixed-blade knife sheathed on her hip.

Connor took a step forward at the same time as the woman did.

"Hannah?" he whispered, the word so soft that Trevor could barely hear him.

"Connor," the woman said, her rough voice seemingly out of place with her soft features. "It's been a long time."

Trevor stood watching the tableau like it was something out of a movie, the one where the kidnapping victim is saved from her attackers, long-separated family members are reunited, and everything is wonderful with the world again.

Hannah turned to the ghouls and made several sounds that seemed closer to barks and grunts than words. One of the ghouls replied in the same language, then as one, the creatures faded back into the shadows and disappeared around the corner again.

"Were you just talking with those things?" Connor asked, clearly as confused as Trevor.

Connor's sister turned back to them, studying him for a moment, and Trevor thought she was going to hug her brother. But instead, Hannah walked past them, heading in the direction he and everyone else had just come from.

"I'll explain everything later," she said. "Right now, Jenna is in trouble."

CHAPTER 19

"It says in here that ghouls have a problem with sand from their ancestral homeland," Jenna murmured, slowly working through the ancient tome Davina had given her, forced to use Google Translate to figure out what each of the Latin words in the book meant. It was a terribly slow process. "Of course, it would help if we knew where their ancestral homeland was before we go running down to the beach to scoop up some."

"Well, your discovery is about as confusing as ours," Esme said from the far side of the office where she sat with her brother, staring down at the pages of a thick leather-bound book that probably weighed as much as she did. "It says here—I think—that certain religious icons can damage their otherwise impervious skin. Unfortunately, it doesn't say which religion or which icon."

"I know it's frustrating," Davina said from behind the laptop on her desk. "But we all need to keep looking. These ghouls have a weakness. We just have to find it."

Jenna sighed but kept translating. She had doubts that they'd be able to find any weaknesses, but at least focusing on this Latin stuff distracted her from thinking about Trevor, Connor, and the others. And the fact that they'd gone down in those tunnels again—without her.

It made complete sense that she stay topside and help Davina with the research. After all, Trevor and the others were merely planning to do some recon and look for a clue on where they might go next. There should be absolutely no chance of them running into the ghouls again. No reason to think Trevor would be in any danger. Although she was a little concerned that he and Connor might get into a fight again.

Still, even as remote as that possibility might be and as terrified as Jenna was of tight, dark spaces—and ghouls—she was still worried about Trevor being down there without her. She was absolutely head over heels into him.

"So you're dating a werewolf?" Esme asked casually, not looking up from the big book on the table in front of her and Isaac. "Something tells me that the sex must be absolutely wild, huh?"

Isaac choked on the iced tea he was drinking, his face and ears turning a vivid red even as Davina laughed. Esme glanced up, brow lifted as she waited for Jenna to answer.

Jenna was rescued from having to answer Esme's question by the office door opening. A second later, Madeleine walked in carrying a handful of takeout bags from the club's kitchen, the thumping techno beat being pumped out of the club's speakers somewhere below them following her inside. Even though the door to Davina's office didn't look that thick, it was remarkably good at keeping sound out of the office. Jenna hadn't even realized the club was open already.

Madeleine closed the door with her hip, then came over to set the food bags onto one of the tables off to the side of the room, well away from any books.

Her friend had been waiting in the hallway outside Jenna's apartment when she and Trevor had come out, wanting to make sure everything was okay. When Jenna had explained that everything had been worked out and they were going to Davina's club to figure out their next move, Madeleine had insisted on coming to help. Neither Jenna nor Trevor had been able to convince her otherwise.

"Davina, I hope this doesn't come as a surprise to you, but there's a guy in your kitchen working the skillet who's covered from head to toe in fur," Madeleine said as she pulled foil-wrapped bundles out of the biggest bag. "I'm not normally such a stickler for the rules, but that's got to be some kind of health code violation. I mean, shouldn't the guy have to wear some kind of allover body hairnet to keep him from shedding in the food?"

"First off, Kia is a woman," Davina said without

looking up from her laptop. "Next, she's an alemis, a South American version of the yeti, and they don't shed their fur—ever. Third, I would suggest you never let her hear you say otherwise or you're in for a stern lecture."

Madeleine turned and gave Jenna a look, lifting a brow. Jenna only shrugged as she joined Esme and Isaac around the table with the food. Jenna unwrapped the foil to reveal a delicious-looking wrap filled with roasted turkey and cheese, along with tomato, arugula, and some kind of spicy mayo.

"Have you heard anything from Trevor or anyone else yet?" Madeleine asked.

Jenna shook her head. "Nothing yet."

"I'm sure they're fine," her friend murmured, her words of encouragement immediately echoed by Isaac and Esme, who added that they'd only been down in the tunnels for thirty minutes or so.

Jenna nodded and nibbled on her wrap. It tasted as delicious as it looked, but it was difficult to eat when all she could think about was Trevor possibly being in trouble.

"I finally got the full report from that STAT mission where the guy claims to have killed the ghoul," Davina said. "Unfortunately, I'm not sure if it's going to be much help. The guy swears he killed the creature with an old steel pipe, but from what you've told me of your adventures with the aluminum softball bats, that doesn't work."

Jenna was thinking about what it had been like to whack those creatures with the aluminum bat and decided it was probably a lot like hitting a boulder when the overhead office lights started to flicker and went out, plunging the room into darkness. A few seconds later, the reddish glow from an emergency light mounted over by the door popped on, dimly illuminating the office.

"That's weird." Frowning, Davina pushed back her chair and got to her feet, then headed for the door. "We lose power occasionally, but the club has a completely independent and automated backup power supply that should have already kicked on by now."

The moment Davina opened the door, Jenna noticed how eerily quiet it was. Well, maybe not exactly quiet, but instead of loud music coming from below, all she could hear was the low murmur of a few hundred nervous people down on the dance floor. It might have been her overactive imagination, but she swore she could feel the fear growing all the way from here.

"You four should stay up here," Davina said, the emergency light directly over her head emphasizing her high cheekbones and making her vibrant blue hair appear almost purple. "Just until I find out what's going on."

Jenna started to protest, but before she could say anything, Davina was out the door, disappearing down the barely illuminated stairs outside her office.

"It's probably some kind of electrical glitch, right?" Madeleine said softly, moving to stand a little closer to Jenna.

"Definitely," Isaac said, though Jenna wasn't sure if she or anyone else in the room believed him. She doubted he believed it himself.

She forced herself to take a deep breath and relax, only to tense again when the first murmur of surprise rippled up from below them. One moment, there was a babble of nervous confusion, and the next, there were shouts of pure panic and terror. Then came the screams of pain.

Jenna was out the door before she even realized what she was doing. Madeleine and Esme both called out for her to come back, but by then she was halfway down the first flight of stairs, looking over the railing at the bedlam below. Even in the heavy shadows created by the club's eerie red emergency lights, she could see people rushing frantically for the exit.

Small figures darted through the crowd, moving so fast they were near impossible to see clearly in the chaotic darkness. But even without getting a good look at the fast-moving creatures, Jenna knew they were ghouls. How the hell they'd gotten into the club and what they were doing here was beyond her, but it was definitely them.

A flash of light along the far side of the dance floor caught her attention as she descended a few more steps. Jenna looked that way, catching sight of Davina standing in the rushing crowd like a rock in the middle of the ocean, unmoving in the face of the raging crowd. Then she swept out her hand, and a muscular ghoul was yanked out of the shadows and thrown across the room, smashing hard into the far wall.

Jenna vaguely remembered hearing Trevor talking to Connor about Davina being a witch. At the time, she hadn't assumed he meant *that* kind of witch. Obviously, he had.

Davina kept moving her hands, sending creatures flying as Jenna reached the bottom of the stairs and the crowd of frantic people. It struck her then that she had no idea what the hell she was going to do. She couldn't do magic like Davina and wasn't even carrying her softball bat.

But when she saw a woman tumble helplessly to the floor, Jenna found herself surging through the crowd toward her, fighting and shoving until she reached the woman's side. She was probably literally taking her life in her hands to lean down and help the woman to her feet, but she did it anyway.

The world around Jenna blurred as she continued moving and shoving, helping people off the floor and nudging them toward the exit. From the corner of her eye, she caught sight of Madeleine,

Esme, and Isaac assisting the other patrons while Davina focused on doing that thing with her hands, throwing ghouls here, there, and everywhere.

As the main dance floor area started to thin out, Jenna followed her instincts and moved through the nearest archway, heading into the next room, and then the one beyond that, looking for stragglers. A part of her knew it was dangerous and that Trevor would be furious at her for putting herself in peril like this, but she simply could not let the ghouls grab anyone else. So she got every person she came across—most of whom were scared and confused—turned around the right way, shoving them forcefully back in the direction she'd come.

She was about to head for the exit herself when she spotted an arch leading to a space not much bigger than her own living room. There was a small bar along one side as well as a few high-top tables scattered around the space. The heavy drapes on the wall gave the room an almost cozy feel. She glanced around to make sure it was empty, then headed for the door.

Then she heard the whimpering.

Stopping, Jenna whirled around, following the sound and realizing it was coming from behind the bar on the other side of the room. She crossed the room and hurried around the end of the curved piece of black granite, peeking her head carefully over the edge until she saw a woman hiding in the corner.

She was wedged so tightly in the space near the fridge that Jenna barely saw her in the darkness. But the soft crying—and trembling shoulders—gave her away.

Jenna quickly walked around the bar.

"Hey," she whispered, kneeling down beside the terrified woman. "I'm going to get you out of here, okay?"

The woman looked up at her, eyes round as saucers and tears running down her face. "Are they gone?"

Jenna considered lying, wanting to offer the poor woman at least some kind of comfort. But lying wouldn't do the woman any good if a ghoul popped out in front of them. So the truth it was.

"I'm pretty sure they're still here," she said as calmly as she could. "Which is a damn good reason to get out of here. Before those things find us."

The woman's eyes widened even more than before. But at least she nodded and got to her feet, though she stayed low, like she wanted to hide behind the bar as long as possible. They were coming out from around the end of the bar when a ghoul suddenly dropped down from the ceiling not more than ten feet away, blocking their escape path to the door.

The woman beside Jenna screamed. Long, high, and piercing. Even the ghoul took a step back, wincing, as if the sound hurt its ears.

Jenna didn't waste the distraction. Reaching behind her along the mirror-lined shelves in back of the bar, she grabbed the first thing she could find—a heavy bottle filled with honey-brown liquid. Grasping it around the long neck, she threw the bottle at the ghoul as hard as she could.

She wasn't sure who was more surprised when the heavy bottle smashed into the creature's chest—her or the ghoul. Regardless, the glass shattered into hundreds of pieces on impact, showering the ghoul with sharp splinters of glass and splatters of alcohol.

The creature took a few steps back, its face registering alarm and disgust more than pain. From the way the ghoul looked down at its wet chest, Jenna got the feeling it was bothered more by the alcohol than the glass shards sticking to it.

But all Jenna cared about was the fact that the thing had backed up after getting hit with the bottle. So she grabbed another and tossed that at the creature, too. She was reaching for a third before the one she'd tossed even had a chance to land, practically slinging it without looking. Then another after that. And another. The odor of alcohol filled the room, and she wished she had a lighter—or better yet, a torch—so she could light the thing on fire.

The woman beside her followed Jenna's lead, picking up bottle after bottle and throwing them at the creature. The ghoul let out a screech and backpedaled until it was pressed up against the far wall. Jenna grabbed another bottle in each hand, then tucked an extra under her left arm before she ran out from behind the bar.

"Run!" Jenna shouted, slinging the first bottle as hard as she could, putting herself squarely between the ghoul and the door. "I'll hold it off."

The woman didn't even pretend to think about staying to help. She simply ran, a bottle in one hand just in case, shoes hitting the floor in a rapid tattoo as she darted away at a dead sprint.

Jenna slung the second bottle, an unbelievably heavy one of carved crystal that shattered in spectacular fashion when it hit the ghoul in the head. The creature snarled in rage and fell back another step, bouncing off the wall behind it.

She launched her last bottle, aiming for the creature's crotch, hoping that area might be more sensitive. She didn't wait to see if her aim was true, instead turning and racing for the door the moment the bottle left her hand. There was a grunt of pain behind her, followed by a long gasp, like all the air was being ripped out of the creature's lungs. She had a few seconds to congratulate herself before the click of hard claws on the floor told her the bottle hadn't damaged the ghoul as much as she'd hoped.

Jenna made it out of the smaller room and through an arch connecting the passageway into the next room, and for a second, she thought she might escape. Then something slammed into the back of her legs, and she went down, hitting the floor hard, breath getting knocked out of her as the ghoul climbed up her back like a demonic monkey.

She flipped herself over, trying to crush the ghoul. But it moved with her, ending up on her chest instead of her back. Clawed hands that reeked of alcohol came up around her neck, squeezing tight.

Jenna fought back, punching and clawing at anything she could reach. But it was like the ghoul really *was* made of stone. The only damage she was causing was to her hands.

But Jenna kept fighting anyway because she didn't have a choice. Her vision was starting to get fuzzy from lack of air when she heard a sound from somewhere behind her. *Footsteps.* Instinct made her crane her head around to look even as the ghoul continued to choke the life out of her, not sure what she expected to see.

Isaac and Esme were sprinting toward her, holding bent pieces of metal that looked like they were from a barstool. But hey, they were metal and therefore had to be better than the booze bottles she'd been using. She caught sight of Madeleine coming right behind the two paranormal investigators, her face full of horror.

Then Isaac and Esme were at Jenna's side, the

pieces of metal in their hands coming down over and over on the ghoul's head. The blows didn't seem to bother the thing much, but at least it distracted it enough that it loosened its grip on her throat. She gasped for precious air, and the feeling of being able to breathe again was like a jolt of pure energy to her soul.

But just as it seemed like her friends were going to be able to get her away from the creature, the concrete floor under her suddenly fell apart, and Jenna was falling as the clawed hands around her throat clenched even tighter than before, cutting off every trace of oxygen.

CHAPTER 20

HANNAH MIGHT NOT BE A WEREWOLF, BUT SHE was definitely fast. Trevor and his pack mates could keep up with her fine as she ran down the alley toward Davina's club. Owen and Maya, on the other hand, were two blocks back, gasping for air.

"Are you planning to tell us what the hell is going on?" Connor asked sharply.

He'd been getting more impatient by the second. Probably because his sister—who'd been missing for ten whole years—hadn't said a damn word to him since they'd run into each other down in the tunnel. Actually, Hannah hadn't spoken to any of them, unless you counted those brief moments when she'd ordered Trevor to drive faster. He'd thought at first that she was angry or something—maybe at Connor—but after a bit, he got the feeling that it was simply because Hannah didn't like to talk much. Then again, she'd been held captive by ghouls for a decade. That had to affect a person's ability to interact with other humans.

"Where's the bouncer?" Hale asked as they took the steps down to the door of the club.

"The neon has been turned off, too," Mike said, pointing at the unlit sign to the side of the entrance. "We might be walking into a problem."

Trevor tried to force down the tension rising in his gut but failed miserably, especially when Hannah opened the big metal door of the club and the scent of blood, panic, and fear all hit him at once. The idea of Jenna being in there somewhere, scared and possibly hurt, was enough to make him push past Hannah and charge down the steps. As he ran, he couldn't miss the fact that all the overhead fluorescent lights were turned on instead of the usual flashy, colorful strobes. There wasn't any music playing either.

It was quiet.

Eerily so.

Even worse, he couldn't pick up more than half a dozen heartbeats in the building.

There was no way in hell that could be good.

His werewolf nose locked on Jenna's scent immediately, and Trevor chased it down the stairs and through the double doors below. But the moment he entered the main dance floor area and realized that her scent wasn't as strong as it should be if she was there, he knew something was wrong.

Jenna wasn't here.

Davina and Madeleine walked into the room and stopped in the middle of the dance floor, interrupting Trevor's panic attack just as it got started. Both women looked shell-shocked and tired, and Madeleine was covered with a fine layer of dust for some reason that defied explanation.

"What happened?" Connor asked, charging in and sliding to a stop beside Trevor with Hannah and everyone else right on his heels.

"It was the ghouls," Davina answered, moving over behind the main bar and pouring herself a shot of whiskey. "They dug their way up through the basement and attacked in strength. It's impossible to tell how many there were, but I'm guessing it had to be at least fifteen of them, maybe as many as two dozen."

"They took Jenna," Madeleine said tearfully. "Esme and Isaac, too. The ghouls came up right through the floor underneath them and then the three of them fell into the hole and disappeared. I tried to get to them, but I was too late."

Trevor's heart seized in his chest, and all at once, he couldn't breathe.

Behind him, Hannah cursed. At least he thought that was what she did. Most of the words came out as grunts and some kind of low vocalization that sounded like someone choking—or trying to throw up. It took him a moment to realize that he'd heard those noises before down in the Prohibition tunnels when they'd first run into her. She'd directed those sounds at the ghouls who'd been with her. That could only mean that Hannah could speak the ghoul's language.

"Show me the spot where they disappeared," Trevor said urgently, moving toward Madeleine,

Connor right with him. "We can catch up to them if we move fast."

Madeleine shook her head, looking completely devastated. "No, we can't. I jumped down that hole a few seconds behind them, figuring I could follow them—though I had no idea what I was going to do when I caught up to them—but the ghouls collapsed the tunnel behind them as they escaped. I couldn't make it more than fifteen feet before the passage became completely filled with rubble. There's no way we'll be able to go in that direction."

Trevor cursed, fighting to keep his inner wolf under control even as the animal howled. He felt like he'd been punched in the gut. "We have to get back to the Prohibition tunnels. Maybe we'll be able to pick up her scent if we're lucky."

"You won't," Hannah said, moving over behind the bar and coming out with a can of soda. She popped the top, then took a long sip, closing her eyes for a moment as if savoring the beverage. "They would have already collapsed the main tunnels that connect to the surface and the outside world. They'll have a single tunnel left for emergencies and oxygen, but it will be damn near impossible to find on your own."

Trevor glanced at Connor and his other pack mates, then Maya and Owen. They all seemed as freaked out as he was. And just as confused.

"How can you possibly know all that?" Connor

asked, walking over to the bar. "Hannah, do you know why the creatures took Jenna and her friends?"

Hannah tool another long sip of soda, pausing to savor it once again. Trevor had to wonder how long it had been since she'd had a soda. For all he knew, it could have been before she'd been kidnapped.

"They took Jenna to use as bait to lure me into a trap," Hannah finally said, staring down at the polished surface of the bar. "I imagine that Esme and Isaac were merely collateral damage. Wrong place, wrong time kind of thing. The ghouls were definitely here for Jenna."

Connor looked like he was about to say something, but Hannah interrupted him. Not by speaking but by reaching behind the bar for another soda and popping it open. The way she'd yet to look at any of them throughout this entire conversation was starting to get a little disconcerting.

"I was held captive by the Umdar—that's what the ghouls call themselves—for almost five years," Hannah murmured softly, gaze still transfixed on the bar top. "I tried to escape over and over, but they always found me and dragged me back. I never gave up, though, no matter what they did to me."

"Five years?" Connor echoed. "Are you saying that you've been free since then? That you had gotten away and never tried to let Jenna or me or Mom and Dad know you were okay?"

"It isn't quite that simple," Hannah said. "But I suppose from your perspective, that's exactly what I'm saying. Because when I was finally able to get away, I made the decision to stay."

Connor didn't say a word. Instead, he collapsed down on one of the barstools, shoulders slumped, his heart so still that Trevor thought it might have stopped.

Hannah swallowed hard. "When I tried to escape the last time, I almost made it to the surface, but they caught me when I was only a few yards from freedom. They were angrier than I'd ever seen them. I mean really, *really* angry. It was…well…it was bad. They left me there to die of dehydration and shock, and I would have too if the Others hadn't come for me."

"The Others?" Trevor asked with a frown, immediately picking up on the significance she'd put on the rather generic term. "Who are they?"

Hannah lifted her head then, but only long enough to glance at Trevor and Connor for a quick second before she looked down at the soda in her hand.

"The Umdar have a very rigid caste society," Hannah continued quietly. "There's a lone ruling voice at the top known as the patriarch, and those lower down in the hierarchy are expected to follow the wishes of that voice. The concept of going against the grain, having independent thought or action, simply isn't supposed to exist for them."

Trevor thought of the ghouls that had been with Hannah earlier, realizing where this was going. "I'm guessing it does, though?"

Hannah nodded. "A rift had been developing within their society for a long time between the members of the Umdar that could only see the old way and the Others, who want to move to a future where they don't treat humans as property or use them for food. Seeing me stand up to the abuse and refusing to accept my captivity or accept the orders of those supposedly above me lit a fire. When I was left for dead in that tunnel on the edge of the clan territory, the Others came for me and took me somewhere safe where they nursed me back to health."

She stopped to search under the bar again, and for a moment, Trevor thought she was looking for another soda. But instead, she came up with a big plastic container of pretzels. Pulling off the top, she took out a large handful.

"It took months for me to heal," she said between bites. "When I got better, the ghouls who'd saved me were more than ready to take me to the surface and give me my freedom. But by then, my entire perspective on the situation had changed. The Others had taken a chance by saving my life, and while I was grateful for that, there were still other captives being held, not to mention people getting kidnapped off the street all the time. I couldn't simply go back to my old life and leave them behind, no more than I could abandon the Others who'd helped me escape and were trying to change their culture. I had become a symbol to them, and I couldn't let them go forward on their own. Not when I could help."

Connor shook his head in disbelief. "So you've been, what, running a literal underground resistance movement in LA and freeing captives for the past five years? On your own?"

"Not only in LA," she said, finally looking up to lock eyes with her brother. "And not on my own. There are over thirty members of the resistance—as you call it—helping me, along with a network of people on the surface who help us. We've rescued captives as far south as San Diego and as far north as Bakersfield. Our human network then gets the captives to safety and helps them recover as well as helps them come to grips with everything that has happened to them."

The room was silent except for Connor's rapid breathing. Looking at his pack mate, Trevor couldn't tell if it was anger or sorrow that was consuming him.

"Why didn't you reach out to me for help?" Connor finally said, expression torn and broken, voice accusing. "Ten frigging years, Hannah. You had all these strangers helping you, but you couldn't come to me for help?"

Hannah winced at the pain in her brother's words, her hazel eyes filling with a pain equal to that of her brother. "Honestly, I didn't think you'd come."

"What? Why would you ever think that?" This time, it was Connor's turn to look like he'd been punched in the gut. "You're my sister!"

"I know." She bit her lip, chewing on it for a moment. "After I made the decision to stay, the first thing I did was go home to see you and Jenna and our parents. No one was home, so I used the key that Dad always kept in that fake rock in the flower bed in front of the house."

Trevor didn't know much about Connor's life in LA, but he knew that four years after Hannah's disappearance, his friend had joined the LAPD, gone through his werewolf change, and then moved to Dallas to join the SWAT pack.

"I found our parents' divorce paperwork on Mom's desk in the home office," Hannah continued in a soft voice. "Along with a handwritten journal where she wrote about Dad living in a condo on the far side of the city, you transferring from the LAPD to the Dallas SWAT team, and Jenna still spending hours in therapy after trying to convince everyone that monsters were real. Mom didn't come out and say it, but she pretty much called Jenna a nut job, and I got the feeling from her journal that everyone else agreed with her. After reading all that, asking for help from anyone didn't seem like a good idea."

If Connor looked gut-punched before, now he looked like he'd been eviscerated. Hale, Mike, and Davina tried to keep their expressions carefully blank but failed. As for Madeleine, she looked like she'd rather be anywhere than there. Trevor couldn't blame her.

"I can understand why you didn't bother contacting the rest of us, but why didn't you ever go talk to Jenna?" Connor asked, voice full of confusion. "If you read the journal, then you had to know how hard your abduction was on her."

"I wanted to see her and tell her everything more than you can imagine," Hannah said. "But at that point, I'd already made the decision to keep fighting with the Others, and I knew that if I told Jenna everything, she'd want to help, too, and I couldn't put her at risk. So I made the conscious choice to walk away from her and everyone else. I've found myself reconsidering that decision a hundred times over the past five years, but with all the danger I've been in, I can't honestly say I would have done anything differently. I would never want her to be in the hands of the Umdar like I was."

No one said anything. After that painful confession, Trevor realized that Hannah had been living under the same kind of crushing guilt as Connor. They'd both made decisions in their lives that had a drastic effect on those they loved.

"I hate to point this out," Trevor finally said.

"But regardless of what you wanted, Jenna is now in their hands, along with Esme and Isaac. We need to focus on getting them back."

At that, both Connor and Hannah nodded.

"You mentioned earlier that the ghouls took Jenna to use as bait to lure you into a trap," Trevor said to Hannah. "Why would they do that? More importantly, how could they have tracked her here to the club? We're miles from the Skid Row district."

"The Umdar clan has known my identity for years now," she said, taking a slow, deep breath as she regarded Trevor. "They've been trying to catch me the entire time but have never come close. When you and Jenna ran into that ghoul in the alley a few days ago, it immediately recognized Jenna as my sister and alerted the rest of the clan. My informants inside the clan told me the patriarch decided to grab Jenna, thinking I would come out of hiding to save her. He's obviously right."

"Wait a second. Back up a bit," Hale said, holding up his hand. "You're saying that this ghoul Trevor and Jenna ran into was good enough with human facial features to recognize that Jenna is your sister after only seeing her for a few seconds? How the hell is that possible?"

"It's not her face they recognized—it was her pheromone signature," Hannah explained. "The Umdar have a drastically different sense of smell than humans do. The scent coming off other living creatures is like a DNA scan to them, with a medical history report on the side. They can tell if you're healthy or sick, who your parents or siblings are, even if you're angry or scared. And once one ghoul in the clan smells a person, the information is passed to the entire clan through some kind of collective psychic mind link and retained in the clan's collective memory forever. Since they know what I smell like, they immediately realized that Jenna and you"—she looked at Connor—" are my sister and brother."

"I can't believe that this enhanced sense of smell and collective consciousness isn't in any of my books," Davina murmured, seemingly more to herself than to any of them. "Though I can see how it might have developed over time as a way to find suitable mates in their relatively closed-off society. Interbreeding could definitively be a problem for them."

"Um, that's all very interesting," Trevor said, though truthfully, it wasn't. "But it doesn't explain how the ghouls were able to track Jenna back to the club."

"When all of you went down in the tunnels and got into that fight with the clan, they ended up putting a scent trace on all of you," Hannah explained. "Ghouls have scent glands on the inside of their wrists. They use them to mark the tunnels that they dig, and it gets everywhere during a fight. All of you were marked, and they used that trace to track Jenna here after the rest of you left to explore the Prohibition tunnels. The trace is so strong they can use it to track you anywhere in the city."

Well, crap. How the hell had he and his pack mates not been able to smell it?

"Is there a way to get the scent off us?" Mike asked. "If we're going back into those tunnels for a rescue attempt, we can't be broadcasting our presence."

Hannah nodded. "There is a way, but it's a long process involving an oatmeal scrub mixed with a dozen different minerals and underground root vegetables. We'll need to get started on it as soon as possible if we're going to get you down into those tunnels in time."

Trevor tensed. "What do you mean...*in time*? Is there some kind of deadline here that we don't know about?"

Hannah let out another long sigh. "Like I said, the Umdar have already collapsed the main tunnels that connect to the surface and the outside world. That's because they view that little sojourn of yours into their caverns the other day as a full-scale invasion. And since they couldn't kill you—which is definitely something we need to talk about—the clan is falling back on its standard backup plan. They're going into migration mode and moving the entire clan to a new, safer location."

"I'm guessing the ghouls won't be leaving their captives behind?" Davina asked with a hopeful expression.

"Definitely not," Hannah said firmly. "When they decide to move, they'll collapse everything, including the family caverns. Any captives who are too weak for the migration will be left behind in the caverns to be crushed. The rest, including Jenna and her friends as well as anyone else who's fit enough, will be used to carry the clan's possessions. Those who can't withstand the journey won't live very long."

"Shit," Connor murmured. "Any idea how long we have before this all happens and they start their migration?"

"Not long," Hannah said, glancing at everyone scattered around the room. "They'll probably wait for a little while to see if I'll fall for their trap, but when it's clear I'm not coming, they'll move fast."

"Then we'd better get moving," Trevor said. "Because there's no way in hell I'm letting Jenna get taken away by those ghouls."

"That sounds great in theory, but have you all forgotten that we still don't have a way to fight the ghouls?" Davina reminded them. "If you go running down into those tunnels without a weapon that works, you're not saving anyone."

Trevor growled in frustration but knew Davina was right.

Hannah walked around from behind the bar, pulling out the rusty, decrepit-looking knife she'd had on her hip. "I think that's something I can help with."

CHAPTER 21

Jenna woke up, her head throbbing so badly she thought she'd be sick at any moment. Forcing herself to take deep breaths, she lay there on the hard ground, scrunching her eyes closed and praying for the pain to go away.

That was when the memories came flooding back in.

She relived the attack in the club—the ghoul coming after both her and that poor woman, the creature choking her, the floor collapsing, Madeleine reaching for her as the blackness overwhelmed everything.

Jenna had no idea how much time passed as she replayed the disturbing memories over and over, but at some point, the nausea receded to a level she could live with, and the throbbing faded to a degree that hopefully meant her eyeballs wouldn't fall out when she finally opened her lids.

Holding her breath, she slowly opened her eyes.

And saw absolutely nothing.

She was blind. She must have hit her head on something during the fall. Something that had taken her sight. That was why it had been pounding so much.

Jenna was halfway into a full-blown meltdown when she noticed an orange glow flickering right in front of her. She stuck out her hand, only to find out that there was a rough stone wall only a few inches away. The glow was reflecting off it.

She rolled over to see three small fires burning nearby. She followed the thin smoke coming up from the flames with her gaze, watching the way it weaved and curled its way up to the ceiling of the large cavern, disappearing from sight in the darkness up there.

It took a few moments for the rest of the scene to finally filter through her still-aching head. Most importantly, the half a dozen figures moving around the fires. A dirty and bedraggled man and woman tended to the heavy earthenware pots hung over the fire while four ghouls sat around content to do nothing more than watch them work.

Jenna probably could have made out more details of exactly what the people and their captors were doing, but a series of twisted wooden poles lined up in front of her made that difficult. She tried to move to the side to see around the poles, only to realize two things. One—the wooden poles were actually the bars of her prison cell. And two—her whole body hurt like she'd been rolled down a long hill inside a trash can.

She tried to stifle a groan but didn't succeed. The sound was still loud enough to bounce off the stone wall behind her and the rough ceiling overhead, echoing in the small space. Two of the ghouls over by the closest fire glanced her way but thankfully didn't bother to come check on her.

"Jenna, thank goodness you're finally back with us," Esme said from beside her, a gentle hand coming to rest on her back. "We were scared when we couldn't get you to wake up."

Her stomach sank at the realization that Esme had gotten grabbed, too. That made her own capture so much worse.

Jenna turned, able to make out Esme's face in the dim light coming from the fires. Isaac was right behind her, his face covered in dirt and a bruise coloring his jaw. Oh, damn. Both of them had been taken.

More people moved closer in the darkness, and Jenna's stomach dropped another few feet when she saw Ada and Nicole. They both looked exhausted and desolate, even if they seemed happy to see her. Behind them were a few other prisoners, many who looked like they'd been there for a while, if the condition of their clothing was any indication. Jenna leaned this way and that, hoping to see Hannah among them. Unfortunately, she wasn't there.

From the quiet conversation among her fellow prisoners, it didn't take Jenna long to figure out that Esme and Isaac had already explained what had happened at the club. That was good, because it kept Jenna from having to talk about it. Hell, she'd prefer if she never had to even think about those moments again. The only thoughts that kept running through her head instead were what Trevor would do when he learned what happened. He'd be devastated and would almost certainly blame himself for her kidnapping. She only prayed he didn't do anything stupid. Like come running down here to save her without a plan.

"Any idea what they're planning on doing with us?" Jenna asked during a lull in the whispered conversation, looking out toward the ghouls standing around the fires and forcing herself to think about something other than Trevor being in danger. "I have to admit that when I fell through the club's floor, I didn't think I'd be waking up again."

"We spent hours packing a bunch of wicker-like baskets today," Nicole grimaced. "At least I think it was today. It's difficult to tell when it's always dark. Anyway, we were packing up everything from food to cooking gear. If I had to guess, I would think we were here to help them move. The same way we'd do for friends at home. Without the free pizza and beer."

Jenna nodded, considering that. "I guess that makes sense. But it doesn't explain why they went to so much effort to get Esme, Isaac, and me. I mean, they attacked a packed nightclub. That seems an extreme way to get three more workers to help pack."

"I'm pretty sure those ghouls were only there for you, Jenna," Isaac said. "Esme and I sort of fell in the hole when we tried to save you and ended up going along for the ride."

She frowned. "But I don't understand why they would bother to kidnap me specifically. What's so special about me?"

Answers to those questions varied, though all of them involved her connections to Trevor or Hannah. Of course, only Esme and Isaac knew that Trevor was a werewolf—though they never said the word out loud during the conversation—so they pushed that theory over the idea that the ghouls had grabbed her because of her relationship to Hannah.

For her part, Jenna had no idea. She seriously didn't think the ghouls would go out of their way to lure Trevor into a trap to get revenge for the way he went up against them in that fight the other day. It also didn't make sense that the creatures would kidnap her because she was Hannah's sister. How could they even know that?

She and her fellow captives were still going back and forth on that when Jenna heard movement outside the makeshift holding cell. She looked up to see five ghouls moving toward them. She didn't have long to wonder if that was a bad thing, since half the prisoners in the holding cell quickly shuffled toward the back wall, tension clear even in the darkness.

One of the ghouls untied the vine-like rope that

held the door of the cell closed, then stepped back as three other creatures shambled into the cell. Prisoners scattered, with a few helping shoves from the ghouls. The things might not be very big, but they were strong, and they had no problem slashing their claws at anyone who didn't move fast enough.

Jenna tried to move aside along with everyone else, only to find that the ghouls changed direction to keep heading straight for her, making it obvious that she was the one they were here for. As scared as she had been waking up in the darkness, knowing the ghouls were coming for her was even worse.

Even though she knew it wouldn't help, Jenna still scrambled backward, hoping to disappear into the heavier shadows along the back wall of the cave. But the ghouls kept coming, grunting and snarling out guttural sounds that clearly showed they were getting angry.

Jenna balled up her fists, ready to fight, even though it would probably do no good. But before she could make a move, Isaac and Esme stepped in front of her, shouting at the ghouls to stay away from her. The creatures slashed at her friends, forcing them back, and Jenna heard them gasp in pain.

"Isaac! Esme! Stop!" she yelled, moving forward to put out a hand on each of their shoulders, pushing her way between them until she was in front. "Let them take me. Please. I don't want you guys getting hurt on my account, especially when it won't mean anything. They'll still get me, no matter what you do."

The ghouls stood there, eyes darting from side to side to scan the cell, as if they were waiting to see if anyone else was going to put up a fight. When Isaac and Esme backed off—albeit reluctantly—two of the creatures stepped forward and wrapped their claw-tipped fingers around Jenna's arms, pulling her toward the door. The way their claws pinched into her skin made her whimper, and she bit her lip to stifle the sound. Memories of the night she'd watched the ghouls drag Hannah away just like this flooded her mind, and her heart began to pound faster.

"You're going to be okay, Jenna!" Esme shouted from behind her. "We'll find a way to get out of this and we'll come find you. I promise!"

Jenna tried to focus on the words—and that promise—telling herself that if she believed enough, it would come true. But as the ghouls dragged her past the cluster of fires and the humans tending them who refused to even look in her direction, she couldn't deny that she was getting more and more terrified with every step. Something told her this situation wasn't going to end well for her.

The ghouls silently led her through a series of dimly lit tunnels. Every once in a while, they'd pass a big cavern with one or more fires burning, but within a few minutes, they moved beyond any sources of light, venturing deeper and deeper into darkness. If it wasn't for the creatures' firm grip holding her upright, she would have tumbled to the floor a dozen different times.

After a few hundred feet, they moved into an area so pitch-black that she couldn't see anything at all, which was more terrifying than she ever would have imagined.

"Where are you taking me?" she demanded, her voice echoing off the walls.

The ghouls didn't answer. Then again, they probably didn't understand a word of what she'd said. Even if they did, she suspected they wouldn't tell her.

A little while later, the ghouls stopped in their tracks so suddenly that she stumbled. She expected the creatures to help keep her on her feet like before, but instead, they let her fall to her knees. She put out her hands to catch her fall, wincing as the rough ground dug into her palms.

Jenna braced herself, expecting one of the creatures to yank her back up, but when none of them did, her already-racing heart began beating like a jackhammer. Being held captive in their grip was scary for sure, but being on the hard floor and at their mercy when she couldn't see a damn thing was even worse. She stayed there on her hands and knees on the cold stone, looking left and right, trying to figure out where the ghouls had gone and what they were up to.

She tensed, waiting for claws to slash through the air and tear her apart or for a foot to slam into her back. Waiting for it to happen was the worst damn part.

Tears ran down her face. She didn't want to die. She wanted to live more than anything, if for no other reason than the simple fact that she didn't want to leave Trevor alone. She thought about the last time she'd seen him. She'd told him that she wanted to be with him regardless of the fact that he was a werewolf, but she hadn't told him why—because she loved him.

Now, she would never get the chance.

She cried out as a clawed hand roughly grasped her shoulder.

"Please don't hurt me," Jenna begged.

This time, she didn't wait for an answer but instead started fighting like her life depended on it—because it did. Whatever her fists came into contact with was as hard as stone, making her hands hurt like hell, but she kept swinging, kicking, and screaming anyway. She couldn't let it end like this.

The ghouls barely seemed to notice her heroic efforts. They simply dragged her to a sitting position and pulled her backward a few feet until something hard slammed into her spine. She only had a second to figure out it was some kind of vertical post set into the floor of the cave before they yanked her arms behind her and tied her to the thing.

Still, Jenna kept struggling, kicking with her feet in any direction she could reach. Her tennis shoes came into contact with the creatures a few times but didn't do much. Within seconds, she was tied to the post so tightly that her fingers were already beginning to tingle. While it hurt, she was more concerned about her inability to stop whatever was about to happen next.

Breath coming so fast she was hyperventilating, Jenna squirmed against the bindings around her wrists and arms. Since she couldn't see anything in the darkness, she closed her eyes and held her breath, thinking that might help her hear something—anything—that would let her know where the ghouls were.

Long moments passed before it struck her that she couldn't hear anything at all. In fact, it was utterly silent. The kind of eerie silence that came only when you were completely alone.

Her breath came out in a rush, but her relief was short-lived as she realized that being abandoned in this desolate section of tunnel might not be a good thing. Why would the ghouls leave her out here like this, staked down to the ground like some kind of offering?

Then she heard it.

A scraping sound somewhere far off in the tunnels.

The noise echoed off the walls so she had no idea which direction it was coming from. But whatever it was, it was definitely something heavy being dragged across stone.

And it was getting closer.

Jenna froze, fresh fear gripping her.

The ghouls had left her tied up here for some other kind of monster.

Like a sacrifice.

CHAPTER 22

It was stunning how fast a handful of ghouls could dig through solid stone. Actually, it was terrifying, because it meant that if they didn't get Jenna and the others back before the clan started its migration, then his soul mate and her friends could be a hundred miles away in a few days.

Trevor couldn't let that happen.

But unfortunately, he wasn't sure what he was going to do to stop it. Even with Hannah's intel on the network of caves and tunnels under the city and the help of the ghouls within her resistance movement, they were still facing incredible odds. Worse, they had no idea if Jenna or anyone else was even still alive.

Panic spread through Trevor's chest, the pain so intense it was like someone had plunged a knife into his heart. Since finding Jenna and accepting that she was his soul mate, he'd started to subconsciously construct a vision of what his life might be like in the future. Every one of those visions had included Jenna. To even imagine that it might not happen, that Jenna might not be there with him, was the most crushing thing he'd ever experienced.

Refusing to let his mind dwell on that possibility,

he turned his attention back to Hannah's ghoul friends (and yeah, even in his head, he realized how weird that sounded), watching as they excavated a four-foot-high tunnel ahead of him. He glanced behind him to see Connor, Hannah, and Madeleine all standing together, the latter two holding flashlights. Tension—and in the case of Madeleine, fear—rolling off their bodies as they waited for the ghouls to do their part in this plan. Madeleine's flashlight was shaking like a leaf, making the beam of light bounce all over the place.

Hannah had been right about the Umdar clan collapsing every passage leading into their territory, which was why they had to create another way in. Two ways in, actually. Hale and Mike—along with Owen and Maya—were leading a second team of ghouls that would come in from a completely different direction. The idea was that if the clan suddenly tried to move Jenna and the other captives, coming in from two directions would double their chances of stopping them. Admittedly, not knowing exactly where Jenna and everyone else were being held—if they were even still here at all—it wasn't much of a plan. But it was the best they had. Hannah hadn't heard anything new from her sources inside the clan, so they were running under information that was hours out of date. Anything could have happened since then.

Trevor turned back around to watch the ghouls

work. Three of them were digging while the other six were busy moving the resultant piles of rubble to the side, creating smaller closet-like alcoves to the left and right of the main path where they stowed the material, somehow compressing it down to occupy less space than it originally had. He didn't understand how they were even doing that. It probably shouldn't have been possible to fit the huge amount of debris into such a small space. Ultimately, he supposed it didn't matter how the ghouls did it. They were getting closer to Jenna and the others with every passing second. That was the only thing that mattered.

Suddenly, all the ghouls stopped what they were doing almost as one, though none of them had made a sound or even a gesture that he could see. Then one turned and started making soft grunting and coughing noises. The sound made Trevor think of a cat hacking up a fur ball.

"He said we're here," Hannah translated, stepping past Trevor to make several grunting sounds of her own at the ghoul that he assumed was the boss of the digging operation. It was unreal that a person could speak their language.

"There's only about four inches of stone between us and the clan tunnel. We need to be ready to move the moment they break through," Hannah said in a soft voice, like she was worried someone would hear her.

Trevor wanted to point out that if no one had heard the three ghouls clawing their way through a mountain of rock, whispering should be okay. But for all he knew, maybe the sound of voices carried farther down here underground than the scrape of claws on stone.

Instead, he nodded and got ready to move. Connor stepped up beside him while Madeleine stayed in the back of the group. If it had been up to him, Jenna's friend would never have come with them in the first place, but the woman had been stubborn, threatening to find her way through the Prohibition tunnel on her own if necessary. Trevor doubted she'd get far, but he knew Jenna would be furious if her friend got hurt, so he'd acquiesced and told her she could go with them. He hoped he didn't regret the decision.

"There shouldn't be anyone in this part of the caverns," Hannah whispered as she drew the rusted hunting knife from the sheath on her hip, nodding for the ghouls to start digging again. "But if there are, we'll need to deal with them quickly and quietly before they can raise the alarm."

Trevor hefted the length of rusted metal in his left hand, pretty sure it had once been used to hold up a stop sign, wondering once again how this could possibly work. He glanced at Connor to see his pack mate holding up a similar piece of rusted steel, maybe from some old piece of farming equipment, all twisty with gear teeth running along one side.

Hannah had told them earlier that steel wasn't the secret to hurting ghouls. Instead, it was the rust sometimes found on that steel that could get through their normally impervious skin.

"I have no idea why, but ferric oxide is like their kryptonite," Hannah had told them. "They avoid it like the plague. On the surface, they won't touch anything that's rusty, and while digging, they'll go miles out of their way to avoid ore pockets containing the stuff. Getting hit with something rusty will break the skin and hurt like hell. Too much of the stuff in their bloodstream will kill them."

Trevor wished they'd had some way to confirm Hannah's claims, because it was seriously difficult to believe that a creature as dangerous as a ghoul could be terrified of something as innocuous as rust. But time hadn't been on their side, so Trevor was simply going to have to trust that Hannah knew what she was talking about. She'd lived among the ghouls for ten frigging years, so if any human knew their weaknesses, it would be Hannah.

"Okay, here we go," Hannah announced softly as their own ghouls broke through the wall ahead of them, catching the largest chunks of stones before they fell and lowering them silently to the floor.

The ghouls immediately backed out of the way, letting Trevor and Connor enter the large space beyond the opening they'd created. Trevor moved in with his rusty steel club held high but quickly realized the tunnel they'd come out in was completely empty. A few sniffs revealed nothing more than the musty scent he'd come to associate with the ghouls, and even that seemed pretty stale. No one had been this way in a while, certainly not Jenna or any other human.

He and Connor quickly strode forward, making room for Hannah, Madeleine, and the team of ghouls. Trevor watched as the creatures began tying pieces of red material around their upper right arm—the signal they'd agreed on earlier to identify which ghouls were on their side.

After tying the red sashes, the ghouls split up and disappeared into the darkness, leaving Trevor to once again worry about whether they could really trust the creatures. It would be incredibly easy for their allies to turn on them. And Trevor and everyone else would never know until it was too late.

"They're going to slip in and warn their family members and the other members of the resistance that everything is coming to a head," Hannah whispered as they began to move through the tunnel. "When the time is right, they'll start creating distractions and lure as many members of the clan away from us as possible."

Trevor understood that had been the plan, but he wasn't sure how effective it would be. "If it comes to it, will the Others fight with us against their own kind?"

"They'll help as much as they can, but if it comes to it, I'm not sure if they would kill one of their own," Hannah admitted. "The Umdar clans are basically one very large family, close in a way that most human families will never be. This resistance movement by the Others has drastically changed how they see each other in ways that even they probably don't understand yet. When the fighting starts, I don't know what's going to happen."

"I guess we'll simply have to live with that," Connor said. "And deal with whatever happens, no matter which way it turns out."

Hannah nodded, turning to shine her flashlight down a narrower tunnel to the left. "Come on. We're heading toward the main gathering area for the clan. That's where the holding pens for the captives are and where I hope we'll find Jenna and the other prisoners."

The entire concept of *holding pens* was enough to almost force Trevor into a shift, fangs threatening to extend to their fullest. Connor reached over to put a hand on his shoulder, squeezing gently.

"Jenna's going to be okay," his pack mate murmured softly, more supportive than Trevor had ever imagined him being. "And so will everyone else. We're going to get them out of here. You have to believe that."

For some bizarre reason, Trevor did.

They moved quickly after that, Madeleine keeping up with them, even if she was still obviously terrified, flashlight bouncing around so much now it was like a strobe. She was breathing faster now, and it had nothing to do with the light jog they were maintaining. She had a small rusty mason's hammer hanging from a loop on her belt, but Trevor knew he'd be stunned senseless if Madeleine ever pulled the damn thing out, much less used it.

"I smell something," Connor said suddenly a few feet ahead of the rest of them, a position he'd taken up after trying to calm Trevor down a few seconds ago. "Humans for sure."

"That makes sense," Hannah said. "We're only a few hundred feet from the main cavern with the holding pens. Two or three turns in the passageway and we're there. How many ghouls do you smell?"

Connor had given his older sister the fifty-cent explanation of what it meant to be a werewolf after explaining that he, Trevor, and the rest of the guys were ones. Having heard the secondhand stories from the Others about their first run-in with the ghouls, she had accepted the whole wolf thing rather easily. Honestly, she'd been more concerned with any abilities he and the guys might have that would help them get Jenna and the rest of the captives back. The fact that they could smell the presence of people and ghouls had been far more interesting to her than the night vision, claws, fangs, and enhanced strength.

"Three, maybe four," Connor said.

Trevor thought was probably right. While the scent of ghouls was nearly overwhelming as they moved into the much more heavily populated part of their territory, several of them were a bit stronger, indicating a fresher source.

"I smell Esme and Isaac," Trevor added a few feet later, his nose working overtime. "There are other people with them."

"What about Jenna?" Hannah asked hesitantly, like she was afraid to hear the answer.

Trevor sniffed the air again, his heart beginning to beat faster at what he found—or didn't find, rather. Out of the corner of his eye, he saw from the expression on Connor's face that his pack mate had figured out the same thing he had.

"She was there," Trevor finally said. "Recently. But the scent is starting to fade a bit, meaning they took her out of the holding pens within the last ten or fifteen minutes."

Hannah cursed that same mix of human and ghoul words she'd uttered back at the club. "We have to get there and hope that one of the prisoners can tell us what the hell happened. And that you two can track her through the tunnels."

Trevor had no doubt that he and Connor could, but that didn't keep his mind from going to all kinds of horrible places as he ran after Hannah. What if they'd dragged Jenna off to some desolate part of the cave system to hurt her like they'd done to Hannah? What if they'd already done something even worse?

Before his thoughts could spiral into darkness any deeper, the four of them rounded a sharp turn in the tunnel they'd been running along, sliding to a stop in front of a large cavern. Three fires were burning around the open space, surrounded by several ghouls and humans. Along the far wall, deep-set alcoves had been dug into the walls and covered with twisted pieces of wood set into the floor and ceiling to serve as bars.

The holding pens.

Even though he knew Jenna wasn't in there, Trevor still took off running across the cavern floor, skirting the fires and heading straight for the door of the prison cage. Around him, he heard the humans scurrying out of the way as the three ghouls turned to fight.

One of the creatures moved to intercept him, bounding toward him on all fours, covering the distance in a blur and leaping straight at him. Trevor's claws and fangs came out instinctively even as he planted his feet and swung the twisted length of steel in his hands.

The sound the ghoul made when the rusted steel slammed into his shoulder was unlike anything

Trevor had ever heard. The shriek was so loud it echoed off the walls as the creature tumbled to the floor of the cavern and scrambled away, clutching its bleeding shoulder as it sped away, glancing back at Trevor a few times like he was some kind of monster.

There were several other shrieks behind him, but by the time he turned around, all he could see were the other two ghouls running out of the cavern with the one he'd whacked, Madeleine chasing them for several strides with her little hammer held high over her head. The humans who'd been tending the fires were cowering on the floor, arms protecting their heads as if they thought someone was going to hit them. It was painful to see them react like that, and he could only imagine the horror they'd been through.

Was Jenna going though that right this second?

Or something even worse?

"We need to move fast," Hannah shouted as she ran over to join him at the door of the holding pens. "Those three will be back soon enough, with help. The rusted steel hurts them, but they can still overwhelm us with numbers if there's enough of them."

Hannah started working at the vines holding the doors closed, but Trevor nudged her aside, having no patience for the methodical approach. Instead, he wrapped his fingers around two of the wooden bars, claws still fully extended, and then heaved backward with a loud snarl.

The whole door came apart in his hands, wood splintering and vines snapping. He tossed the remains aside, ducking down to step inside the space beyond, only to see a group of terrified people in front of him. Even Ada and Nicole, who'd at least met him before, were staring at him like he was more dangerous than the ghouls.

Didn't these people understand he was here to rescue them?

Shouldn't they look more relieved?

Then he abruptly remembered his claws were still extended. In a panic, he ran his tongue across his teeth, feeling razor-sharp fangs. *Crap.* No wonder they were freaking out.

Then, from somewhere in the back of the cell, Esme and Isaac shoved everyone forward.

"Let's go, people!" Esme shouted.

"He's here to help," Isaac added. "Let's not make him wait."

Trevor stepped out of the way, and with a little more nudging, everyone was quickly moving out of the pens. Some of them—almost certainly the ones who'd been there the longest from the looks of them—seemed as terrified of leaving as they were of staying. But Esme and Isaac—along with Hannah—got them all headed in the right direction.

"Where's Jenna?" Trevor asked Esme, Connor right there at his side as the last of the prisoners were herded out of the pens.

"I don't know for sure," Esme said as she helped an older man take his slow first steps to freedom. "Three ghouls came to get her about fifteen minutes ago. They took her down that smaller tunnel over there."

Trevor looked toward the passage Esme motioned at. He closed his eyes and breathed through his nose, picking up his soul mate's scent. He turned that way, ready to follow, only to realize Connor was about to go with him.

"We both can't go after her," Trevor told him. "We can't leave all these people without protection."

"Hannah can lead them out," Connor said, his heart beating faster and his eyes already starting to glow yellow gold. "She has a weapon and knows how to fight."

Trevor bit back a growl but didn't say anything. Didn't his pack mate realize the impossible position they'd been put in? He understood what Connor was going through, but he needed his friend to recognize this was simply the way it had to be.

After a moment, Connor nodded, even if it looked like the last thing in the world he wanted to do. "You're right. I'll go with Hannah and everyone else, then get them to the surface and the vehicles that Davina has waiting. But then I'm coming back. So you'd better not get yourself killed before you find Jenna, or I'll kill you myself. You got that?"

The threat sounded stupid, but Trevor didn't

point that out. "I'm not going to get killed. I'm going to find Jenna and then we're all getting out of here together."

Without another word, Trevor turned in the direction of his soul mate's scent and started running.

CHAPTER 23

THE SCRAPING SOUND GOT LOUDER.

Jenna yanked at her bindings harder, ignoring how much it hurt. Her mind tormented her, showing her images of a gigantic monster dragging itself across the rough floor, it's horny carapace gouging grooves into the stone as it came toward her.

Blood ran down her arms. The bindings were cutting into her skin as she struggled, but she didn't care. Something was out there, and it was coming this way, and she definitely didn't want to be here when it arrived. The thought of being attacked while still tied to this post made her stomach twist into knots.

There was a crunching sound from somewhere nearby, quickly followed by a soft clatter, like pebbles hitting the ground—or bone fragments falling out of some horrible creature's mouth as it chewed. She stifled a sob at the thought and fought even harder to free herself.

She stared into the darkness around her as she tried to escape, willing her eyes to work better, to reveal the creature coming her way, to let her see those teeth at least once before they locked down on her body. But nothing came except tears.

"Jenna, what's wrong?" a familiar voice said suddenly from only inches away. "It's just me. Calm down. You're okay."

The adrenaline drained from Jenna's body so fast that it felt like she was a balloon that had sprung a leak. She collapsed back against the post behind her, feeling dizzy from the relief.

"Hale!" she finally managed to say, the words barely making it out through all her gasping and wheezing. "Why didn't you say who you were sooner? And what the hell was all that noise? I thought you were a frigging monster coming to eat me!"

Bright beams from two flashlights suddenly flared in her face, overwhelming her eyes that had become completely accustomed to the pitch-black void of the cave she'd been left in for what felt like hours, and she blinked.

"Sorry about that," Hale whispered as he sliced the bindings around her arms with his claws. "I guess we made more noise digging our way in here than we realized."

Jenna looked around for Trevor, but instead, she found Mike, Owen, and Maya. And behind them, barely visible in the glow of Maya's flashlight, were four ghouls, crouching down on their haunches like a bunch of little kids. She fell back on her butt and crab walked in reverse to get away, expecting the ghouls to come charging straight at her. But they merely stayed where they were, tilting their heads and staring at her curiously.

"Relax," Hale said, kneeling down by her side. "These ghouls are friends of Hannah's. They're part of her resistance movement. They're the ones who dug the tunnel so we could get in. They're helping get you and all the other captives out."

Jenna's head spun, attempting to unpack all the crap Hale had unloaded on her. "Ghouls...Hannah resistance? Wait...what?"

"I'd love to explain it all in exquisite detail, but we don't have time." Mike leaned over his teammate to tell her. "I have no idea why the ghouls left you staked out here in the middle of the cave like this, but it can't be for any good reason. We need to go—now. Where are Esme, Isaac, and the rest of the prisoners?"

Jenna still had a hundred questions of her own but accepted that they'd have to wait. "They're back in that direction," she said, pointing the way she thought the creatures had brought her. "The ghouls are holding everyone in a kind of prison carved into the side of one of the larger caverns. They pulled me out of the cell and brought me here, but I think everyone else is still back there."

"That's good," Hale said.

Taking Jenna's hand, he helped her to her feet, then guided her in the opposite direction she'd pointed out a few seconds ago. She stumbled a few times since the only light they had to see by came from Owen's and Maya's flashlights, and they were already a dozen yards ahead of them.

"Where's Trevor, Connor, and Hannah?" she asked worriedly.

"They headed for the holding pens near the center of the clan territory along with Hannah's ghoul buddies while the rest of us came in through the back door," Hale told her. "If the bad ghouls heard them, we figured they'd take the prisoners and run this direction, where we'd be waiting for them."

Jenna didn't consider herself any kind of master strategist, but even she could see about a dozen ways that plan could have gone wrong. Apparently, it had since she was the only one who had been rescued by the scheme, while everyone else was still trapped in the holding cells.

"Okay, but why are we heading this way?" she asked. "Shouldn't we go toward the holding cells so we can help Trevor and everyone else?"

"Not right now," Hale said. "Trevor would want us to get you out of here first. Then we'll come back to help him, Connor, and Hannah."

That was a stupid idea if she'd ever heard one.

Jenna stopped in her tracks, turning to tell Hale exactly that, but before she could unload on him, some rocks clattered to the floor of the tunnel not more than twenty feet ahead of them.

She and everyone else froze…ghouls included.

"What was that?" Owen whispered even as the ghouls looked back and forth among themselves, soft grunts creeping out from deep in their chests.

She would have asked them what was wrong, except for the obvious language barrier. Still, even without having a clue what they were muttering about, she knew it had to be something bad. More rocks started falling all around them, and her stomach clenched as she remembered the cave in which they'd been trapped in a couple of days ago. Crap, they were going to bring the entire ceiling down on their heads.

"The entrance to the tunnel we came in is right ahead of us," Mike yelled, shoving both Maya and Owen into motion. "We need to move!"

Jenna didn't want to leave without Trevor, her siblings, and everyone else who could very well still be trapped in the other tunnel, but more rocks falling from the ceiling convinced her. They definitely couldn't stay here.

But she'd gone barely more than a single step before it seemed like the whole world was falling apart around her. Chunks of rocks were dropping all around them, hitting the floor and shattering, the noise incredible. Then amid the falling chaos came larger shapes that fell to the ground with no sound at all.

"They're dropping on us from the ceiling!" Hale shouted.

Growling, he swung at one of the swiftly moving shadows with a flat length of metal with rags wrapped around the bottom of it. It didn't look that sharp, but when it hit the ghoul coming at them, the shriek of pain was unlike anything Jenna had ever heard before. It was so unnerving it brought the hairs up on the back of her neck.

"They're all around us!" Mike shouted over the noise of shrieking ghouls and falling rocks. "This was a frigging ambush! Hannah was right. They used Jenna as bait."

Jenna almost asked what that meant until the implications of the ghouls tying her to a post in the middle of nowhere hit her. They'd done it because they'd somehow known somebody would come for her. And they'd laid in wait for them. She immediately felt bad that everyone had been lured into a trap on her account, but a moment later, all she could think about was the fact that she had so many people who were willing to risk everything for her. She couldn't deny how good that felt.

Suddenly, there was a ghoul running straight at her in the darkness, mouth opened incredibly wide to show off more razor-sharp teeth than any creature had a right to possess. Jenna froze, not sure what she could possibly do to defend herself. Then Owen was in front of her, flashlight flailing as he swung his own piece of rusted metal like a madman. The ghoul took several swipes at him, but Owen stood his ground. The creature let out another one of those horrifying shrieks as Owen clipped its arm with his thin club, and the ghoul abruptly backed off.

Way off.

"Here, take this!" Maya shouted, showing up out of nowhere and shoving something into Jenna's hands. "They're deathly afraid of rust because it will hurt them."

Jenna stared at the thing in her hands, having a difficult time making it out in the wavering flashlight. But after a few seconds, she realized it was a piece of bicycle chain that was so rusted that the links could barely move. She had a difficult time believing something like that could protect her, but she nevertheless twisted one end of the chain around her right hand, ignoring the blood staining it, then turned to face the oncoming hoard of ghouls.

Fear immediately overwhelmed her when she saw how many there were. It was impossible to get a clear count because the tunnel they were in was too dark, but there seemed to be dozens upon dozens of the things moving around out there in the shadows. And every few seconds, another one would drop down from one of the holes in the ceiling.

"There are too many for us to fight our way through!" Mike called out even as one of the ghouls that was on their side got dragged to the floor of the cave by his own kind and torn apart. Apparently claws that could tear through stone could also tear through flesh as hard as stone. "Fall back to the wall so they can't surround us."

But even with the wall at their backs and all of them arranged in a semicircle facing out, Jenna knew they were screwed. The ghouls were coming at them all at once now, and there were simply so many of them. Maybe if she, Owen, and Maya were werewolves like Hale and Mike, it might have been okay. But she and her friends were about as far away from werewolves as people could get, and given how the ghouls kept trying to get at them first, it seemed clear the creatures knew that as well.

"They're about to charge," Mike warned. "Stay close together. Don't let them lure anyone out away from the group."

Jenna's heart sank. She would fight, that was for damn sure, but she had no delusions of what would happen after that. With so many ghouls, the outcome was obvious.

Why the hell hadn't the ghouls left her in the holding pens with everyone else a little while longer? The outcome might have been the same, but at least then she could have been with Trevor when it happened.

"Here they come," Hale murmured.

He edged closer to Jenna like he intended to protect her all by himself. She would have glanced over and smiled at Trevor's friend, but then the mob of ghouls started moving toward them and she forgot about everything but swinging the rusty bike chain in her hands.

Out of nowhere, a long howl suddenly tore through the air, cutting right through the grunts and snarls of the ghouls surrounding them, the eerie noise bouncing off the walls and ceiling, freezing everyone, including Jenna. The ghouls looked around, confused and nervous, grunting and chattering to each other with something that almost sounded like concern.

The howl came again, closer and full of rage, sending shivers down Jenna's spine. While the ghouls definitely seemed disconcerted now, she wasn't sure if she was hopeful at the thought of what might be coming or terrified.

Trevor had locked on Jenna's scent before he even left the large cavern with the holding pens, so tracking it wasn't a problem. No, the only issue he had now was Jenna's growing fear. He could smell it clear as day, the scent becoming more and more potent with every step through the tunnels, and it was making his inner wolf pace back and forth like a caged animal. From the scuffs he could make out along the stone floor, it was clear that his soul mate had fought her captors every step of the way. It was equally obvious that her efforts hadn't done any good. The thought of what those creatures might have done to her was damn near driving him to shift even as he ran.

Trevor's guilt grew with each passing second. If he'd gotten to the cavern fifteen minutes earlier, he could have stopped the ghouls from taking Jenna. He would have saved her and already gotten her out of these damn tunnels. If anything happened to her, it would be his fault, all because he hadn't been fast enough.

He had no idea how long he ran, but the sound of fighting abruptly dragged Trevor out of his downward spiral of self-recrimination. He slid to a halt, looking around wildly in an effort to pinpoint the source of the noise. The musty scent of ghouls was so strong it made his eyes water and kept him from being able to smell nearly anything else. He couldn't imagine how many of the creatures it would take to generate an odor that strong.

He sniffed the air again, finally able to filter out the stench of ghoul after a few moments and focus on the scents he was really looking for. Hale and Mike must have partially shifted because the scents of their inner werewolves were more obvious than usual. Trevor smelled Maya and Owen, too. But stronger than any of those scents was the familiar and soothing scent of honeysuckles.

Jenna was alive.

The realization nearly made him dizzy with relief.

But then the fear that was pouring off her in waves hit him, and everything else faded into the background. The only thing that mattered right then was getting to his soul mate and saving her life.

Trevor heard the piece of metal from the sign pole he'd been carrying clatter to the ground before he even realized he'd dropped it. But before he could wonder why he'd done that, his knees were slamming into the stone floor of the cave, the bones and muscles all over his body beginning to twist as he started to shift.

Undergoing a full shift was uncomfortable at the best of times. With the sheer amount of physical reshaping going on, there was no way to avoid the pain. But going through the change from human to wolf while wearing clothes was frigging awkward.

His boots slid off without too much of a problem, but the belt and pants were the worst. Which was why, at any other time, Trevor would have at least popped his belt and shoved his jeans down. Unfortunately, in the midst of worrying about Jenna, he'd forgotten about any of that. So as soon as his jawline elongated enough to allow it, he dipped his head down and bit right through the leather of his belt and the front of his jeans. Finding something to wear later was going to be a problem, but he'd worry about that burning bridge when he got to it.

His T-shirt tore right up the back at the same time as he shook free of his pants, and then he was focusing on the change to his wolf form, pushing the transformation faster than he ever had. Doing that made it hurt worse, but he couldn't take the chance that he'd be too late.

Again.

The part of the change where his fingers blurred together and became part of his extremely large front paws had always amazed him, but this time he wished the transformation would hurry the hell up.

He took off running while his fur was still settling in. It was uncomfortable as all get out to move while his skin was spasming and sprouting the thick, furry stuff, but he didn't want to waste any more time. He realized absently that he was leaving the rusted length of metal behind—the only weapon he knew for sure would hurt a ghoul. But there was nothing to be done for it now. He only prayed it wasn't the worst mistake of his life.

Trevor still had a few hundred feet of tunnel ahead of him when he first caught sight of the huge crowd of ghouls around Jenna and his friends. As he watched, they charged forward, ready to kill.

He howled in anger, rage, and fear as he raced forward, eager to take out every single creature between him and his soul mate. The ghouls froze at the sound, but it didn't change anything. They'd been half a second away from killing the woman he loved.

Trevor howled again in a subconscious challenge to all of them.

He was running so fast that by the time he reached the outer ring of ghouls, stopping wasn't even a consideration. So instead, he simply lowered his head and slammed into them at full speed. Claws dug into his chest and shoulders, but his thick fur turned them away for the most part.

After bowling through a half dozen ghouls and sending them flying, Trevor snapped out left and right with his huge jaws, chomping down on anything he could reach. He had very little faith that he would be able to actually damage the ghoul's stone-hard skin, so he was kind of shocked when his fangs sank in a couple of inches and then gouged a path as he flung away one ghoul and moved to the next target.

The creatures grunted and shrieked in alarm, pulling back in pain. But then they charged at him again, attacking him over and over, no matter how many times he knocked them back.

Shit, there were so damn many of them.

One of the ghouls jumped on his back, sharp claws digging in deep. Trevor snarled at the pain, but before he could even think about shaking it off, a second one joined it, and then a third. His legs began to buckle from both the weight as well as the agony of their claws burrowing into his flesh.

Right as he was about to go down, Hale and Mike jumped in the middle of the cluster of ghouls, swinging their rusted metal weapons. Creatures went flying, including the three on his back.

Hale and Mike were pushing the crowd of creatures back, leaving some unmoving on the floor of the tunnel. Three other ghouls with pieces of red material tied around their upper arms were helping, and Trevor could almost sense the battle turning in their favor. Given a moment to catch his breath, he turned to scan the rest of the area, his nose leading his eyes right where they needed to go.

Jenna was standing with her back to the wall of the tunnel—Maya and Owen to her left—and she was swinging a rusty length of bicycle chain to hold off a determined ghoul that kept trying to edge around her defenses. She was yelling at the creature, daring it to come at her. If Trevor hadn't been so terrified at the sight, he would have cheered.

Damn, Jenna was such a badass!

But even as he finished that thought, Trevor caught sight of three other ghouls skirting along the wall in Jenna's direction, heading straight for her. Based on the numbers of necklaces the creatures had bouncing against their chests, something told him they were older than their brethren. Maybe they were the ghouls in charge of the clan.

Regardless, from the way they were moving, it seemed clear they were targeting Jenna for something specific.

Trevor surged forward, slamming his way through the few remaining ghouls that seemed willing to put up a fight. But even as he slashed and snapped, creating a clear path, he knew he was taking too long. He glanced in Jenna's direction again, letting out a howl of rage as the three older ghouls reached his soul mate and quickly overwhelmed her.

His worst fear was realized when two of the creatures dragged Jenna off her feet and yanked her kicking and screaming into the darkness. The third ghoul trailed behind, obviously there to keep anyone from following.

Snapping his jaws closed on the shoulder of another one of the creatures trying to block his path, Trevor bit down hard, giving the thing a savage shake before tossing it aside. That violent move, as well as the shriek the creature let out, discouraged the last few ghouls from attacking him, and the path ahead of him quickly cleared.

Trevor took off running at full speed, letting his nose lead him through a maze of twists and turns that had him wondering where the hell the three ghouls were taking Jenna.

He caught up with the creatures just as they were dragging her across a small cavern with an even smaller fire burning in the center. The flames provided enough illumination to allow him to see Jenna clearly fighting and kicking to get away from the creatures holding her.

Trevor didn't even slow as he approached, momentarily bunching his four legs under him and then bounding over the third ghoul—the one still lagging behind the others like some kind of rear guard. He covered a good fifteen feet, his forelegs slamming into the two creatures holding Jenna, sending all of them sprawling across the floor.

Trevor was on his feet in a flash, but the third ghoul moved in even faster, heading straight for Jenna. Whether the thing wanted to use her as a hostage to get away or kill her outright, Trevor didn't know. But he wasn't going to let either of those things happen.

He shouldered Jenna aside as gently as he could, then quickly turned to face the ghoul that had been coming her way. The creature slashed at his face, claws moving so fast they were little more than a blur. He immediately jerked back but still felt two deep scratches across his muzzle.

Trevor ignored the pain, lunging forward to snap down on the junction of the ghouls' neck and shoulder, giving a few hard, savage shakes before dropping the unmoving creature.

He spun, keeping himself between Jenna and danger, expecting to find the other two ghouls poised to attack. Instead, both were standing there, staring at the one he'd killed. After a few seconds, they turned their gazes to him, their big eyes flat and expressionless.

Time froze as Trevor stood there in his wolf form, staring at the two ghouls who remained completely still. It took him a moment to realize that they were waiting for him to deal with them the same way he'd dealt with the first ghoul.

He glanced down at the dead creature to see an inordinate number of necklaces lying on its chest...a mix of bones, teeth, and roughly polished stones. Based purely on the quantity of the things, he assumed the ghoul had been important to the clan.

Now it was dead, and the two remaining ghouls seemed to be leaving their own fates up to Trevor.

Not understanding any of this, nor having the time to worry about it, Trevor simply turned his back on the two creatures and padded over to Jenna. She was regarding him wide-eyed, her wondrous gaze taking in his huge fur-covered body and fang-filled mouth.

"Trevor?" she asked softly. Taking a step toward him, she slid her fingers through the ruff of fur around his neck. "Is that really you?"

He wondered how she could possibly know it was him. Perhaps it was because they were soul mates. Because he doubted his furry face resembled anything like his human one. But ultimately, he didn't care how she knew it was him. She did and that was all that mattered.

Trevor closed the last few inches separating them, then pressed his broad forehead against her stomach, letting out a soft chuffing sound. Jenna's fingers sank deeper into the fur to either side of his neck before sliding up and down his ears. This kind of contact in his wolf form was a first for him, but truthfully, it was the most amazing thing he'd ever felt.

He let himself sink into the sensation, exhaling out all the tension that had been locked in his body for the past few hours. If he could, he'd stay locked in this moment forever.

But soon enough, Jenna took a step back, telling him that they needed to get back and check on Hale, Mike, Maya, and Owen. "We need to make sure they're okay. Then you have to fill me in on what happened with Connor and Hannah and everyone else."

Trevor chuffed again, less than pleased when her hands stopped caressing his ears. But he knew Jenna was right. Everyone else could still be fighting for their lives while he and Jenna stood here having a moment. Looking around, he realized that the two ghouls had disappeared somewhere while he'd been standing there with Jenna. He only hoped that letting the creatures go didn't turn out to be a mistake.

Knowing that staying in his wolf form would

make any future communication impossible, Trevor decided to go ahead and shift back now, before they headed off to check on everyone. Dropping to his belly, he started the shift, hoping he didn't freak Jenna out too badly.

To his relief, she didn't seem bothered at all, even when his bones cracked as they reformed. She simply stood there watching with an interested expression on her face. Something told him that knowing her, Jenna was memorizing the scene so she could sculpt him in wolf form later.

As soon as he completed the transformation and stood, Trevor immediately found himself wrapped up in Jenna's warm embrace, her arms around his neck and her face pressed against his bare chest. He wrapped his own arms around her, holding her close.

"While I do love your big furry wolf self," Jenna murmured softly, "I have to admit to enjoying the feel of having your arms wrapped around me. By the way, it goes without saying, but thanks for coming to rescue me."

"Always," he murmured, pressing a kiss to the top of her head. "You ready to see what's going on with the rest of the team?"

Jenna pulled back, looking him up and down with a smile. "Definitely. But before we head back, maybe we can find you something to wear? You're naked."

CHAPTER 24

"So that's it?" Jenna asked as she led Trevor, Hannah, and Connor into her apartment a few hours later. "The patriarch of the ghoul clan is dead, and now they're simply going to give up kidnapping and eating people?"

No one answered as they headed straight for her kitchen, yanking the fridge and cabinets open, taking out food and stacking it on the counter. Jenna left them to it, flopping in exhaustion on the couch, too tired to care about the mess she was probably making with her filthy clothes.

Trevor walked into the living room a little while later with two glasses of almond milk in one hand and two plates of food balanced in the other. He handed one of the glasses and a plate to Jenna, then sat down beside her. She glanced at the peanut butter and jelly sandwich he'd made for her, smiling when she saw a stack of five PB&Js on his plate.

Connor and Hannah came out of the kitchen a few seconds later with their own plates of sandwiches. Her brother also had a bag of Doritos and a package of cookies to go with his half dozen PB&Js while her sister was carrying a big bag of peanut M&M's. With all the food, Jenna almost wondered if Hale and Mike, as well as Madeleine and the peeps from HOPD, had changed their minds and decided to join them but knew they hadn't. Everyone had figured that this was going to be a family discussion and had decided to give them some privacy.

Jenna supposed she was going to have to get used to how much werewolves ate considering she was dating one and related to another. Surprisingly, Hannah ate almost as much as Trevor and Connor, devouring two sandwiches, half a dozen cookies, and a few handfuls of candy.

"To answer your earlier question," Hannah said, reaching for another cookie. "When a patriarch of the clan dies, the members of the clan's ruling class come together to elect a new one. Normally, this would be a completely meaningless exercise since the ruling class is composed of all the old farts who all think totally alike. It doesn't matter who wins because they all behave the same."

"But it's different this time?" Jenna prompted.

"Yeah," Hannah said with a nod. "Quite a few of the previous rulers were wiped out in the fighting, and those who weren't killed were demoted to a lower level of the hierarchy. As in all the way to the bottom. The new ruling class will be composed entirely of members of the Others—the ghouls who are on our side. With new leadership comes new rules and new customs. In this case, that means no more kidnapping people."

Connor looked dubious as he helped himself to more chips. "They'll change decades of behavior simply because someone tells them that's what's going to happen, just like that?"

Hannah nodded, her eyes rolling a little in pleasure when she bit into the chocolate chip cookie. Jenna had to wonder when her sister had last eaten one. Ten years ago?

"It is the way of the Umdar," Hannah said after she finished the cookie. "Those below obey those above. They don't usually think about it because they're discouraged from having opinions of their own. That's why it took me so long to change the beliefs of the ones I spent time with. I had to get them to see the value of the individual first and then build from there."

Jenna sat and stared at her sister, awed beyond belief. To go through everything Hannah had experienced and still be able to dedicate herself to a goal as unobtainable as changing an entire culture was more than amazing. It was unreal.

"So what's going to happen to all the captives we rescued tonight?" Jenna asked, thinking of all the people currently bedding down in Davina's club. "I mean, while we were still down in the tunnels, Trevor told me that you've been getting people to freedom for the past five years. But that was one or two people at a time. This is different. Won't the world notice if over thirty missing people all show back up at once?"

Hannah gave her a small smile. "You'd think so, but in reality, most of the people we rescued tonight were never on anyone's radar. And the ones who were have fallen off long ago."

Jenna shared looks with Trevor and Connor, seeing the same expression on their faces that she knew was on hers. Was that the way her sister thought of herself, as someone who'd fallen off the radar? That no one would care—or notice—that she was back?

"What about you?" Jenna asked. "Now that the ghouls aren't going to kidnap people anymore, you don't need to go back to living underground."

Her older sister looked over, and for a moment, there was such a look of panic on her face that it took Jenna's breath away. It was as if the question had caught Hannah so off guard that there was no possible way she could answer it.

"Right?" Jenna prompted.

"I don't know," Hannah said, her voice so low it was difficult to hear it even though the room was so quiet they could have heard a pin drop.

"You can't leave us again," Connor said, his expression devastated, as if it had just come to him that could be a possibility. "Not after we've finally got you back."

Hannah's gaze went back and forth between Jenna and Connor, looking lost and alone one moment, and the next, like she was the strongest woman in the world.

"What else am I supposed to do?" Hannah finally asked, her expression settling into the lost and lonely one. "I was sixteen years old when the ghouls kidnapped me. Since I escaped, I've taught myself to drive and can act the part so I can blend in—at least on the edges of society—but sometimes, I don't even think of myself as human. I never graduated from high school, can barely use a computer, and haven't used my Social Security number for something as simple as getting a job in so long that I can't even remember it. I don't know much about current events, much less who the current president is, so I'm pretty sure that anyone who talks to me for more than five minutes will realize there's something off about me. Hell, I haven't watched a TV show or seen a movie in ten years." She shook her head. "How am I supposed to step back into your world like nothing ever happened?"

Jenna didn't realize she was crying until she felt something wet running down her face. Stifling a sob, she got up and moved over to sit by Hannah, wrapping both arms around her.

"I know it won't be easy," Jenna murmured into her sister's hair. "But I didn't spend the past ten years looking for you to give up now. I'll be there to help you with anything you need, no matter how long it takes."

"We'll *all* be there to help you," Connor said firmly, leaning forward in his chair. "Now is as good a time as any to confess that I gave up on you, Hannah, which is something I don't know if I'll ever forgive myself for doing. And while I'll never be able to apologize enough to you, I can promise that I'm here for you now. Jenna and I will do whatever we have to do so you can get your life back—whatever kind of life you decide you want."

Hannah nodded, a small smile curving her lips even as she blinked back tears. Holding on to one of Jenna's hands, she reached out to grasp Connor's with her other one.

"Thank you," she said, then took a deep breath. "Since I'm going to be rejoining society, maybe you guys could start by catching me up on what's been going on the past ten years."

Jenna and Connor filled her in on everything, including how he became a werewolf, revealing it was the reason he'd left LA and moved to Dallas, while Jenna told her about being a special effects artist. In return, Hannah told them what it was like living most of her adult life underground. She even clarified why she'd run away from Jenna that night in Skid Row a couple months back, explaining that she'd been in the middle of a rescue operation that couldn't be delayed. After seeing what it was like for the poor people held captive by the ghouls, Jenna completely understood.

The conversation prompted more tears from all of them—Connor included—but Jenna decided it was cathartic. For all of them. It was especially worth it when Hannah and Connor hugged for what seemed like the first time in forever, both of them trying to look like they weren't crying. Jenna almost grabbed her phone to take a picture but then realized she didn't need it. This moment would live in her memory forever.

In the end, Hannah still had no idea what she was going to do with her life, but at least their sister had promised she'd accept everyone's help when it came to figuring it out. And that help started with moving into Jenna's guest bedroom, sculptures and all.

Figuring everyone could use something stronger to drink after that, Jenna offered to grab some beers from the fridge.

"I'll give you a hand," Connor said, quickly getting to his feet and grabbing the empty plates from the coffee table.

The moment they were in the kitchen, her brother set the plates on the counter and turned to look at her.

"All the confessing and apologizing I was doing with Hannah made me realize I've never apologized to you," he said.

She shook her head, too emotionally drained by everything that happened over the past few days—not to mention that evening—to worry about anything more. "You don't need to apologize."

"Yeah, I do. And you know it," Connor insisted.

"I need to apologize for everything from how I abandoned you after Hannah's abduction to leaving LA without considering you, and then for not believing you when you came out to Dallas and said you'd seen our sister. I screwed up at every turn over and over again. But as bad as all that was, I feel even worse about the way I treated your relationship with Trevor. The connection between you and him is obvious, but I thought I knew better. I thought you weren't ready to deal with a soul mate because of everything you'd been through, but I know now that was bullshit. Like all the excuses I made for my shitty behavior. And I'm sorry. I'm sorry for all of it."

Jenna wasn't sure how she ended up with her arms around her brother, but that was where she was, hugging him tightly and crying against his chest as she accepted his long overdue apology.

But then something he said struck her as odd.

"Soul mate?" she asked, pulling back to look up at him, pausing for a second to wipe a few tears away from her cheek. "What's that supposed to mean?"

Her boneheaded brother looked baffled for a second, as if he had no clue what he'd said to her. But then his eyes widened and he got this guilty as hell expression on his face.

"Um…I think that's something you need to talk to Trevor about," he mumbled. "But first, let me ask you something. Have you ever had this bizarre feeling that pops up out of nowhere telling you that you and Trevor are simply meant to be? That you've felt like the two of you clicked since the moment you met?"

Jenna must have answered those questions without saying a word because her brother flashed her a quick smile, then nodded.

"I'll take that as a yes. So talk to him about it. Seriously. You'll need to bring it up, though, because he's hesitant to do it."

She wanted to know why that was, but Connor was already turning and walking into the living room. Jenna finished tossing the last of the garbage into the trash can, making it out to the living room in time to see Trevor standing up and Connor and Hannah hugging again, her brother saying he was heading back to his hotel room and that he'd be back first thing in the morning—with doughnuts.

The damn coward was running away, Jenna realized even as Connor slipped out the door with a wave. She would have gone after him, but Hannah stepped in front of her, giving her another hug.

"Thanks again for asking me to stay here," her sister said for probably the tenth time. "I have a thousand things I still want to talk to you about, but I'm wiped out, so I was hoping you could show me that guest bedroom?"

Jenna smiled. "Sure."

Telling Trevor that she'd be right back, she led Hannah down the hall.

"Forgive the mess," she said as she reached out to flip the light switch in the guest room. "I usually use this space for my workshop, but the bed is pretty comfy."

Hannah glanced around, her gaze settling on the sculptures along the wall, lingering on the most recent one of Trevor in mid-transformation. Jenna thought her sister would say something about them, but instead, she kept scanning the room, stopping on Trevor's weekender bag that was still sitting unzipped in the corner.

"I hope I'm not putting anyone else out," Hannah said, turning to regard her with a curious—albeit downright knowing—expression. "I could sleep on the couch."

"No, that's not necessary," Jenna said quickly. "Trevor was sleeping in here when he first arrived, but he doesn't use the room now."

"Because he's sleeping in yours?" Hannah prompted, brow lifted to go with the matching smile. "And don't bother denying it. It's obvious there's something serious going on between the two of you."

Jenna laughed. Hannah may have been missing for a decade, but they were still sisters. There was nothing they couldn't share. There never had been.

"Yeah, it's serious," she admitted. "But it's kind of new, so we're still figuring everything out."

"Well, I want to hear all the details in the

morning. Just to make sure this guy is good enough for my little sister," Hannah said, giving her a grin. "I wish I could hear the story right now, but if we sit down and start talking, I'd probably be asleep in five minutes, I'm so wiped out. I'm definitely looking forward to sleeping in the first real bed I've seen in a long time."

Jenna hugged her sister again, even more tightly this time, hating the reminder of the life Hannah had been forced to live. But never again, that was a solemn promise. From this moment on, Jenna would make sure that her sister had whatever she needed.

She walked back into the living room to find Trevor sitting on the couch again. He looked so exhausted that she wondered whether it was the fighting that had worn him out so much or shifting into a full wolf, something that still amazed her.

"Hannah get settled in okay?" he asked softly as Jenna sat beside him.

Jenna rested her head on his strong shoulder as he wrapped an arm around her. "Yeah. She's absolutely exhausted."

It was so warm and comforting snuggling against Trevor's body that Jenna thought she might fall asleep herself until she felt him turn toward her a little and clear his throat.

"I don't think I ever got around to mentioning this, but one of the abilities that comes with being a werewolf is enhanced hearing," he said. "So even though I wasn't eavesdropping or anything, I was still able hear you and Connor talking in the kitchen earlier. I heard when he mentioned the soul mate thing."

She sat up straighter. "Yeah, my brother mentioned that term to me. But he didn't explain what it meant, other than that it had something to do with the way I feel about you. He said I should talk to you about it, then ran off like a big ol' chicken."

Trevor chuckled. "Yeah, that sounds like how Connor would choose to handle the situation."

"So soul mate?" she prompted when Trevor didn't say anything else after a while. "I'm assuming it means what I think it means?"

Trevor appeared at a loss for words for a moment before simply nodding. "There's this legend among werewolves saying that for each of our kind, there's one and only one person out there who we are meant to be with—*The One* who can accept us for what we truly are. For years, everyone in our pack assumed the legend was just that—a legend. A desperate folktale kept alive by lonely werewolves who could never find someone they trusted enough to tell their biggest secret."

"Being alone with that kind of secret sounds horrible," Jenna said softly, knowing exactly what it was like to have a secret she'd never been able to share. "What changed to make you think the legend might be more than that?"

Trevor smiled. "Two and a half years ago, Gage Dixon, the commander of the SWAT team and the alpha of our pack of alpha werewolves, met this extremely nosy journalist who was investigating us and intended to expose our identities as werewolves. Long story short, she and Gage fell in love—extremely fast and extremely hard. It nearly broke the Pack apart, but in the end, we had the first confirmed soul mate connection that any of us had ever witnessed firsthand."

"How can you know for sure they're soul mates?" Jenna asked. "Maybe the two of them simply have good chemistry and are great in bed."

Trevor chuckled softly. "Oh, I expect there was good chemistry and sex, but finding *The One* is more than that. The second you meet that person, there's this immediate sense of knowing you've found someone special...someone who's perfect for you. You get this excited feeling in your gut, like you're on the world's biggest roller coaster. It's terrifying but exhilarating at the same time. And that person's scent—which is impossible to explain to anyone not having a werewolf's nose—but trust me, that scent is unforgettable."

Jenna felt a quiver in her stomach, realizing she'd experienced many of those same phenomena herself. Okay, maybe not the whole scent thing, but definitely everything else.

"So I have a distinctive scent that's unforgettable to you?" Jenna asked.

She felt her face grow warm as she realized it probably sounded like she was fishing for compliments.

"Honeysuckles," Trevor said without a moment's hesitation. "Sweet, fruity, and warm with hints of honey and a touch of citrus and vanilla. It makes me think of the hottest part of summer back in Virginia. When you just sit out on the porch and relax with a big glass of Grandma's homemade lemonade."

"That's oddly specific," she murmured. "It makes me wonder how much time you spent thinking about how I smell."

His mouth curved. "A lot. Hours and hours actually, especially right after we met, when I still wasn't sure this was really happening."

"But you're sure now?" Jenna asked, though she suspected she already knew the answer to that question. That didn't mean she didn't want to hear him say it out loud.

"Yeah. I've known for a while that you're *The One* for me," he said. "You're the person I'm meant to spend the rest of my life with."

She took a deep breath, letting it out slowly, trying to cover up the fact that her insides had suddenly gone all mushy like a marshmallow.

"If you've known all this time, why didn't you tell me earlier?" she asked. "There were so many times since you arrived here in LA that you could have told me."

"I suppose I could try and convince you that I was waiting for the perfect time to tell you, but to be honest, I think I was scared that you wouldn't be able to see beyond the claws and fangs to even listen to the soul mate part."

Jenna considered that, remembering how upset she'd been. Not that Trevor was a werewolf but that he hadn't told her. But there was no way he could have understood the difference.

"Okay, I guess you're right," she admitted with a sigh. "I'm not sure how I would have responded if you'd come out with, *I'm a werewolf...and oh, by the way...we're soul mates, too.* I probably would have freaked out a little."

He studied her face. "Now you know that there's more between us than chemistry and compatibility in bed, are you still going to freak out?"

"No," she said without hesitation. "Like you, I guess I've known for a while that we were meant to be together. Heck, maybe even before you did. I might not have known about the soul mate thing, but I've known I love you. And that was enough."

Jenna didn't realize she'd said the "L" word until Trevor's eyes widened, a stunned expression on his face. She started to stammer, wondering how the hell that particular four-letter word had slipped and whether she might be able to take it back. But as she opened her mouth to try, Trevor leaned forward and kissed her.

All the static in Jenna's head disappeared the moment his lips touched hers, and she stopped worrying about what she should or shouldn't have said. She simply let everything go, melted into his arms, and kissed him back.

At some point, Jenna found herself straddling Trevor's thighs, his hands tightening in her hair as they kissed until she was dizzy from lack of air. Only then did Trevor pull back, a warm smile crossing his face.

"I got the feeling you needed a distraction," he said, his hands sliding out of her hair to cup her butt. "It seemed like you were about to slip up and go for a retraction, and I couldn't have that. Not until I had a chance to say *I love you* back anyway. But now that I've had my say and told you I'm completely in love with you and can't imagine a life without you in it, do you still want to take it back?"

Jenna had no idea how he could have possibly known that she'd been about to say anything like that, but she supposed it didn't matter. They'd both said it, and for something like that, there were no take-backsies.

She shook her head with a smile and leaned forward to kiss him again. "No, I think I'll stick by my original statement," she said softly against his lips. "I love you, and apparently, you love me. I guess that makes it official. We're soul mates."

He chuckled. "That we are."

"So what do we do next?" she asked. "Are you going to move out here to LA? Am I moving to Dallas with you? And what do we do about Hannah? Because there's no way I'm letting her go again now that I've finally gotten her back."

Trevor kissed her as she began to ramble on about a dozen other major issues they needed to figure out. Once he got her quiet, he gently kissed her nose and smiled.

"I have no idea what we do next," he said softly. "But we'll figure it out...together."

CHAPTER 25

Jenna couldn't help but laugh at the scene in front of her. The training area behind the SWAT buildings was a complete madhouse filled with kids, pets, and more than a few members of the Pack running around laughing like they'd each recently consumed a five-pound bag of sugar. But it was the sight of Tuffie, the team's beloved pit-bull mix/mascot, playing with Connor and Kat's adorable new addition to their family, a little black kitten they adopted—appropriately named Kitty—that she couldn't get enough of. They were absolutely precious together.

"I think moving here was a really good idea," Hannah said, coming over to stand beside her, watching the kids and the adults play as Hale worked the grills off to the side of the volleyball court. "Thank you for talking me into coming with you and Trevor."

"I'm glad you agreed to come with us," Jenna said, nudging her sister with her shoulder. "So let's call it even, okay?"

Hannah laughed. "Deal."

They wandered over to one of the many coolers to grab two bottles of cold water. Even though it was mid-October, the day was almost unseasonably warm. Along the way, they stopped to chat with some other members of the Pack, werewolves and mates alike. Jenna was thrilled to see Hannah having such a good time, glad to have one less thing to worry about when it came to her sister. Jenna had worried that since Hannah spent most of her life living underground, she might not be comfortable in social situations, but thankfully, that wasn't the case.

While Mike and Hale had left Los Angeles the day after rescuing everyone from the ghouls, Trevor and Connor had stayed for much longer, both of them committed to helping Hannah any way she'd needed. In the end, most of that help revolved around getting her established in the modern world, including obtaining a driver's license, passport, bank account, credit cards, cell phone, email address, and various social media accounts.

The next big milestone on Hannah's reintroduction to the human world was a visit to see their mom and dad. Truthfully, Hannah had been somewhat ambivalent about the prospect of seeing them again but had agreed to do so, more for closure than anything else.

The visit had gone...okay. Scratch that. Actually, it had been weird as hell. Their parents hadn't even known Connor was in town, and Jenna hadn't bothered to mention him or Trevor when she'd called to set up dinner. When all four of them had walked into their mother's house on their parents in the middle of yet another argument—this one about Jenna asking to see them when she hadn't spoken to either of them in months—the silence had been awkward. Luckily, Mom and Dad had bought the story they'd all come up with about Hannah being held captive by a cult outside the Mojave Desert. It wasn't like they could ever tell them about the ghouls, after all. They'd obviously been happy and relieved to see that Hannah was alive and well, but any thought that they could somehow be one big happy family again was simply not meant to be. Too much time had passed and too many bridges had been burnt for that to ever happen.

They'd been there for barely over two hours when Dad had announced he needed to leave to avoid traffic. Mom had suggested Jenna, Connor, and Hannah get together with them again for Christmas...or maybe a Skype call instead. That comment had effectively put a fork in the reunion.

The idea of moving to Dallas had originally been Connor's. While it had been Trevor's preference as well, he'd been content to stay with Jenna in LA if that was what she wanted, even though that would mean leaving his pack. She loved him even more for that, which was why she'd never ask him to do something like that. For werewolves, a pack was like a family, only stronger, the bond between its members tighter. Asking him to give that up was something she hadn't even considered.

As for Hannah, her sister had been directionless for a while, not sure what she wanted to do with her life now that she had it back. Then the director of STAT had shown up at the apartment, saying he thought that Hannah had all the makings of a good field agent and that they could use her help rescuing other people whom ghouls had captured all over the world. But Hannah had only taken the job with the understanding that she'd be spending the majority of her time trying to get these other clans around the world to change their perspective on how they treated humans. It seemed like a hopeless task to Jenna, but her sister seemed really excited at the possibilities.

Connor had absolutely hated the idea of Hannah putting herself in danger again, but joining STAT had given their sister a purpose in life, and that was the most important thing in the end. And in between missions and her efforts to change the ghoul world, Hannah could come back to Dallas to visit them. She'd even helped Jenna and Trevor pick out a new three-bedroom apartment that she'd share with them when she was in town.

"Jenna! Hannah! Over here," Kat called out, waving at them from a nearby picnic table. "I've been saving a seat for you guys."

Jenna had met Kat Davenport, Connor's soul

mate, when she'd visited Dallas the first time, and since moving here, Kat had become close friends with her and Hannah. Part of it was her willingness to reveal all their brother's most embarrassing secrets, but the bigger part was how easy it was to talk to her about nearly anything.

"Hey," Jenna said, giving Kat a smile as she and Hannah joined her. "Any idea where Trevor and my brother are? They said they'd be here when we got to the compound."

Kat nudged an open bag of chips in their direction. "They were supposed to be, but they went on a call earlier this morning. It was some kind of shooting, but apparently there wasn't much SWAT could do to help since the assailants were long gone before they arrived. Trevor and Connor stayed for a while to help out but are already on the way back."

Jenna let out a sigh of relief. Trevor and Connor might be werewolves and could handle a lot of damage, but they weren't indestructible, so she couldn't help worrying every time they went out on a call.

While they waited for the guys to show up, Jenna, Hannah, and Kat chatted about the new apartment as well as she and Trevor visiting an animal rescue to adopt a dog soon and Hannah's new job. Her sister would be leaving in a few days to start her field training with STAT, which Hannah couldn't be more excited about.

"What's going on with Madeleine and those paranormal investigators who helped you guys out in LA?" Kat asked, nibbling a corn chip while they waited for Hale to finish grilling. "Have you talked to them since moving?"

While Kat had been as eager as the rest of the Pack in the part Jenna, Trevor, Connor, and Hannah had played in what had happened out in Los Angeles, she'd also wanted to hear about what Madeleine and the HOPD peeps had done during the rescue.

"Owen is talking to STAT about HOPD doing some part-time work for them," Jenna said, relaying what the paranormal investigators had told her when they'd Skyped a few days ago. "Nothing dangerous, of course. Just some research and occasional recon. They're pretty hyped about the idea."

"And Madeleine?" Kat prompted. "She still working as a private chef?"

Jenna nodded. "Yeah, she's still doing the private chef gig, but not nearly as much since she's also started working at Davina's club, adding a little haute cuisine to their nighttime menu. It turns out that she and Kia not only work together really well but are also becoming besties. Madeleine spends almost all her free time hanging out with Kia and her girlfriend. She's also picked up where I left off handing out meals to the unhoused in Skid Row and giving me updates on all my friends who live there. She even got two of my closest friends—Nicole and Ada—into a job training program that includes housing. Madeleine is doing amazing work out there."

Before Kat could say anything, Trevor and Connor appeared at the table, along with Mike. Trevor slid a paper plate in front of her with a Jenna-sized cheeseburger on it with a side of baked beans and just enough coleslaw so she could lie to herself about having a veggie with the meal. Of course, Trevor's plate held more food than three non-werewolves would be able to eat, including four Trevor-sized cheeseburgers. On the other side of the table, Connor placed a plate in front of Kat as he sat down.

"What kept you guys so long?" Hale asked, joining them at the table with his own mountainous pile of food as well as a plate for Hannah. "Gage said it was a shooting?"

Mike nodded. "Yeah. It looks like another gang-related turf war might be starting. There was an attack on a large outdoor party near Terrace Grove. A dozen dead, all with ties to the Hillside Riders."

"So we're thinking it's the Locos?" Hale questioned. "Did anyone get a look at the shooters?"

"The Locos makes the most sense," Trevor said, picking up on the narrative, and Jenna could only assume they were talking about two competing gangs here in Dallas. "All we know about the shooters is that they were five big guys. No one got a look at their faces but said they were wearing tactical gear of some type. At least three of the assailants were shot during the gun battle and barely even stumbled."

"At least no innocents were hit," Connor said. "The attacker only went after heavily armed gang members."

"I don't think we can notch that up to anything more than pure luck," Mike said, and to Jenna, it seemed as if the rest of the guys agreed.

Thankfully, there wasn't much shop talk after that, as everyone started talking about their favorite movies and TV shows of the past ten years, trying to help Hannah come up with a list of things to catch up on. That left Jenna and Trevor free to talk quietly to each other.

"So have you decided which job offer you're going to take?" Trevor asked as he leaned over and scooped up some chips from the bag on the table.

Jenna took a small bite of her burger, savoring the juicy taste and trying not to smile too much with her mouth full. "I've decided to take the job with the effects house on Dyer Street. They do more graphic and CGI work than I've ever done so it's way different from what I'm used to, but they love my work and are willing to train me, which was a major factor in my decision."

Beside her, Trevor visibly relaxed at hearing

that. While he hadn't said anything, of course, she knew he felt badly about her leaving a job she had in LA that she not only enjoyed but that paid well. She knew he'd been nervous she wouldn't be able to find anything even close to that in Dallas. And while it was true she'd never find a job that paid as much as her last one, it was also true that almost everything in Dallas was cheaper than it was in LA, so money here definitely went further. Not to mention the fact that she now had Trevor, which was worth all the money in the world.

As they ate, she and Trevor talked about when she'd start, her work schedule, and how her days off would line up with his and how they would start getting involved with helping the unhoused population here in Dallas. The simple mundane act of planning for future getaways was enough to turn her heart to mush all over again. Yet one more example of what it meant to have a soul mate, she supposed. Or maybe this was simply what it was like to be in love?

A few minutes later, Hannah slipped down to their end of the table to tell them that she was heading inside with some of the Pack to watch a bunch of the Marvel movies on DVD that she'd missed. "Since I saw all the Phase One movies, we're going to binge-watch all the Phase Two movies starting with *Iron Man 3* up to and including *Ant-Man*," she said, clearly excited. "You two wanna join us?"

Jenna threw a glance Trevor's way, immediately knowing what he'd rather do from the quirky smile tipping up the corners of his lips.

"Actually, I think we're going to head back to the apartment and finish unpacking some boxes," Jenna said, realizing this movie marathon would give her and Trevor hours and hours of alone time. Something that had been in short supply since her sister had moved in with them. "Maybe we'll neaten up the cabinets some, too."

"Neatening the cabinets?" Hannah flashed them a broad smile. "Is that what people started calling it while I was away?" Laughing at Jenna's blush, she leaned over and hugged her. "Go home with your soul mate and have fun. I'll spend the night at Connor and Kat's place. You two have fun."

Trevor was already tugging her up from the table before Jenna had a chance to reply. "You heard your sister. Let's go home."

Home.

She liked the sound of that.

ACKNOWLEDGMENTS

I hope you had as much fun reading Jenna and Trevor's story as we had writing it! We knew Trevor was going to fall for a pack mate's sister from the beginning, but we didn't know which pack mate. Connor clearly wasn't thrilled his sister was going to be *The One* for his best friend, but he finally came around. Admittedly, it took a little while to get Jenna and Trevor together, but I think it was worth the wait!

This whole series wouldn't be possible without some very incredible people. In addition to another big thank-you to my hubby for all his help with the action scenes and military and tactical jargon, thanks to the editors at Sourcebooks (who are always a phone call, text, or email away whenever we need something) and all the other amazing people there, including my fantastic publicist and the crazy-talented art department. The covers they make for me are seriously drool-worthy!

Because I could never leave out my readers, a huge thank-you to everyone who reads my books and Snoopy danced right along with me with every new release. That includes the fantastic people on my amazing Review Team as well as my assistant, Janet. You rock!

I also want to give a big thank-you to the men, women, and working dogs who protect and serve in police departments everywhere as well as their families.

And a very special shout-out to our favorite restaurant, P.F. Chang's, where hubby and I bat story lines back and forth and come up with all our best ideas, as well as a thank-you to our fantastic waiter-turned-manager, Andrew, who makes sure our order is ready the moment we walk in the door!

Hope you enjoy the next book in the SWAT: Special Wolf Alpha Team series coming soon from Sourcebooks and look forward to reading the rest of the series as much as I look forward to sharing it with you. Also, don't forget to look for our other series from Sourcebooks, STAT: Special Threat Assessment Team, a spin-off from SWAT!

If you love a man in uniform as much as I do, make sure you check out X-Ops, our other action-packed paranormal/romantic-suspense series from Sourcebooks.

Happy Reading!

ABOUT THE AUTHOR

Paige Tyler is the *New York Times* and *USA Today* bestselling author of sexy, romantic fiction, including the X-Ops series, the SEALs of Coronado Series, and the Alaskan Werewolves Series. She and her very own military hero (also known as her husband) live on the beautiful Florida coast with their dog. Visit www.paigetylertheauthor.com.

Also By Paige Tyler

STAT: Special Threat Assessment Team

Wolf Under Fire
Undercover Wolf
True Wolf

X-Ops

Her Perfect Mate
Her Lone Wolf
Her Secret Agent (novella)
Her Wild Hero
Her Fierce Warrior
Her Rogue Alpha
Her True Match
Her Dark Half
X-Ops Exposed

SWAT: Special Wolf Alpha Team

Hungry Like the Wolf
Wolf Trouble
In the Company of Wolves
To Love a Wolf
Wolf Unleashed
Wolf Hunt
Wolf Hunger
Wolf Rising
Wolf Instinct
Wolf Rebel
Wolf Untamed
Rogue Wolf
The Wolf Is Mine